Pure Angst

Stephen Scarcliffe

Published by Stephen Scarcliffe, 2018.

PURE ANGST

First edition. December 30, 2018.

Written by Stephen Scarcliffe.

I dedicate this novel to my partner Angela, who was always there to lend an ear, provide advice, and offer unwavering support and encouragement any time self-doubt crept in. My old dear for all the hours she spent scouring over content to assist with spelling and grammar, not to mention the rest of my family and close friends for their support. My editor Claire Wingfield, my proof-reader Sophie Wallace and my cover designer Domi from Inspired cover designs. And last but not least I dedicate this novel to the memories of Frankie Mcewan and Pete Tinlin, two legends taken too early.

1

"£2.48, pal." A dark hand appeared at the bottom of the cage. Billy wiped the sweat away with his sleeve before sticking a clammy hand inside his joggers pocket and pulling out a battered five pound note. After handing it over he took the change, before dumping the Jelly tots, Frosties and Irn Bru inside a plastic bag.

He snatched a look over his shoulder as a tall laddie began tapping a heavy metal wrench against the shop window. He had a maroon hood pulled down over his head, covering half of his eyes, and he let out a toothy grin as his friends paced restlessly behind.

"Do you know them pal?" said a voice from behind the bars.

"Naw."

The dark skinned man smiled. "You're no from round here are ye?"

"Jist moved."

"Well, here's a bit of advice fer ye. Wrap yer arms tight around yer face, crouch as small as ye can and hope they get bored. Ah'd help ye pal but there's a reason this cage is here. Godless little bastards."

Is that all ye've got? Jist gaunnae stand there?

The taunts seeped from his subconscious and began digging underneath his skin like the wooden splinters still there from the previous night's beating. A sharp fire ignited in his gut as he gripped the glass Irn Bru bottle, clenched his teeth and let the rest of the bag drop to the floor. After putting his foot through the door, he slammed the bottle hard into the side of the laddie's head as his pals stood back in shock. By the time the glass had shattered on the ground, the orange liquid fizzing up and spraying everywhere, Billy was already flying down the street for his life, the curses shooting past his ears like darts as the gang regrouped and took chase.

Weaving in and out of back streets that he didn't recognise, he tried desperately to shake off the wild dogs on his tail, finally tumbling into someone's back garden. He lay as still as he could at the bottom of the hedge, gasping for breath as they hovered with menace on the other side.

"You're fuckin deid ya little CUNT! Cannae hide forever!"

2

"BILLY."

He felt a jolt up his spine as the old man clicked his fingers hard in front of his eyes. "Aye, Dad?"

"Away tae the shops an get yer auld man some milk will ye? Ah want a coffee."

His head dropped as his mother Angie appeared in the living room doorway, cutting a trembling figure. "I'll go Jack. It's no safe fer him."

Jack pointed a stiff finger at his wife. "Stop fuckin mollycoddling him you! Billy, ye see these?" He clenched his fists and aimed a grim stare at his only son. "If you see those laddies, ye use thum. Yer a Wright. So man up and act like one."

Billy's stomach churned as he passed through his gate and onto the street as a police siren sounded nearby. There was an air of rage and frustration hanging over Muirhouse as thick as the grey clouds up above that never seemed to budge. It was etched on the angry faces of passers-by that daggered you for looking unfamiliar, and entrenched in derelict corners where gaunt-eyed zombies paced. Trampled syringes littered back passageways adorned with jagged graffiti, and many of the flat windows were either smashed in or boarded up. From the looming high rises that seemed to hold their inhabitants trapped within their hideous structures, to the dreaded shopping centre itself, he could feel it everywhere. It was a different kind of hell to the one Billy endured at home, and yet for some reason it made him feel alive and on edge instead of suffocated.

He picked up a boulder as he reached the railing at the edge of the centre. To his relief there were no tooled up mobs, and he could feel his jangling nerves calming as he approached. An Alsatian came trotting past, its tongue hanging out, its chin caked in hardened saliva. He gave it a pat on its mane and then backed off as the straggly mutt growled deeply, as though it sensed the approach of danger. It barked several times in the direction of the large vennel before turning and trotting off down the street as a rusty Ford Escort spluttered past. The sound of boys shouting and a ball being kicked against the stone walls echoed around the centre. His heart pounded hard as they emerged, dribbling a tattered old ball about. There was a small ginger laddie with a freckled face, decked out in torn, denim dungarees, flanked by the tall one that he had clattered the previous day in that same maroon HMFC hoodie. The third was the biggest of the group, the ringleader it seemed, an absolute tank bounding about in a Scotland strip that served to accentuate his oversized belly, and light grey joggers with black knee-patches.

They were too engrossed in their frenzied kickabout to notice him. All he needed to do was turn around and follow the Alsatian's lead.

Wee shitebag. Call yersel a Wright?

He took a quick breath, flung the boulder as hard as he could, and braced himself as it cracked against the wall behind them.

The tallest one tore his way toward him, his gangly body making itself as large as possible as it flew at its target. Billy met him head on and they tumbled to the pavement, both trying to seize the upper hand as the other two circled. After overpowering him, Billy mounted him and pounded him with lefts and rights, bursting his nose open as he put every ounce of his weight behind the onslaught. He felt a sharp stinging sensation, first in his side, then in his arm. He looked up to the sight of the snarling wee ginger lad taking pops at him with a rusty screwdriver. He rolled out the way in a panic as the tool flashed past him and stabbed into the concrete, falling right into the path of the big man who brought the boulder crashing into his skull. He slumped to the deck, everything went blank. By the time he came round the three of them were laying the boots in at will as the shopkeeper appeared. "He's had enough! Leave um be or Ah'll phone the Polis!"

A set of angry glares forced him back within his cage, peering fearfully through the mucky glass. Billy tried to catch a breath as he spat out a tooth and clutched at his stinging arm that was leaking blood. As they walked away laughing, joking, and recounting the scene with pride, Billy pulled himself to his knees, blowing hard. "Where are ye's gaun!? Come back here ya cunts!"

After looking at one another with disbelief, the small one came steaming at him, aiming a wild kick at his head which he managed to anticipate and catch before pulling him down to the ground. Billy lost all control, bashing him about the head with the rock as he pictured that screwdriver plunging into his arm and puncturing his side. He bounced to his feet as the other two edged forward. "MON THEN!"

He ran straight into a powerful right hand. After wobbling backward, he threw himself at the big lad in the Scotland strip again, now running on pure adrenaline and pride, before finding himself bear hugged hard against the wall. He slumped to the deck again and covered up. When he moved his arms away from his eyes seconds later, the big lad was standing over him with a wide welcoming grin covering his sweaty face.

"You can fight like fuck wee man. What's yer name?"

"Billy Wright."

3

George Donaldson grinned at the steaming fish supper as he emerged from Drylaw chippy. The fish was huge, wrapped in that chewy batter he loved, drenched in chippy sauce, perfect.

He reluctantly parted with a few chips as the scavengers circled before pulling away, making sure no-one touched the crusty bit at the end of the fish that he loved. The problem was George liked his chippies a little too much.

"Want a chip Billy?" said George as he took in the sight of the new kid on the block shuffling about awkwardly in his upturned jeans and scuffed old Nikes that looked ready for the bin. On closer inspection they were Nicks, not Nikes.

"Nah."

Billy spat on the ground before looking into the distance with a sharp glint in his eye. He was a loner, that much was obvious. Clearly didn't want anything off anyone.

"George asked ye if ye wanted a chip so have a fuckin chip, you," barked wee Jimmy Thomson, the vicious little terrier. Within seconds they were nose to nose, both faces still bearing the cuts and bruises of the previous day's scrap.

Just as George stepped in between to defuse the situation that was threatening to go off like a lit aerosol can, he stopped dead at the sound of the motorbike. He stared, with mouth gaping open, as a big, broad shouldered biker with a skin tight leather coat covered in patches pulled up in front of the chippy. George had fallen in love with motorbikes the moment he stole his first, a wee shitty 50cc which he razzed around Ferryhill field all day long before buzzing the last of the petrol, lying down and staring up at the clouds through hazy eyes.

His dad Dougie had promised to buy him a top of the range Honda as soon as he hit eighteen, and yet here it was, bright red, shining and gleaming at him. Screaming out to be snatched.

"That's mine."

"Ah want a backy!" shouted Jimmy, igniting a crazed pushing and shoving match. George barged through the crowd as he observed Billy's balled up fists clenching themselves tighter and tighter.

"Ye up fer it?"

His angry blue eyes softened slightly, revealing a glimmer of vulnerability beneath the fierce front. "Goan then."

"He can steal it. He can prove umsel, eh!" shouted Joe from behind. Joe Harrison was a thin, lanky, pigeon-chested character with a mouth that knew no limits, and he was still smarting from Billy gaining the upper hand on him not once but twice.

Billy attempted with great difficulty to pull himself onto the bike but the pain from his patched up arm was telling.

George peered inside the chippy, and then sighed as he looked at what was left of his supper before dumping the remains on the concrete. He mounted the bike, kicked off the safety, and started the engine as Billy pulled himself on and clasped himself to his back. George felt a wide grin stretch across his face as it roared beneath him, sending a surge of adrenaline shooting up his spine like an electric bolt as the furious biker charged through the chippy entrance.

The rest of the gang scattered as the bike kicked into gear, hurtling them off the pavement with a force that George barely managed to contain, leaving a livid madman ranting and raving in their wake.

"HUD OAN!" yelled George. They screamed their heads off with delirious excitement as he ripped the arse out of the engine, flying past a line of parked cars as Billy grasped onto him, his scuffed, untied trainers and laces flailing in the air. He powered his way along the railway line, past the overgrown gardens of Crewe Road, and grassy verges littered with everything from strewn toilet roll to abandoned shopping trolleys and smashed up dolls' houses. He felt his insecurities blur into the distance behind him as he surrendered himself to a sense of reckless abandonment. The sense that just for the moment, nothing mattered anymore. No longer was he the big one lagging behind, trying his damnedest to keep up, but an oblivious juggernaut spurred on by the thrill of the steal.

As they reached Ainslie Park School, he dropped the speed and brought it under control, before turning it around as it hummed away impatiently beneath them.

"Ye Ready?"

"Aye!"

Upon reaching Telford Park at the other end, George jumped off and let Billy take control after quickly showing him the ropes. He ended himself with laughter as Billy razzed it round the field, nearly bursting his way through the fence that sealed off the swings, as concerned mothers clutched at their bairns.

By the time the others appeared, clamouring for a shot, George and Billy had turned the top of the field into a mud patch. Just as Jimmy was eagerly trying to pull himself onto the bike, the siren pierced the air. They scrammed in the direction of the railway, as George tried his hardest to keep up with his smaller, nippier counterparts. No longer could he move like the wind but like a carthorse, his weakness laid bare as he puffed and panted. The bull, that's what they called him. Everyone in the playground knew that George Donaldson was the hardest. Everyone knew he hit like a young man not a boy, with the build of a bulky teenager and hands like small shovels. Add to this common knowledge a fearsome family reputation and his loyal following, and it rendered him practically untouchable. Still, the aura he had built around himself was nothing more than a means of disguising the demoralising complex he carried around like a dead weight. What George saw every morning when he looked in the mirror before school wasn't a bull, but a fat cunt.

His legs buckled as he reached the edge of the field, collapsing under his own weight and that of at least one police officer.

George looked up to see Billy, Joe and Jimmy disappear up the path that led into Easter Drylaw, before hearing a large clattering of bodies followed by screams and shouts. Seconds later he watched as they were marched out through the railway line and onto the field, kicking and struggling.

George bit his lip as he felt his arm getting twisted up his back, determined not to give them the satisfaction of hearing his pain. He felt the thud of the bodies hitting the ground and turned to the sight of Jimmy screwing up his bare toothed, rodent like face.

One of the officers, a barrel-chested man with thick sideburns and a jaw like Desperate Dan, planted his feet in front of them. George felt the tight grip release itself and sat up in the mud, clutching his arm in pain.

"Right. Who was it? Ye better make this easy on yersel's boys cause we'll stay here all day if we have to. I want to know who it was right now. An I've got no qualms about slappin it out of ye if Ah have tae. Got more important things tae be daein with my working day than wasting time on little arseholes like yous. Always the bloody runaround fae you wee thieving schemies. Bloody scum off the bottom of my big size 11 so ye are! Never amount tae fuck all, none of ye! Little bloody wasters."

He was met with a wall of silence as he towered over them, laying it on thick, his face reddening as spit flew from his mouth, increasingly frustrated by their lack of interest.

"Cunt, Ah've no even hud a shot yet..." said Joe, igniting a barrage of giggles. Giggles that were stopped in their tracks the moment the big ranting moron stood on his leg and applied all his weight.

"Aaah, ya!"

"Jist fer yer bare-faced cheek, Ah'm gonnae stand here until either you or one of yer pals owns up tae stealin that bike. And fer every minute no-one owns up I'll apply more pressure. We've got plenty of time haven't we guys?"

He turned to his colleagues, who offered smug sneers in response.

"It wis me who took it."

George's eyes widened as he turned round and looked at Billy, his casual, careless stare flanked by dirty blonde curtains.

The officer stepped off of Joe's leg and grinned. "There. That wisnae so hard now was it? Guys, get that wee scaff in the back of the car. The rest of ye can fuck off, before Ah change ma mind."

"Wis both ay us," said George.

"Well what do ye know. These little bams actually have a conscience after all. Awrite big yin, you're in the back of the car too."

"Big yin? Look who's talkin, eh." Now the sniggers weren't just coming from George and his pals.

"Got another smart arse here have we? What's your name?"

"Donaldson. George Donaldson."

George watched as the surname registered on each of their faces. Desperate Dan didn't look too fazed, but the wanker who had just been twisting his arm like it was a pipe cleaner was visibly shaken. George looked up with an empowered grin, as the visibly shaken policeman looked down at the floor, knees wobbling, shitting it. George's Dad, Douglas Donaldson was the most feared and respected figure around. From loan sharking to gambling, protection to drugs, Big Dougie had it all sewn up. When smack flushed the area at the start of the 80's, it hadn't taken long for him to seize control, solidifying his status as number one kingpin in the north side of Edinburgh. He had enforced his brutal regime on Muirhouse with such authority and conviction that every local business was now paying him protection, and it was fast becoming clear that the apple didn't fall far from the tree.

"Another bloody Donaldson. The joys. Come on, both of you little thievin bastards, shift it. NOW!"

4

The first thing that struck Billy was the size of the place. The living room was dominated by two black leather couches and a big coal fireplace. There sat Dougie with his feet up in a leather recliner, an *Evening News* splayed across his lap, while Lorraine scurried about in the kitchen. He was wearing big heavy dark brown doc martens that looked like boats and his thick gristly forearms were decorated in faded tattoos. He sat there, puffing away on a cigar, whisky in hand with seemingly not a care in the world.

"Oh hiya son! This yer wee pal that ye've told me about?" said Lorraine eagerly as she appeared from her domain. She was a plump woman with a warm, friendly demeanour, yet when Billy looked at her he saw the same fear and raw nerves that had plagued his mother for so many years. She had a pretty face, rosy cheeks, and a head of permed brunette hair. "Dougie, we've got a guest."

"Hiya pal."

"Dae ye wantae stay an have somethin tae eat wae us darlin?"

"Aw naw, Ah wouldnae want tae put ye out Mrs Donaldson." He shuffled about nervously.

"Nonsense! There's plenty tae go round. George, away an set up a place fer yer wee pal."

The rich smell that came from the oven as Lorraine Donaldson served out the plates was like nothing Billy had ever experienced in his own house. He could have sat for hours just taking in that scent.

"Dae ye like steak, Billy son?" said Dougie as he chewed on a juicy piece of meat.

"Never had steak before Mr Donaldson."

"Dougie. Call me Dougie, son. Make me feel like a bloody school teacher here. Ye need tae eat lots ay meat at this age. Git some meat on those bones ay yours."

"Dougie stop it. Ye'll give the laddie a complex."

"What? He's a growin laddie. He needs his meat. How long ye steyed in Muirhouse Billy son?"

"Just a few weeks."

"Aw aye. Where did ye stey before like?"

"Wester Hailes. Ma dad got a joab at the pipes jist along the road so we moved."

"That right? An what is it ye wantae dae yersel then? In life."

"Dunno," said Billy bashfully as he looked down at his plate. "Fireman mibbe."

"Aw aye. So ye like puttin out fires rather than startin thum?" said Dougie as Billy turned to George who had begun sniggering. It didn't take him long to work out the source of amusement, given they had lit up a pile of tyres along the railway line a few days earlier, a stunt that had drawn three fire engines.

Dougie turned to Lorraine with a confused look. "Was it somethin Ah says doll?"

"Obviously a private joke."

Once the hilarity subsided there was a comfortable silence as they began tucking into their meals. The boiled potatoes were a far cry from Angie's efforts, hard as doorstops, and the meat melted in his mouth, wasn't tough or dry, just perfect. At twelve years old Billy had never tasted anything like it. It didn't take long for the conversation to progress to Lorraine's most popular topic, Maggie Thatcher. Billy looked up at her as she droned on about the Falklands and the mining industry, the loss of jobs. It was the same tiresome talk that he endured at home, boring him half to death. He noticed George quietly giggling away next to him, before looking across the table where Dougie was pretending to fall asleep at Lorraine's side, his stubbled jaw resting against her shoulder. As Dougie pretended to snore, Billy coughed, trying his hardest not to laugh. Lorraine gave her husband a slap on the arm. "Ocht Dougie. It's important these young laddies know what they're dealin with."

Dougie threw his napkin on the table and groaned heavily. "They're young laddies doll. They wantae talk aboot fitba, Star Wars, girls. No bloody politics."

"Okay Dougie, maybe better they bury their wee heads in the sand then eh?" She stood up and began huffily gathering up plates as Dougie called after her.

"Aw come here you!"

Lorraine ignored him as he tried to grab hold of her waist, and disappeared into the kitchen. Dougie took a sip of his whisky before flashing a grin at the two young boys who were now in fits of laughter without Lorraine in the room.

"Right laddies come oan. Dinnae wantae upset yer Mother, she means well."

"It was you that started it Dad."

Dougie threw his son a steely glare that was enough to silence him in an instant.

"Anyway she's got a point. Closin down aw these factories, killin off joabs fer the workin man, raisin unemployment. Puttin the squeeze oan us so they are. It's up tae us tae take a stand. Fight tae build somethin better fer ourselves. By any means necessary at that."

Billy drained the last of his orange juice as the words rang true in his mind.

"Got nothin against folk like yer father Billy son. Good honest hardworkin folk. That's good. A man needs tae provide fer his family. It's important. Question is whether ye settle for that or strive fer more, ye know? Take risks. See how far ye can push it." Dougie shrugged his shoulders as he aimed a sly back-glance toward the kitchen. "Break the odd rule if ye need tae. Cause if ye want that wee bit extra naeone's gonnae hand it tae ye."

Dougie sat forward and clenched a sturdy fist, exposing a faded, blueish anchor above his misshapen knuckles, in order to illustrate his point as he glared at Billy. "Got tae take it."

Billy held Dougie's stern stare for several seconds. He could smell the alcohol on the gangster's breath as he took in the wicked glint in his squinting eye.

"Awrite son?" Dougie grinned widely, ruffling Billy's blonde curtained hair as Lorraine appeared at the door.

"Puddin boys?"

5

He didn't notice her till it was too late. They collided at the gate, her going one way, him the other. It was a sight that was sadly all too familiar. The red eyes stained by sobbing, cheekbone puffed and swollen. Jack had obviously been at it again. Billy wondered what the excuse was this time. Was dinner shite? Moaning too much? Was she breathing too hard? It didn't take much for him to loosen his hands. It never had. Whether it be fists, leather belt, or Jack's favourite weapon of choice, the stick, it was something Billy had been forced to accept as part of his existence since he had been old enough to walk. Yet still, it didn't make it any easier to take in the sorry sight that stood before him. Part of him felt guilty that he hadn't been around enough of late, not that it would have made the slightest bit of difference if he had been. He looked up at her, feeling the temptation to ask if she was alright before stopping short in the knowledge that the words would be empty and pointless. Then just like that she had barged past him and she was gone. Probably away to spend the night with a friend or relative who would tell her over and over that she needed to leave. And Billy knew she'd be back within a day. Part of him wanted to grab hold of her himself and scream at her to leave him.

He eased his way through the doorway, hoping he'd be able to get in and out without the old man noticing. He tiptoed down the hall and into his room to grab his striped turtle-neck sweater, the one he hated, but kept him warm all the same. It was still fairly light outside but the nights were coming in fast and he knew that it would be cold before long.

He dragged the sweater over himself before slipping out of the bedroom and back down the hallway, but froze as he reached the front door.

"BILLY!"

His head dropped and his heart sank as he loosened his hand on the door knob, contemplating pulling it open and making a bolt for it.

"Ah'm jist away oot Dad," he responded as he tightened his grip, desperately seeking an escape.

"No yet yer no. C'mere." Jack was sitting on his favourite armchair, a glass of whisky in hand and a sad twisted look on his red face. Billy couldn't tell whether it was shame, guilt, anger or a combination of different feelings.

He didn't doubt that his father might regret his actions from time to time, in quiet moments when there was time to reflect. He'd even overheard him weeping tears of embarrassment and desperation in an effort to prevent Angie from leaving him. But when it boiled down to it Billy wasn't sure what he found more difficult to take, his mother's weakness or the old man's rage.

"Where you gaun?"

"Back oot tae see ma pals."

"That right? This hoose no good enough fer ye? These meals? Ah bust ma back tae pit a roof over yer heid an food in yer belly an yet yer never bloody here anymair." Jack sat forward as his eyes darkened. Billy could tell he'd been hitting the whisky hard. It was in his voice and etched on his face. He knew he had to play his cards very carefully or it could be him getting skelped around the room next. He shuddered inside.

"It's no that... it's, it's." His voice began quivering.

"It's what? Spit it oot son. Man up!"

It's you ya evil, cowardly, wife battering Fuck. YOU.

"Mon then, out wae it! We no good enough fer ye anymore? That ye have tae run tae the Donaldsons every night? Well ken what?" Jack sat forward, slurped down the last of his whisky with his bruised and shaking hand and slammed it down on the coffee table. "Me an you are gonnae go up tae The Gunner an spend a bit quality time. Ah think it's about time I introduced masel tae yer Uncle Dougie don't you?"

The air was thick with the fog of cigarette smoke as Billy wandered into the local Muirhouse haunt, The Gunner, behind his old man. The ceiling was low, the walls had little decoration other than a few framed pictures of the pub's football team in action. There was an underlying feeling of tension and anger beneath the wisecracks and banter. It felt like his whole life had been a training ground preparing him for places like this. An elderly couple sat in silence, looking on as a grizzled, weary looking old-timer with a battered old acoustic guitar set up in the corner. Billy looked across to the other side of the pub where three laddies barely of drinking age huddled round a juke box, frantically pressing at buttons. A burly looking bartender bounded over as they entered the pub, halting Jack as he looked around.

"Nae kids in here efter seven pal."

"What's that?"

"Ah says nae kids efter seven. It's like the OK Corral in here. If a fight breaks out an he gets caught in the crossfire its ma licence they're lookin at. Either send um on his way or leave."

"Bobby." A gruff voice bellowed from behind. The bartender's stern eyes softened as he turned and saw Dougie standing there.

"They're fine."

"But Dougie, ma licence."

"Ah says, they're fine." Dougie repeated himself and held the bartender's stare, forcing him to drop his head in defeat before wandering back to the bar like a schoolboy on his way to detention. Billy looked up at Dougie's grinning face.

"Awrite Billy son. This must be yer old man Jack, that right?"

"That's right aye," said Jack as Dougie extended a hand.

"Dougie." They exchanged a firm handshake.

"Wee Billy here comes over for dinner fae time tae time don't ye son?"

"Aye so Ah hear," said Jack as Billy opened his mouth to respond.

"Ye'd think he'd never had a meal in his puff the way he wolf's doon they roasts." Dougie turned for the bar. "What's yer tipple?"

"Thanks, but we'll pay our own way." Jack smiled cheaply, as Dougie stopped and turned, with an expression that suggested he wasn't used to his offers being turned down too often. "Thanks all the same."

"Suit yerself. Billy see ye around wee man eh." Dougie threw Jack a questioning look before retreating to a spot at the bar where his associates were standing. Billy glanced across the table as Jack sipped his whisky, staring up at the bar.

"Cardboard gangster. I've eaten bams like that fer ma breakfast. Think he's tougher than yer auld man dae ye?" Billy sighed. "Not a chance ye hear me?"

"Aye Dad."

"Aye you would say that. Give it time."

Billy looked across at the old guitar player as he began plinking away at his rusty looking strings.

For a brief moment Billy lost himself as he tuned into the words of a song he was sure he had heard somewhere before. He wondered who the old bearded stranger with the sad eyes was. Wondered what he was doing singing in a pub like The Gunner. He looked around the pub as people stopped their conversations to join in with the scratchy old voice. There was a chorus coming from the bar area where Dougie Donaldson was standing.

Some of the women had a hard look about them. Three of them stood by the jukebox, wearing fed up expressions that suggested the guitar bored them, itching to get the latest hits back on. They had matching permed hair propped up with headbands, fags hanging from their lips, and large bangles dangling from their earlobes. They all chomped hard on gum as they struck fed up, cross armed poses, their brightly coloured jumpers all hanging off the one shoulder, with wide shiny black belts and leggings. They all looked so different to Angie, with her long dark skirts, and knitted jumpers. Dark, drab colours to match her sad features. Billy could only imagine what Jack would do to her if she turned up looking like these fascinating sorts. As the song drew to a close over a small chorus of claps, Billy jolted out of his daydream as Jack slammed his empty glass on the table. "Mon let's go an get a chat with Dougie. Think it's time Ah introduced maself. *Properly*."

Dougie was leaning against the bar as they approached, listening to Willie Graham, a 19-year-old loose cannon and one of Dougie's main dealers. Willie had a pair of beady eyes that bulged out of a veiny cranium, with curly hair creeping down at either side. He stood there with his foot against the back of the bar wearing a look of pure menace, his thumbs tucked behind a set of black braces as he rocked back and forth on his black steel toe capped right boot. He had on a white and black skin tight striped top that complemented his black trousers well. He looked restless, ready for action as he chewed at his lip, flashing angry glares around the bar area.

Gordon Trevor looked down and nodded at Billy as they appeared, having been introduced to him at George's once. Gordon Trevor, or Big Goggs as he was known, was Dougie's trusted enforcer. Standing at least 6 foot with a skinhead, a deformed nose, a set of broad, hulking shoulders and large spade-like hands it wasn't hard for Billy to see why as he stood there lumbering slowly in a knee length brown leather coat. Willie turned to Dougie and began jabbering away.

"So Ah wis like that tae um Dougie, where's the fuckin money!? He says, Ah've no got yer money pal, fucko! Cracked um again wae this big vase man. One ay they big thick fuckers ken? Jist wouldnae smash Ah'm tellin ye..."

Gordon nudged Willie firmly. He continued. "So Ah'm like, listen, Dougie's wantin is money, cunt. Fucko, hit um again eh…" Gordon nudged him harder still.

"Willie, we've got company ya wee faggot. A bit ay discretion eh?"

"Ah dinnae ken who they are dae Ah?"

Dougie turned as Jack stood there staring back at him.

"Listen Ah didnae wantae come across rude before. It's just Ah like tae pay ma own way ye know? Ah'll take that whisky though if the offer's still open."

"Sure. Nae problem."

After accepting his drink Jack turned to the restless stranger whose story he had interrupted. "Don't mind me son, carry on. Finish yer story."

"Nah ye killed the moment didn't ye." Willie spat on the ground and looked away with disinterest.

"So Jack Ah hear ye used tae be a boxer that right? Wee Billy wis sayin."

"Amateur champion up at Clovey, aye that's right."

"Aye so why didn't ye turn professional then? No good enough?" mouthed Willie.

"Fergive him eh. Petulance of youth an all that."

Jack smiled as he sipped back more whisky. "Ah've seen ye in here before, as I blended intae the background in a corner somewhere." There was a pause as they applauded another song, the old stranger wiping some ale from his beard as Billy arched his head round. "Of course you wouldn't notice a nobody like me would ye?"

Dougie turned to the barman.

"Bobby get this poor bugger another whisky will ye? Dinnae be so hard oan yersel Jack."

"Ach well seein as ye are all in such a story-telling mood. Ah've got a story fer ye."

"Ach hit the road Jack eh?" Willie's laughter was silenced in a heartbeat by the back of Dougie's hand stopping an inch from his jaw.

He coiled back as Dougie daggered him. "Go'n then Jack, tell us a story."

"Well there's this guy. He stayed up at Wester Hailes. Was a bit of a name up that way. Folk knew not tae fuck aboot. Then all of a sudden he gets a job, has tae uproot his family an leave fer the money. So he moves tae Muirhouse.

Nobody knows who he is, he carries on goin aboot his daily job. Meanwhile his son strikes up a friendship. Starts spendin mair an mair time oot the hoose. Tae the point where the poor guy starts wondering whether beneath it all, his own cunt son is startin tae look up tae his friend's faither wae mair respect than he does his own. So it's round about this time that the man in question realises that life's gotten boring. An he's no longer interested in just blending intae the background. Realises that if he's gonnae get some proper respect fer himself in this new area, he's gonnae have tae go right tae the front ay the line, and earn it." Jack fixed a stare on Dougie as he clenched his fists.

Billy felt dizzy as he looked up to see Willie Graham edging forward clutching an empty bottle and Gordon Trevor standing there, arms crossed.

Dougie smiled as he took a long draw from his cigarette. "Is that right."

"Aye."

Billy watched as a smiling Dougie stubbed his fag out in the heavy ashtray and barely had time to blink before the same ashtray came crashing into his father's face, tiny bits of glass flying everywhere. His heart skipped a beat as Dougie brought the ashtray crashing down on the top of Jack's head with all his might, forcing his knees to buckle. As he crumpled to the floor an eager Willie Graham tore in from the side and unleashed a dull boot to the face, bursting Jack's mouth wide open as a string of blood and saliva sprayed the pub floor.

Billy looked down at the sorry state before him. He wanted to feel sympathy, he wanted to feel anger, but all he felt was satisfaction. Satisfaction at seeing him on the receiving end for once, forced into the same pathetic beaten state both him and his poor Mum had been forced into so many times. He felt a smile forcing itself at the corners of his mouth as Willie Graham shattered an empty beer bottle over the back of Jack's head, before putting the toes to him with venom as Billy felt the urge to lay one in himself.

"Thought ye were a fuckin boxer? Should have seen that ashtray comin then eh?" said Dougie before grabbing Willie Graham and dragging him back toward the bar. He pulled a cigarette from his packet, stuck it between his teeth and lit it before turning to Gordon Trevor. "Goggs get that shite out of ma pub will ye?"

Billy stared on as Gordon Trevor hoisted his beaten, bloodied father up off the ground and rammed him head-first through the doorway. He turned and locked eyes with Dougie who looked down on him, his face clouded by smoke.

"Well? What ye waitin fer!? Go on follow yer father. OUT! An don't come back tae my house cause yer not fucking welcome anymore! What's happened tae the bloody music anyway!?"

As Billy turned to leave he caught the eye of the old guitar player who had begun strumming again with shaky hands.

4 Years Later...

6

They stood over him, bewildered.

"Is he deid?" said Joe, prodding at the lad's limp body with his foot.

As Billy looked down he saw the muddy Stanley blade lying just inches from Craig MacDonald's hand. George had wiped him out with the golf club before he had had the chance to use it. He turned and offered his pal a nod of recognition for saving him from a tan down the face, but George was too busy prodding at the boy himself with that same four iron, checking for signs of life.

"He's jist knocked oot," said George, kneeling to turn him over.

The day had turned into a whirlwind from the moment the final bell had sounded on the final day of fourth year. School was out and neither Billy, George, Joe or Jimmy had any intention of returning. Between them they had racked up more detentions and referrals than the rest of the year combined and had been hanging on by the skin of their teeth since first year. A few bottles of cheap cider, copious amounts of glue fumes and a few joints later and they had found themselves at Craigroyston playing field, high as kites, along with the rest of the Muirhousers, doing battle with a mob from neighbouring Pilton. Now, however, the whirlwind had been dragged kicking and screaming to a halt as members of the two mobs gathered round Craig MacDonald, who lay unconscious on the floor with a hefty lump on the side of his head. MacDonald was the youngest member of a notorious family from Pilton, so reprisals were inevitable.

Billy stopped and stared through bleary blue eyes as a clapped out grey Lada swerved toward the shopping centre later that afternoon. It nearly collided with a railing as it ground to a halt, forcing a group of young lassies to scatter amidst frightened screams. He tried his hardest to focus as the car door swung open. His eyesight was blurred and hazy, leaving tracing shadows behind all figures and objects. He pulled a thin Stanley of his own from his backtail and extended the blade as a furious Kevin MacDonald approached, followed by two bat-wielding friends.

Billy steamed forward, thrusting his blade, but his co-ordination was completely gone. He didn't feel the first blow as it bounced off his head, and as soon as the second blow struck the lights were out. He came to, in what seemed like seconds later, and looked up to the sight of Kevin MacDonald swaggering back to the motor followed by his two grinning friends. Mac-Donald turned to point a dagger-like finger at George, who stood there puffing and panting, blood spilling from a fat lip and a cut above his eye.

"That's for Craig ya cunt! Next time I'll get ye somewhere where there's nae witnesses ya fat wee bastard, do ye proper. Young Pilton Derry ya wee cunts!"

7

Sean Donaldson grinned as he checked himself out in the side window, admiring his chiselled jawline as he pulled up slowly at the side of The Gunner.

"Lookin good san." he said to himself cockily as he pulled a small coke filled vial from his shirt pocket, unscrewed the top and tipped some onto the side of his knuckle. It felt good getting his hands on gear reserved for the privileged, out of reach for the cunts on the streets. Came direct from the top boy in Glasgow who his Uncle got his drugs from and it didn't come cheap. He tipped his head back after sniffing it up in one go, wondering what the occasion was that had prompted Dougie to demand everyone be at The Gunner for seven on the dot that evening. Sean had sold the last of that week's swag earlier that day so he could finally relax. The Ted Baker polo tops had sold like hot cakes and the Ralph Lauren Harringtons were always in heavy demand. The best fakes in Edinburgh that was for sure, a great little earner on top of the hash and speed, and as long as the big man was cut in he could charge whatever he saw fit. It was a win-win situation as he got them every week off the back of a lorry at such a good price that at fifteen quid a pop for the polos, tenner for the tees, and thirty for the coats, he was guaranteed a tidy profit. Folk were happy to pay, knowing that the real deal was way over the budget for most, and besides, when it came down to it who could tell the difference? Might end up shrinking after a few washes. That yellow might fade to an off-white colour after a while, but by that point hopefully they'd have the dough to top up the collection. Of course he would always hold back a few freebies for the boys every week.

When it came to his own dress sense, Sean fashioned himself like he was a proper businessman. Suits. Long overcoats. Cufflinks. The works. Often he was the butt of the jokes for this bold dress sense, especially for a young man who had just turned twenty-three, but he didn't care. *Godfather 2* was his all-time favourite film and the birds lapped it up, the ones that were dizzy enough to fall for his charms, that is. It enabled him to create a persona for himself that set him apart from his more rough-edged partners in crime. Even the police had caught onto it, greeting him sarcastically as the young Al Pacino when they turned up to search his flat, a comment that planted a grin on his mug for close to a week. To Sean's friends, however, his nickname was Preemo. The handle had came about from his insistence on labelling everything he deemed to be of high quality whether it be women, clothes or coke, Preemo.

Sean bounded into The Gunner with a spring in his step, still grinning from ear to ear over last night's ride, getting a semi just at the thought of it. "Why the long faces, has someone died?" he joked, pulling several tops out of a Safeway's bag. "Right ladies, take yer pick." As Willie eagerly rummaged through the freebies, Sean grabbed a beige cardigan and lobbed it at Bob Callum.

Bob was a close confidante of Dougie's. The two had known each other since high school and it was this trust that had led Dougie to place Bob in charge of the bookies when he had taken it over a year earlier. Bob was a bulbous red-faced man with a pot belly. A man of simple pleasures.

"There ye go Bobby, double XXL just fer you big man!"

Sean hadn't noticed Dougie as he appeared behind him flanked by Gordon Trevor.

"What the fuck's goin on here?"

"There Uncle Dougie, try that on fer size."

Dougie snatched the jacket and stuffed it back in the Safeway's bag before doing the same with Willie's. "Now's no the time fer fucking fashion parades. Yer cousin was attacked at the shopping centre the day by Kevin MacDonald. We think we might know where the little cunt's holed up so time tae strike while the iron's hot."

Sean shuddered as Ryan Lockhart ghosted into the pack, grinning at him deviously.

As Sean pulled his car into Boswell Terrace with Dougie in the passenger seat glaring into space and big Goggs and Ryan in the back, he felt the sweat seep into his shirt collar. Perhaps now he was twenty-three, Dougie felt it was time he cut his teeth with the darker side of the operation, prove that he could fully live up to his father Davy's shadow as he sat in his Barlinnie cell. Truth was, Sean saw himself as more of a lover than a fighter. His charismatic charm, slick, dark brown hair, sharp jawline and intense, hazel eyes gave him license to change his birds like the weather, and it wasn't unusual for him to have at least three or four on the go at any one time. As he sat there trying to loosen his top button enough to draw breath, the coke making him all the more agitated, last night's ride suddenly seemed months ago. That semi was now inverted.

The only sound in the street was the voice of Tim Booth booming out of the third floor flat window as they exited the motor followed by Willie. Dougie barked at Bob to stay put and keep watch as he led the pack across the road. Sean could feel the butterflies buzzing around his stomach as they approached the service door. Normally coke made him feel confident, ready to face the world, but right at that moment it seemed to be having the opposite effect. He nearly jumped out of his skin as Willie Graham jumped on his back and shouted in his ear.

Dougie turned, jammed a finger against his lips and ordered Willie to the buzzer, his eyes wild. His pal's encouragement had produced the desired effect, shaking Sean out of his frantic state. He took a deep breath and focused.

You're the man Sean. You're the fucking man. You can handle this.

The door swung open and the pale-faced stranger appeared to shrink into his own body at the sight of the entourage that stood before him.

"Look like ye've seen a ghost pal. What's wrong wae ye?"

"N-nowt Willie."

"Brought a few friends. Dinnae mind do ye? Would've said but Ah knew fine well ye wouldnae have buzzed me up if Ah had."

It was a sparsely decorated flat with a Bob Marley poster on one wall and several Playboy centrefolds pinned up on the other. The charcoal carpet was covered in fag burns and hot rock holes, not to mention tobacco, empty cans, skins and lighters. Willie Graham swaggered into the middle of the room and pointed at a picture of a blonde Playboy model on all fours with a large grin on her face, as Jamison turned his speakers down to a murmur with a trembling hand. "Check the fuckin erse oan that by the way." He turned and raised his eyebrows at Jamison. "Bet ye hud a few ham shanks over her when ye were inside ya cunt!"

Aye an wae a room like this that's the only action this cunt's getting...

"Aw aye what's this then?" Graham pointed to a pile of base speed sitting on a record case in the corner of the room, the crystals scattered across the cardboard.

"Ye dinnae mind do ye Ray?"

"Naw Willie. Go right ahead." Jamison's face dropped as Willie proceeded to dab away at the base, smothering his gums with it till there was none left.

Sean glanced at his uncle who looked close to losing patience with the pleasantries. It was clear as he looked around the room that there was no sign of Kevin MacDonald, just Ray Jamison the speed freak and two shifty looking lads sitting on the edge of a bed. One was gnawing away at his knuckles the other was rubbing his hands together with discomfort. Both were wearing matching Lacoste jumpers that had no doubt originated from his counterfeit ring. He smirked to himself as he pondered how he had transformed the fashion sense of the local headcase and nutter. Suddenly, everyone was dressing like they were football casuals or mods. Everyone except Sean that is, he had a style all of his own, that was the way he liked it.

"Need tae calm doon oan this shit man. Yer lookin like a zombie! Aw skin an bones." Willie looked Ray up and down with disdain before grabbing an opened bottle of beer and swigging it till there was none left. He burped loudly before wiping his mouth with his sleeve and casually dropping the empty beer bottle on the carpet. "Kevin MacDonald, Ray. Been hearin he's been comin doon here quite a bit since he got oot. Would that be right son?" He locked his hands behind his back before fixing a stare on him.

"Who? Kev? Naw." Jamison shook his head nervously. "Seen a bit of um when Ah wis in the jail. That wis it. Seen um aboot once since ees been oot. Bit of a radge. Ah try an avoid um."

"Funny how ye refer tae um as Kev, an no Kevin. Ye must be friendly wae the cunt?" Goggs shifted restlessly.

"Wouldnae lie tae me would ye Ray?"

"Naw Willie of course no. Ah've known ye fer years man. Why would Ah do that?"

"What dae ye ken aboot the scrap at Pennywell shops earlier the day?"

"Ah dinnae ken anythin about that Willie, honestly."

"Laddie's talkin shite Dougie. Ah can read um like a book," sneered Lockhart as Dougie stood silently, eyes switching their way around the room like they were set to a timer.

"How about these two? No fuckin sayin much ur they?" said Goggs through gritted teeth. "Where are you two fae then?"

"Pilton," replied one of them.

"Aw aye, that's fuckin interestin. What dae yous ken aboot Kev's where-abouts?"

"Fuck all," he replied defensively while his friend stared down at the floor, his whole body shaking with fear.

"What wis that? An look me in the eye this time."

He sat up straight, looked him straight in the eye and responded twice as defensively. "Ah said fuck all. Ah dinnae ken where he is awright? Fuck all tae dae wae me anywey."

Sean cringed, knowing fine well what came next.

"We got a cowboy here have we? Some balls on you son. Shouldae taken a leaf ootae yer pal's book an kept yer wee gub shut." Goggs pulled a wooden bat from the back of his jeans and prodded it against the young man's chin. His speed-fuelled courage appeared to evaporate in seconds. He raised his hands, pleading for mercy.

Sean began to feel the adrenaline pumping in his veins.

"Look, Ah dinnae want any trouble Ah..."

"How many of thum were there the day Willie?" Goggs asked, not for a second taking his eyes off the youth.

"Three or four Ah think."

"Three or four aye? Well Ah dinnae like the look ay this mouthy wee bam sittin oan the bed."

"Ah-Ah've got fuck all tae dae wae this."

"Aw aye. Is yer arse fallin oot now ye ken we're fuckin serious is it? Shoul-dae known tae begin wae shouldn't ye. You cunts like tae hit young laddies in the heids wae sticks dae ye?"

"Wisnae me, Ah swear!"

Sean glanced around at the faces in the room that were all fixed on the boy who had been crazy enough to try and mouth off to big Gordon Trevor.

"Do um Goggs!" barked Lockhart, with spittle flying from his mouth.

"Ah'm gonnae gie you one chance tae redeem yersel ya little cunt. You tell me where Kevin MacDonald's holed up an Ah might consider givin ye a pass. Now, what's that? Ah cannae hear ye!"

A few seconds hesitancy was all it took for Goggs to rattle him on the side of the head. His temple burst open as he slumped sideways onto his friend who started shrieking in shock as blood spilled onto his stonewash jeans.

"Too late!" Goggs grabbed the knocked-out Piltoner and yanked him off his friend, dumping him onto the floor as Ryan Lockhart dropped to his knees and stared up at the other one who looked like he was having serious trouble breathing.

"What about you, Princess?" Lockhart grabbed the boy's chin and thrust his tear soaked face upwards. "Anythin tae proclaim?"

"Ah'm beggin ye. Ah dinnae ken anythin..."

Lockhart sat back before launching himself at the terrified youth with a powerful head butt clean on the nose. A sickly snapping sounded as he fell back onto the bed clutching his face. Within seconds Lockhart was on his feet, dancing back and forth on his tiptoes with a Samurai sword which he aimed in the direction of the broken nosed lad.

"Please Willie make thum stop! We've no done nowt! We dinnae ken where Kevin is!" shrieked Ray Jamison, before finding himself shoved up against the window by the scruff of his neck by Dougie, whose eyes were now bulging with rage. He pulled a machete out of his leather coat and forced it up against Jamison's groin area.

"Either you deliver that prick tae me oan a silver fuckin platter, or Ah'll cut your fuckin balls off right here! Ye hear me?"

Sean couldn't tear his eyes away. His body throbbed with excitement.

"Someone open that FUCKIN WINDAE!"

Sean bounded forward, and snapped open the latch. The large window swung open and in a moment a petrified Ray Jamison was hanging out of it, Dougie's bear-like grip the only thing stopping him from a fall three floors down.

"Ah'm gonnae gie ye five seconds tae spill the beans or yer oot this fuckin windae. One! TWO!"

Sean noticed him trying to mouth something but the words weren't coming out. He grabbed a handful of hair and yanked his head upwards.

"The cupboard. He's hidin in the cupboard. Please just do um an let me go. It's nowt tae dae wae me, honest."

After finding nothing but an empty cupboard, Sean burst through the door at the urging of his Uncle with Willie close behind. His legs could barely carry him as they clambered down the stairs frantically, the adrenaline and cocaine flowing in his system, the paranoia having vanished. After Willie flung the door open at the back of the stair they searched amidst the nettles, litter and weeds, wondering if he had taken toes through the gardens at the back, but neither was prepared to go on a chicken run through the angry looking overgrowth to find out. As they swaggered out the front Sean stood still as he heard a yell from above. The sickening thud that followed was muffled only by the hedge and the damp grass. Sean held his breath as the limp body slumped half into view.

"Oh ya cunt ye," said Willie as he crept forward, halted only by Sean's wary hand. As Sean looked up he caught sight of Dougie staring down on them grimly. The search was over before it had even begun. It was time to get out of dodge – and fast.

8

Sean brushed away the coke residue from his dashboard as he emerged in the eerily quiet Western General car park. He was honoured Uncle Dougie had tasked him with this latest role, seeing it as a sign that bit by bit he was being trusted with more responsibility within the firm.

After checking his Rolex, Sean tensed up, fidgeting in the agonisingly slow lift as it crept its way up to the correct floor. Dougie had stressed he needed to be there for seven on the dot as any wandering doctors might grow suspicious if he turned up after visiting time, and it was now creeping on for ten past. He inhaled the dank hospital smell and strode purposely down the hallway towards Ray Jamison's hospital room. Ronnie Slater, Dougie's bent scum, eyeballed him angrily as he appeared, tapping frantically at his own watch as Sean slipped inside the doorway.

The ironic thing, Sean thought to himself, as he stepped up to the hospital bed, was that Ray Jamison actually looked healthier than he had done when he'd appeared at his flat door a couple of weeks earlier. Less speed, more food, Sean deduced as he grabbed an apple from his bedside table and took a large chomp.

Jamison's eyes began to flicker open as Sean chomped harder and harder.

"Awright Ray."

As soon as Jamison opened his eyes fully he opened his mouth to scream, halted only by Sean's hand, which he clasped firmly around his mouth, jamming a finger against his lips as he took in the panic in his eyes.

Sean clenched a fist and aimed it at his face, grabbed a chair, dragged it across the floor and took a seat right in front of him.

"How the fuck did you get in here? There's police outside."

"Aye funny that eh? How ye holdin up anyway? How's the back?"

"Ah could be in a wheelchair fer the rest of ma life. Ah'm twenty-five year auld."

"Aye well ye've got Kevin MacDonald tae blame fer that, no Dougie, awright?"

"He threw me oot a windae. Look Ah need tae sleep."

"Plenty time fer sleep Ray. Yer in hospital, all ye do is sleep. A bit of stimulatin conversation won't do ye any harm eh? Besides there's somethin Ah need tae talk tae ye aboot. Word on the street is you're thinkin about goin up in court against a man you really shouldnae be testifyin against."

His face drained of all colour as the gravity clearly set in.

"Look, what happened was an unfortunate occurrence indeed. My uncle's got a temper, what can Ah say."

"Please, Ah'm tired." bleated Ray. "Ah cannae cope wae this. Leave me alone please."

Sean sat forward, rapidly losing patience. "Ah'm no going anywhere until you give me the answer Ah'm after. Do you think the polis give a fuck about you? They couldnae care less whether you walk or no, as long as they get what they want. You're just a fuckin pawn tae them ye ken that? Ye might think they're after yer best interests, ye might think they're tryin tae help ye but yer wrong. You ever thought about what happens afterwards? We're no in America pal an Ah cannae see you gaun intae the witness protection programme. An that's what they'll have tae dae tae protect ye. If Dougie was tae go doon dae ye think we're just gonnae crawl under a rock and ferget this ever happened? Do you really want tae spend the rest of yer life lookin over yer shoulder, paranoid? That's if you even make it tae the trial. Dougie can get you just as easily in here as he can out there." Sean snapped his fingers. "Have yer lights turned out. Have you thrown outae this fuckin windae tae. This isnae some run of the mill joker you're dealin wae son. This is a heavy fuckin guy, a major player in this city. Do you think he's gonnae let you or anyone else jeopardise his business?"

Sean sat back in his chair, calming down on the hard press. "Look, Ah'm the nice guy awright? Ah'm the nicest guy yer gonnae meet, believe me it gets worse. Ye were in the wrong place at the wrong time. If Dougie could turn back the clock an dae things differently he would, but he cannae. What's done is done. Ye've just got tae make the best of the cards ye've been dealt. Ye see this?" Sean pulled a small powder-filled vial from his top pocket. "Top quality cocaine straight off the rock, preemo gear, rare as fuck. Beats that base ye've been takin." Sean grinned. "That can be yours. All the best gear, all the best clothes. You name it, Dougie will look after ye. I'll look after ye. We'll even help pay fer yer back treatment, get ye back on yer feet again. Make sure no-one fucks wae ye. All ye need tae do is tell the police ye've had a big change of heart."

Sean adjusted his collar as he entered The Gunner that night, before wading through the heavy handshakes and pats on the back as he felt a chuffed smirk pushing at the corners of his mouth. The man of the moment it appeared. He accepted a pint from Gordon Trevor before finding himself synched into a powerful headlock from the big Frankenstein bastard. He surfaced, with gritted teeth, to the sight of his best mucker Willie Graham grinning like a maniac with two shots lined up.

The place was rammed for a change. It felt like the regulars were filtering back in now that the firm were back in good spirits. They could relax and breathe easy without the frightening prospect of an angry, unpredictable Dougie/Goggs combo hanging off the end of the bar like timebombs ready to go off in everyone's face. The mood had changed, for now at least. That, and it was karaoke night. Big Agnes was belting out Sweet Caroline, her many chins wobbling, prompting Sean to spit a mouthful of beer out in laughter as Willie dug him in the ribs and laughed along. Even the young team were there in force, making a nuisance of themselves, hassling the older crowd for pints and vodkas, their shifty eyes darting around for fear of getting collared and flung out onto the freezing streets. Still, it was just the same old Gunner, Sean thought to himself as he threw back his shot and took a swig of his pint. Same old Gunner, nothing new. He scanned the vicinity, and quickly realised there was nothing worth taking home, not by a long shot. This meant town would fast be beckoning. Buster Browns, bright lights, cheesy Wham hits, peroxide blondes in their tacky outfits, cheap and nasty glamour. All ended one way and that was with Sean battering his end away in triumph, sweat dripping from his clenched jaw as he went at it like a sewing machine.

"Few drinks tae be polite then we're up that toon Willie mate, fuck this. Fuckin auld guys' boozer man, what action we gonnae get in here? Besides some dirty fae the scheme."

Willie looked about before leaning in close.

"Sort me oot wae a line ay yer gear, an Ah'll take a dirty fae the scheme all night long Preemo."

Sean smiled.

"Aye an then a trip up the gum clinic oan Monday tae check the damage."

A couple of minutes later they were holding down their favourite cubicle as Sean tipped a pile of coke onto the cistern and began swiping out the rock-stars.

Suddenly there was a loud slapping at the door, forcing Sean to instinctively throw a barrier around his precious gear.

"Hey! Who's in there?" Sean rolled his eyes.

"George, what ye wantin?"

"What ye's up tae?"

"Grown-up shit, nowt fer you tae worry about."

"Let us in."

"Away an hassle someone else George, come oan eh?"

"Just let us in."

Sean lost his patience and flung the door open to reveal George and his pal Billy poking their noses into the cubicle with curiosity. Willie gave George a light skelp on the back of the head.

"Beat it ya wee cunt."

"What ye's wantin? There's nowt fer ye in here," said Sean.

George tried to edge his head in to see what they were doing, just to feel it being pushed backwards by his cousin's hand.

"What ye daein Sean?"

"Like Ah says George, grown-up shit, nothin you can afford anyway. No fer a good few years."

"Here ya wee cunt." Willie handed him a barely touched pint of Tennent's. "Make do wae that ya nippy wee bastard."

George grinned as he began necking the pint, halted only by his pal Billy as he yanked it from his hand mid swig, forcing some of it to spill on the toilet floor as they both started giggling.

Sean slammed the toilet door shut and directed his attention back to the coke, swiping out another couple of lines with his bank card. As he did so he was distracted by the noise of taps running and the sound of more childish giggling outside the cubicle.

Two seconds later a soaked ball of toilet paper smacked against the wall just above, forcing them to duck for cover. By the time Willie had opened the door to chase after them, they had scurried back into the pub.

"Wee fannies eh?" said Willie between sniggers as Sean pointed down at his tracksuit with a confused look on his face.

"Anyway what's this all about man? Fuckin tracksuits an that, it's a night oot, no a game ay five a sides."

"Hey dinnae knock this man. This is a proper original Adidas tracksuit man, fuckin quality gear."

"Ye started coachin like?"

Willie grabbed hold of Sean's suit jacket. "Ye gaun tae a weddin?"

"Ah've a wardrobe of suits even better than this one in the hoose. Ah'll hook ye up mate." Sean sniggered before eagerly rolling up a twenty and snorting his line.

"Cunt dae ye think Ah want your cheap shite eh? Least this is proper authentic shit, know what Ah mean? No a fuckin garden rake!" sneered Willie as he snatched the note. As Willie bowed his head to take the line there was another thump at the door, this time heavier.

"Fer fuck sake, what now?" groaned Sean with frustration.

"Sean, your uncle's wantin ye through the back, pronto," said Bob Callum.

"Sounds serious," joked Willie as he wiped the powder away from his nose.

Sean felt a palpable state of anxiety descend on his gut as he stood watching a grim faced Dougie, a glass of whisky clenched tightly in his hand as he drummed a fist on his left thigh.

Lighten up Uncle Dougie, fuck sake. Only saved yer bacon...

Dougie poured more alcohol onto the degrading rocks of ice sitting at the bottom of his glass. "Enjoyin yerself are ye?"

Dougie smiled dangerously. "Ye swagger in here like yer a big shot, lappin up aw that praise, but nobody realises that you could have cocked up the whole fuckin thing."

"Eh? Everything's sorted is it no?"

"Ah told you tae be in that hospital at seven on the dot. Ronnie Slater says you turned up at twenty past wae yer eyes poppin oot yer heid!" Dougie smashed the tumbler hard on the ground, Sean jolted backwards, pressing his clammy palms hard against the keg as his heart thumped against the buttons of his shirt. "Call that sorted, son? Cause Ah fuckin dinnae! Now Ah've got tae work hard on that cunt tae git um back oan side! Fuckin gettin right cauld feet! Your father, my brother, is currently serving fifteen fuckin years in Barlinnie. Do you want me tae end up in the tin pale an aw!?" He rose with menace, as Sean felt his insides gripped with terror. "You'd better pray that none ay the hospital staff reports that they saw someone walk in aboot twenty minutes efter visitin hours. You better pray that this shit doesnae go south, cause if it does, if I get fucked up all because you had better things tae dae than get through those doors at the time I told you to, you'll be dealt with, family or no fuckin family. Think yer a big man jumpin aboot flashin the cash, takin aw that ching? Dinnae forget Ah'm the one who makes aw this possible! The money, the drugs, the birds, Ah'm the one who lines they pockets, ME!"

"Ah-ah know that Uncle Dougie," stuttered Sean.

"If it wisnae fer me ye'd be just like the rest of thum. A lowlife scumbag, hangin aboot street corners, you and fuckin Willie! Takin smack every day, an stealin off yer ain!"

Sean felt himself flinch as Dougie stepped forward and placed his hands on his shoulders, looking him square in the eye. "You've got a clever head on those shoulders, use it."

"Aye Uncle Dougie. Ah will. Ah promise..."

"Ah cannae have unreliable people behind me. Stakes are too high son."

"Nae mair fuck ups Uncle Dougie, ye can count on me, ah promise."

Dougie stared through him with stony eyes, before easing off to Sean's relief.

"Sit."

Sean sat down with caution, unnerved at Dougie's switch like changing of the guard. After Dougie took a swig from the bottle of whisky he passed it to Sean who glugged it back graciously, feeling it ease his paranoia some.

"Been speakin tae John Spencer over the last few days. Turns out there's a hefty shipment of Pakistani Smack comin intae Scotland. Far purer than the pharmaceutical shite we're used tae gettin. Johns gettin edgy about lookin af-ter so much ay it fer any longer than he needs tae, wants tae get it offloaded quick." Dougie sat forward. "A far stronger product, at a seriously knocked down price Sean. This is a fucking goldmine." Sean watched Dougie's greedy eyes mulling over the profits at stake, as he wondered why he was being made privy to such high level chat.

"We can't hang about an risk missin the boat though. Ah want you an Willie tae go an pick it up an bring it through." Sean gulped.

"An Ah want ye both tae run the distribution."

"Both of us?"

"Aye. Its time tae move ye up son. Willie knows how tae cut the stuff and handle the dealers, easy enough fer ye tae pick it up but there's gonnae be far too much ay it fer him tae handle on is own. An Ah don't trust a Lockhart wae that kindae weight. So that's why Ah've decided tae bring you in. Ye's can run it together."

"Ah-Ah dinnae ken what tae say."

"How about, *aye*?"

"Of course Uncle Dougie. Like Ah says ye can count on me."

"Good. Now what ye waitin fer, git yer arse through there. Have a drink. Enjoy yerself." Dougie grinned. "You's have got somethin tae celebrate as well now."

9

The jagged black fabric scratched and rubbed at Billy's face as he pulled the balaclava over his head in the back of a rusty old van at the back of Pilton AstroTurf. They had made a united decision that the balaclavas were necessary, given the fact there would be at least nine witnesses on that pitch, and anyway they hadn't cost a bolt. Joe Harrison had managed to conceal them within his Reebok hoodie, with the dopey old shop tender at Leith Army Store none the wiser earlier that day.

Billy had been as surprised as the rest of the young team when Kevin MacDonald had resurfaced, swaggering about Pilton, boasting about his conquest a month earlier. Well there were no glue fumes, or merrydown to confuse matters this time around. Billy was stone cold sober, as was George and everyone else in that van, with nothing but adrenaline, nerves, and the thought of revenge to spur them on, on MacDonald's own turf as well.

As they took to the pitch Billy clocked him amidst the shouts and screams. He was doubled over, coughing up phlegm, and mopping sweat from his brow as they darted towards him. Billy's vision was just fine this time around. All he could see was one Kevin MacDonald, not two or three, as the terrified Piltoner tried in vain to pull his broad frame up the fencing, with all colour draining from his panicked features. Billy plunged him as hard as he could right in the arse, and by the time he had been dragged down to the Astroturf by his hair he had been sliced down his arms, under his armpit, and down his two calves as they circled him like a group of small piranhas, taking pieces at will.

Billy stood, poised, as George prised open Macdonald's arms with force, before crouching over him and slashing him right down his face as he kicked and struggled in vain. MacDonald's demented girlfriend screamed her lungs out from the sidelines as they slowly calmed their assault. He turned onto his side, writhing about, his ripped old *Stranglers* T-shirt now drenched in blood as his teeth gnashed in the night air, with condensation coming in bursts.

Wee Jimmy Thomson stepped up to the fencing and pushed his face against it, aiming a cold stare through the mesh at Kevin MacDonald's distraught girlfriend, silencing her in an instant, the screams replaced by silent terror.

As they turned to leave, Billy looked about the pitch for any sign of the rest of the two teams, but there was none, with a streak of vomit and the scattered contents of an Umbro sports bag the only things left of them.

They banged their fists against the side of the van, denting it as hard as they could in unified glory as Danny Walker drove it away from the crime scene. Word soon got out that the Muirhouse young team were coming of age.

Another 4 years later...

10

Billy could barely make out any blue in and around his black pupils in the mirror behind the optics as he muscled in to the front of the bar and demanded a round at Carbolic Frolic. He cringed as Vanilla Ice came on the speakers, before cringing some more as he took in the sight of several boys dancing about in their massive, baggy jeans and tie-dye tops like complete fannies. They had no grit, no balls. They wouldn't dare set foot anywhere near Pennywell Shopping Centre on a Saturday night, or even a Tuesday afternoon for that matter. They were fresh faced, sheltered and untouched by the hardships of life. As Billy turned back to the mirror behind the optics he took in his own sharp features. Intense, fierce, hardened, as he swept back his blonde curtained hair and felt the hairs on the back of his neck beginning to stand on end from the speed. Mummy and Daddy would no doubt pay for their college fees, their houses, then later on their weddings too, but Mummy and Daddy wouldn't buy them the gold chains that hung round his neck, resting loosely against a skin-tight Calvin Klein T-shirt that showed more style than any of those phantoms could shake a stick at.

It was 1991 and fashion was changing rapidly, but Billy's stayed the same. Smart, tight fitting Levis, none of these baggy jeans, and smart, simple, well made designer shirts and T-shirts all the way. The base he had gubbed half an hour earlier was coming on strong and by the time the barman came back with two pints and two vodka and cokes he was bobbing his own head to Ice Ice Baby as his leg rattled away, his jaw chomping with force at the three Wrigley's he had stuffed in his mouth moments earlier. He nodded his head at the barman with a hint of aggro as he gathered up the round and barged his way through the crowd to the edge of the dance floor.

George had barely noticed him as he approached. He was standing there fixated on the huge tits of Lucy, a red-headed nurse who looked like she would give you a diddy ride you'd never forget. As Billy handed out the drinks he turned to his own focus for the night, Cherie, an office bird in a sleek backless dress, with blood red lipstick, a devilish smile and frizzy blonde hair. What a body.

"There ye go gorgeous."

"Better no be spiked." She flashed a cheeky grin and he grinned back as he sipped his pint.

"Nae need fer that is there?"

"Awfully sure of yerself you eh?"

Billy laughed as he took in the strobes that were sending the rushes up the back of his neck into overdrive. Wouldn't be sleeping tonight, that was for sure. He checked his watch anxiously, wondering where the rest of the cavalry was. The job should have been done and dusted by now and he was down to his last fiver. He realised he needed a cash injection, and fast. She didn't look the type to hang around for long otherwise.

"So what is it ye said ye did again?"

"Construction. Me and George run our own firm. Set up jobs all around Edinburgh, eh. Got a couple of our boys comin along any moment. They've been on a joab the night just along the road."

"Aw aye doin what?"

The job Billy was talking about was the mugging of a known high roller who had been taking thousands on a weekly basis in the casino just off Lothian Road. It was a casino they had been scoping out for a couple of weeks and by now they knew roughly what time he would leave and what route he would take home. It was just another of many ploys to make money from one week to the next. Wee Jimmy practically lived off stolen credit and switch card details. Joe had a line on pirate videos that proved popular in the local boozers till he was kicked out for violating the instructions on everyone's latest hired tape cassette. Billy's strength lay in the planning and delivery of house and shop break-ins. George on the other hand split his time between collecting debts for his old man and getting up to this and that with the rest of the Muirhousers. Between the lot of them there was always some kind of scheme in the pipeline.

As Billy moved in for the kill, having softened her up with his relentless speed-fuelled chat, wee Jimmy appeared out of nowhere, puffing and panting, his freckled forehead red with sweat. The moment was ruined.

"Ye fancy giein us a minute?"

"There's been a problem," said Jimmy.

"Eh?"

"We tried tae catch the cunt but he wis too fuckin fast."

Billy pushed a confused looking Cherie with a tweak of her arse before taking Jimmy to the side, where a frantic looking Joe was already explaining to George.

"Dinnae tell me yous fucked it up?" said Billy, prompting Joe to stop in his tracks. They looked at one another before looking sheepishly back at Billy and George. Billy threw his head upwards, staring at the ceiling in disbelief as the implications of the fuck-up sank in.

"Ah'm tryin tae get a ride here, Ah'm doon tae ma last fuckin fiver. Ah wis countin on that fuckin dough!"

"Me too," George said as he stamped his heavy size ten with frustration.

"Aye awrite fer yous, sittin in here bevyin on while we dae the dirty work eh?" said Joe bitterly.

"It wis a two man joab, ye said it yersel! This was yours Joe, yours an Jimmy's, an yous would ay taken the lion's share an all. But now there's fuck all fer any cunt. Fuck!"

"Cunt how dae ye think Ah feel? Ah would have been doon at the pro's right now gettin ma welt sooked. Instead Ah'm standin here without a bolt, starin at yous cunts," said Jimmy.

Billy glanced over at Cherie and Lucy, who appeared to be growing restless.

"Fuck it." He swaggered over, riding on an impulse that was bulging as heavily as what was inside his pants. By the time he surfaced after whispering in her ear, she had an expression on her face that suggested she wasn't impressed.

"Do you think I'm some kind of tart?"

He laughed out loud. "Only windin ye up darlin."

She smiled. "Get us another drink and we'll see."

"BILLY!" He turned his head as he heard Jimmy's yell. By the time he bounced back over to the lads the mood had changed.

"Here! Just dipped the pocket ay some fannie at the bar. Piece eh piss! Cunt had 60 quid in his wallet," said Jimmy as he handed him a score.

"Jimmy Ah could fuckin kiss ye ya ugly wee bastard! Perfect timin!"

Billy's luck had taken a rapid upswing, and so had the music as *The La's* belted out *"There she goes"*. As he stood at the bar anxiously waiting for his two drinks, he felt the rushes circulating again around his neck area now that he was able to relax. He was conscious it was George's round, but George was too busy snecking the face off of Lucy and Billy didn't have time to hang about. The note would cover a pint and vodka, with hopefully enough left to cover a taxi back to his flat in Muirhouse where he would bang the arse off Cherie till the sun came up. Speed cock had never been too much of an issue for Billy. He'd heard friends moaning about it but if anything, for Billy the good old Lou Reed had the opposite effect, with the only downside being a frustrating difficulty when it came to the vital climax. As he turned, his face dropped as he noticed three bouncers circling Joe and Jimmy.

Fer fuck sssss...

"4.20 please," said the barman.

Billy slammed the fiver down on the bar, grabbed the two drinks and prepared himself.

"Listen we have it on good information that your friend stole someone's wallet. It was witnessed, and it's been reported at the door," said the bouncer as his colleagues stood behind him with their arms firmly crossed.

"Well where's yer proof?" said Billy, as he locked his hands behind his back defiantly.

"If he lets me search him, I'll have my proof. If he hasn't taken it he's got nothin tae hide has he?"

"No danger. Your no searchin nae cunt. Ah havnae stolen fuck all."

Billy turned and watched his hopes of a ride for the night slowly but surely smoking away. Cherie was staring on in disgust, as the dog's abuse spilled from Jimmy's angry lips like second nature. As if the fact he had lifted a wallet right out of someone's pocket wasn't enough to put her off. George reappeared from the toilets, wondering what all the palaver was about.

"Listen, I don't need to put up with this shite. If you won't let me search you then we're gonnae need to keep you all here while we phone the police and report a theft."

"Here girls, dinnae listen tae him. We've no stolen fuck all. Been stitched up!" shouted Billy, but he knew it was pointless. That ship had sailed.

"Listen, ma mate says he never stole no fuckin wallet, so he never stole no fuckin wallet. Now thanks tae yous cunts ma ride's just gone oot the windae, so what we gonnae dae aboot it?"

Said George. The head bouncer stepped in front of him.

"Listen, I'm losing my bloody patience with you bams. My colleagues are tryin tae be nice about this, but I'm no so nice. So here's the score, if that wallet's not in my hand in five seconds with all the money intact, then forget the police, I'll be servin up my own justice."

Billy exploded with laughter at the statement. He was some size, standing about six four with large sloping shoulders that formed a pyramid shape, atop which sat an egg shaped bald head with a hook-like nose that was just itching to be burst. He reminded Billy of the big angry headmaster from that Pink Floyd video, but his cringy statement could only draw one comparison.

"Who's this, the big boss man?" said Billy, as Joe edged forward in his usual goofy fashion, keen to get involved.

"Aye man all the way fae Cobb County Georgia eh?!" Joe's laughter was cut short by a heavy spade-like hand that clattered his jaw sideways. The bouncer's smugness didn't last long as George launched himself at him with a powerful head butt on the chin which sent him sprawling backward into his stunned accomplices. Within seconds they all waded in, sparking a full scale brawl that sent bystanders diving for cover. It careered its way to the front doors, where wee Jimmy got himself launched over a table before vaulting back over like a relentless little terrier whilst Billy used the heavy red rope to clatter another bouncer with the steel railing that was supposed to divide off the queue.

After the bouncers managed to force them out into the street Billy stood in front of them with his arms outstretched in defiance. They watched as the head doorman's colleagues restrained him with great difficulty as he kicked and screamed at the doorway. The moment of glory was short-lived however, as the familiar sight of a meat wagon powering it's way down Princes street prompted them to scatter in all different directions.

11

Billy flew down George Street as fast as he could with two bizzies on his tail, the thought of a night in the cells, speeding out his nut providing ample motivation. After snatching a look over his shoulder to see he had created enough distance for himself he took a sharp turn onto North Castle Street and zigzagged across the road, forcing a black Volkswagen Golf to halt in his tracks and beep its horns as he stuck his V's up in passing. After taking a right onto Queen Street he spotted an opportunity as the long row of sand-stoned terraces with their black fencing came into view. The image of some sorry bastard landing arse first on top of one of the similarly blunt spikes at Flora Stevenson's primary flashed through his mind as he fixed his hands to the spaces in between and propelled himself over. Luckily it wasn't to be his fate as he landed on the concrete at the bottom, the moment of hard impact taking him off his feet as he collapsed to the deck next to the bins. He lay there, puffing and panting as the sweet sound of the two bizzies flying past registered. He pulled himself up against the wall, conscious he needed to keep out of view in case anyone from the property had heard or seen him.

He emerged cautiously after a good fifteen minutes of waiting and ensuring the danger was gone, breathing a sigh of relief the moment he landed on his feet at the other side of the fencing. After brushing his Levi's down he made his way round the corner and back onto North Castle street before stopping dead the moment he saw her on the other side of the road. She was standing there in a fitted white top and tight blue denims with a small matching denim coat. Long tousled brunette hair, a shapely figure with child-bearing hips, and long legs. But it was her bright shining eyes that were sucking him in. He hesitated. She looked too good to even consider acknowledging a scumbag like him, and yet she had flashed more than one glance across the road at him as he stood there, dumbstruck.

"Are you lost?" She shouted across at him. He felt his face glow, for once lost for words.

"Eh, naw! Naw Ah'm jist." She pointed to her earlobes and raised her hands in the air as the sound of passing traffic rendered his words pointless. He wandered across the road, feeling awkward, a bag of nerves. There wasn't a hint of badness in her eyes, just pure honesty and kindness the likes of which he had never encountered. He stood in the heat of her gaze, feeling exposed, unworthy, as if he would melt away to nothing but a puddle of muck if he stood there too long.

"Ah, I'm Billy." She shook his hand lightly just with her fingers, before eyeing him curiously.

"Lyndsay. So..."

"How ye doin awrite?"

"I'm fine." She said in soft tones, before peering about the street. He was losing her, he needed to step up his game, and fast.

"So, whats a stunning Bird, Ah, Ah mean girl like you doin standin in town on her ain? You should have a queue ay guys right up tae George street there."

"Cheesy." She chuckled awkwardly. Shot down in flames. "But nice all the same."

Phew...

"If you really want to know, I've been stood up."

"What absolute clown has stood you up?" She tucked a lock of hair behind her ear as she smiled, revealing dimples that had been obscured till now.

"Ah'm serious. He needs a slap whoever he is."

"Doesn't really matter now does it. What's your excuse anyway?"

"Aw me? Ah- Ah lost ma pals." She giggled.

"Lost your pals? You look a bit too old to be losing your pals? They get lucky and leave you stranded?" He grinned.

"Naw, nowt like that. Ah-Ah dont suppose ye fancy grabbin a..." She looked over his shoulder as a taxi pulled up behind.

"That's my taxi." He stood there trying to find the words as she stepped past him and climbed in, but simply didn't have it in him to ask if he could join her. Who was he kidding? She was far, far too good a sort for him.

Aye that's right. Too good fer you. Waster that ye are, dinnae kid yerself...

"Fuck you Dad." He muttered to himself as he watched the taxi moving off, her smiling face disappearing before him. He turned with bowed head, stuffing his hands inside his pockets, wondering where the rest of the gang had got to, and whether or not they had been as lucky as him. He stopped mid stride as a car horn sounded, and turned to see the taxi was at the bottom of the street.

He ran as fast as his legs would take him to the sight of the unknown beauty still smiling at him as she wound down the window.

His heart leapt in his chest as she handed him a piece of scrap paper with the name Lyndsay and a telephone number scribbled underneath.

"Not in the mood tonight. But give me a phone and who knows. Maybe some other time."

Then like that the taxi was gone. He marched back up the street, feeling so light on his feet and swept away in the moment that if the meat wagon was to pull up in front of him right now and whisk him away to St Leonards it wouldn't matter a fuck, because he had her number. Lyndsay, the most stunning creature he had ever laid eyes on.

12

George had been doing the collections and enforcing rackets for his old man since the age of seventeen. At first it had proven a rush, and a major ego boost. Going out with big Uncle Goggs, rattling cages, proving his worth as a Donaldson to be reckoned with, but as he kicked a rusty old bicycle frame out of his path, with shite and litter surrounding him on either side at the foot of Burney's Court, he realised he was growing restless. The money wasn't great to say the least and whilst Dougie had him set up with a wage at the bookies, at the age of twenty he wanted more. He had been hitting the gym the past couple of years as a way of trying to keep his stomach down, this nagging insecurity having proven a secret thorn in the side since youth. The base amphetamine he ingested on an average weekend bender was another strong contender in the weight control stakes. His downfall was the ability to throw back ten to twenty pints or more over the weekend at a rate friends and family found staggering, not to mention his penchant for the chippies. Nevertheless, he soldiered on, challenging himself on how many 60/70/80 kilo reps he could hammer out on the bench press, and how many of the same weight or more he could squat. What he really enjoyed however was rattling those bags and pads. Big Phil McKenzie was always trying to get him along to his boxing club in Leith, figuring that if he got half a chance to mould that ferocious brute power into a sharp well tuned machine he might have a champion on his hands. George wasn't overly fussed though. What Phil didn't grasp was that George had scored more KOs up the town and on the streets than Iron Mike himself and that was where George's interests lay, on the streets and within the underworld, not in a boxing ring. But George wasn't all brawn, he had more than that to offer, and he was anxious not to fall into the category of "The Muscle" like Goggs had over the years.

As they stood at the door of the latest money dodging chancer on the list, Derek Rennie, he realised he would need to make his feelings known to the old man and pronto. "So, who is this cunt?"

"Derek Rennie. Full blown junky, been on it fer aboot ten year eh, right fuck up. Used tae punt gear fer yer auld man years ago on account of the fact he was shovellin so much intae his veins."

"Ten fuckin year man."

"Aw aye, this cunt's a veteran. His bird Shirley croaked it off an overdose a few months back. Cunt came hame an found her lyin face doon in a pool ay her ain shite, nae colour or nowt. Best ay it is, he wis makin a good go ay givin up the stuff at the time an aw. He'd started goin tae some church up the road. They had um involved in some project, helpin cunts that had been in his situation. What's the first thing he does when he finds her? Straight tae Ryan Lockhart lookin fer some gear. Since then he's been takin it non stop. Problem is now he's that fucked up oan the stuff he can barely even gather is thoughts the gither as tae how he's gonnae git is hands oan is next hit. Cunt's fucked eh."

"What's the score wae Willie nowadays? Dinnae see um fer dust an when ye do he looks like a fuckin vampire."

"Aw dinnae get me started on him George son. Spendin aw that time wae the Lockharts shiftin gear that's what's done it. Once some cunt gets the taste..."

"Ah hear he's joined the darts club now, is that right?"

"Aye but no a fuckin word tae yer auld man George. Dougie would go crazy if he found oot. Ye ken what he's like. Willie's been like a son tae um aw is life."

"Aye," George reflected as Gordon thumped his fist against the front door several more times.

"Just you make sure you stay away fae that stuff awright? Use yer fuckin heid son, it's bad news ye ken that."

"Nae chance, dinnae worry aboot me."

"Deek! Open up!" Gordon thumped the door with authority several more times. "NOW!"

Gordon waited several seconds. "Open up now or Ah'm gonnae boot this fuckin door down Derek! Right!"

Gordon gave the front door a stiff boot which splintered the lock away from the swamp green door as it swung wide open. A gust of rancid air escaped from the flat, repulsing George as he jammed his bicep hard against his nostrils to block it out. There wasn't a spot of furniture in sight, just a few bare walls covered with manic felt tipped scrawls in memory of Shirley. A vile looking grey mattress lay on the ground and there were flies everywhere.

"Come oan Deek we've no got aw day! Come oot an face the music. Ah've no got time fer games of hide an seek."

After checking the rooms they walked into the bathroom. George looked down and noticed a quivering, shaking heap in the bathtub, pathetically hidden by a ragged towel which looked more like an oversized dishcloth.

"Come on Derek pal the game's up. Oot ye get."

The pitiful junky wearily lifted his head out of the bathtub.

"Did ye think we'd jist ferget aboot yer little debt?"

"S-s-sorry Gordon, really Ah, Ah um."

"Ah'm sure ye are. Get yersel ootae that bathtub fer fuck's sake, have some dignity eh."

Deek crawled out of the bathtub trying desperately to cover his face. It was clear he hadn't shaved in weeks. His face was covered in thick, dirty brown hair with nervy bloodshot eyes darting around full of fear and paranoia.

Gordon shook his head with disgust. "What a fuckin sight you are eh? Ye got nae fuckin pride? Stand up, git through tae that kitchen, an make us a fuckin brew."

"P-p-please dinnae hit me Gordon, please."

"Dinnae worry, Ah'll no hit ye." Gordon turned and raised his eyebrows at George with a demented grin on his face.

Rennie slowly made his way to his feet. He was a tormented looking creature with an arched back. His spine was twisted and humped like that of an eighty-year old even though he was still in his forties. Ten years of hardcore heroin abuse had clearly taken its toll. As he stumbled out of the bathroom and turned his back on the menace that had invaded his foul flat, Gordon gave him a heavy kick in the backside, forcing him to crumple to his hallway floor. Gordon laughed as he observed the sight that lay before him.

George reminisced about times gone by, sitting at the dinner table with Gordon as Lorraine served up the food, viewing him as a truly well mannered gentleman. He was under no illusion that his old dear knew how her husband provided a roof over their heads, yet he wondered what her opinion would be if she saw him now, surrounded by the true horror of it all. Rennie struggled through to the kitchen before filling up a pan and sticking it on the cooker. He spilled half its contents as he shook violently in fearful anticipation.

Gordon pulled out a fag and lit it up before blowing a cloud of smoke in Derek's direction. "Aw aye did Ah ferget tae introduce ye? This is Dougie's laddie George."

Rennie extended his hand, unveiling an arm covered in red blotches and needle marks. It was clear his veins had taken a wasting over the years. George had seen smackheads like this wandering about the scheme since he was a young boy, baldies they used to call them. But up close and personal like this was almost too much to bear. He pondered the fact that it was his father that had introduced heroin to the area and with it all the suffering that stood embodied before him, before swiftly blotting out the shameful notion by reminding himself that if it hadn't been Dougie it would only have been someone else. Someone had to cash in.

"Awright pal," said Rennie as George looked him up and down with repugnancy. Neither his lips nor his hands budged an inch.

Rennie gazed despairingly at the cigarette that hung from Gordon's fingers. "Ah- Ah- dinnae suppose Ah could have one ay those oaf ye could Ah Gordon?"

Goggs blew a stream of smoke into his face before pulling out a cigarette and dropping it on the floor. Rennie bent over with great difficulty and picked it up with his trembling hand.

"So what's the deal wae this cash then Deek? Ye were supposed tae cough up the readies a couple ay weeks ago. Yer makin Dougie look like a fuckin bam. That's no very clever now is it?"

"Ah know Gordon Ah'm sorry pal. Ah-Ah've jist hud a really bad back an that eh."

"Bad back?" Gordon laughed. "Hear that George? He's got a bad back! Been in hospital wae the virus, payin the bairns' school lunches, bad back? Best excuse Ah've heard in a while that."

George stood silent, eyes fixed on Rennie who nervously fiddled with his right ear.

"What ye daein Deek, searchin fer a vein? Think ye've used thum aw up by the looks ay things. On a serious note now, dinnae insult ma fuckin intelligence. Where's the money yer due?"

"Ah- Ah've been meanin tae pay it. It's jist money's been a wee bit tight an that."

"Derek are you tryin tae take the piss outae me? Ah'm gonnae ask ye one mair time. Where's Dougie's money?"

"Look jist give me until next week Gordon, come oan."

Gordon stood there for a moment staring a hole through Rennie with that cold dead eyed stare of his. He flicked the half smoked cigarette in the junkie's face, before grabbing the full pan of water and cracking him square on the forehead with all his might. Rennie dropped to the floor, trying desperately to avoid the inevitable punishment.

"Gies yer hand."

"Naw Gordon please pal!"

"Gies yer hand, NOW!"

Rennie folded his arms stubbornly.

"Right." He grabbed his wrist and yanked him back up to his feet, before slamming his right hand down on the surface of the cooker, forcing it hard against the scalding pod.

"AAAAAAAAAGGHHH!! AAAAAAAAAGGHHH!!"

"Are ye gonnae git the money?"

"AAAAAGGHHH!!"

"What was that? Did ye hear somethin George? Did ye hear somethin?"

"Didnae hear a thing Goggs."

"AAAAAAAGGHHH!   AAAAAAAAAAGGHHH!!"   Trevor cranked the cooker up to full heat as Rennie shrieked for mercy.

"Are ye gonnae git the money? An stop treatin Dougie like a silly cunt!?"

"Aye! Aye! Aye! Let ees go! Ah'll git yer money!! Ah'll git it!"

Gordon finally let go of Derek's arm. He dropped to the floor, pulling the burning flesh off the red hot cooker as he went. He held his hand as he rocked back and forth on the dirt ridden kitchen floorboards, weeping uncontrollably.

"Right answer. Now I'll be back here, nine am sharp tae collect the cash, an if ye dinnae have it, yer face goes oan that cooker awright? Dinnae make a cunt ootae me Deek. Think yersel lucky Ah've given ye any time at aw, must be gone soft in ma auld age." Trevor readjusted his leather gloves, not for a second looking at the fallen mess that lay in front of him. "Ah dinnae gie a fuck if ye have tae rob yer ain granny tae git it, ye'll have that money. Now get yersel the gither an smarten up! An fer fuck sakes get yersel checked up if ye havnae done so awready. Dinnae wantae wind up in the morgue wae yer beloved dae ye? Dinnae ever bite the hand that feeds ye Derek. It bites back a hundred times harder."

As they began to leave, Gordon stopped for a second on the way out of the door to fire a parting warning. "Aw aye an dinnae think about daein nae runners Deek! Ah've got eyes oan ye! Try anythin stupid and they'll find ye in a ditch wae holes up an doon yer body, an Ah'm no talkin aboot needle holes. See ye in the morning!"

"Dae it now! Put me ootae ma misery!"

They made their way from the stairwell, and once they were out of sight of the block Gordon turned to George.

"What's eatin you the day?"

"What ye talkin aboot?"

"Normally you would have done a bit ay roughin up yersel. Ye seem pre-occupied."

George sniffed. "It's sixty quid we're talkin aboot here, an the cunt looks like he's practically on his last legs anyway. You had it handled, hardly worth me breakin a sweat is it?"

Gordon stopped in the street. "Doesnae matter if it's sixty quid or if it's six grand laddie, it's this kindae enforcin that's helped us keep a fuckin cast iron grip oan this area fer close tae a decade son."

"Ah ken that, it's jist—"

"Spit it oot son. Ye can tell yer Uncle Gordon."

"Ah've been doin the collections for what, three years now? Does he really need the two of us oan the job? You're big enough an ugly enough tae take care eh business by yersel, Ah'm jist thinkin its time Ah wis used in other ways is all."

"Ah hear ye son. But it's no me ye need tae be tellin is it?"

George could barely make the old man out as he sat in his familiar spot at the end of the bar in The Gunner. He had the last part of a Hamlet chugging between his teeth, half hidden by the *Evening News* he was engrossed in, his specs perched on the end of his nose. The place was dead and that was just how Dougie liked it when there was any business to discuss, not that a single soul who entered the pub would dare repeat a word they had heard. Not if they knew what was good for them anyway. Dougie slapped a hand against the paper and slammed it down on the bar as they approached.

"See that? Another bloody recession they're sayin. That's all we fuckin need. Government starts puttin the squeeze on all these local businesses, then what does it leave fer us? Bloody peanuts." Dougie shook his head as he attempted to wipe away the strain before dropping his specs down on top of the paper. "So, what ye got fer me?"

"There." Gordon dropped a roll of notes on the counter. "Only cunt that didnae cough up was Deek Rennie, but we'll have his tomorrow, rest assured."

Dougie chuckled. "Derek fucking Rennie. He no deid yet?" Gordon smiled. "Calendar material by the looks ay things."

Dougie shook his head as he untied the notes and proceeded to count out the two shares before handing them over and demanding three pints. "So anyway. Next line ay business we need tae discuss." Dougie glanced up at his son. "Your good friend, Curtains, Billy Wright."

"What about um?"

"Ah've been hearin he's been very busy recently. In particular a jewellery store in Stockbridge that got turned over a couple weeks back. Him an is pals Joe an Jimmy so Ah hear, maybe Danny Walker too. You wouldnae ken anythin aboot that would ye son?"

"Naw why would Ah?" said George defensively.

"Well, pals or no we all ken what happens when someone fae this area starts plantin their own flag an makin money oan ma watch. Needs tae be taxed before he starts gettin too big fer is boots."

"Come oan Dad eh? The cunt's just tryin tae make a livin like everyone else in this shithole. What's it got tae dae wae us?"

"Got everythin tae dae wae us. If Ah turn a blind eye an leave thum tae roost what's next? Loans? Drugs? Ah'm daein um a favour clippin is wings a bit before he starts thinkin he's a serious name. If he wants tae operate he needs tae pay is dues like everyone else."

"Steady Dad, he's ma fuckin best mate…"

"An we're family. Besides the order comes fae me. All you an Gordon need tae do is go over there the morn an lay it down in plain English. Make sure he gets the message."

"Fuck that."

Dougie's eyes widened. "What did you say tae me?"

"Ah says fuck that, the orders no comin fae me. You wantae start takin his money you go an tell um yersel."

"Ye know son if Ah didnae ken any better Ah'd think maybe you're in bed wae them."

"He's a mate awright? Ah work fer you but they're ma fuckin mates. Ah dinnae fuckin agree wae it." George glugged back the full pint in one go before slamming it down on the bar, gathering up his cash and making for the door.

"Hey! Son you fuckin come back here!"

"Handle this one yersel!"

13

Billy jumped awake when he heard the loud banging at his flat door the following day. And the moment he heard "POLICE, OPEN UP!" coming through the letterbox he knew it was time to panic. Both he and Joe arrived back at his flat the previous night after a two-day bender on the speed, swallowed some valleys and said good night to the world, but now that same world was in danger of coming crashing down around them.

Billy dived underneath his bed as the banging continued, snatching up a gold watch that he'd kept. Not a thing was getting flung until he found out if they had a warrant or not. He hadn't put all that planning into the jewellery store job just to flush it down the toilet the moment there was a knock from polis that were probably trying to put the shitters up them in the hope that their arses would fall out. And besides, this little visit could be to do with any number of things.

"OPEN THIS DOOR OR WE'LL KICK IT IN." Again the deep voice bellowed through the letterbox as Billy scrambled through to the living room where Joe Harrison lay crashed out on the sofa with half an unlit joint hanging between his fingers. Billy trampled barefooted across the empty bottles on the floor before yanking at Joe's leg to wake him up. "Fuckin wake up ya cunt! The polis are at the door!"

"What? The polis? Fuck!"

"Where's the hash?" Billy frantically gathered up several loose wraps of speed from the mantelpiece and a block of hash that lay on the coffee table, swiping away any loose powder as he went. "We're gonnae have tae swallow this shit."

"Here gie me a couple ay wraps then!"

"Go tae the door, have a word wae thum through the letter box, stall thum."

"What am Ah gonnae say tae thum?!"

"Ask thum if they've got a warrant cause if no they're getting telt tae fuck right off!"

Joe hurried to the door whilst pulling on a T-shirt and stuffing two wraps of speed down his throat at the same time. He shuddered before addressing the situation, as the bittersweet and heavily sour taste of base and glucose slid down his throat.

"Hello?"

"Open the fuckin door! We've no got aw day. That Billy Wright?"

Joe peered through the spy hole in disbelief at the two figures standing with hands clasped to their mouths trying desperately not to laugh. As soon as he unbolted the door and reluctantly opened it he was met by a barrage of laughter and the sight of Dougie and Gordon doubled over in the stairwell.

"Ye invitin us in sweetheart?" said Gordon, struggling to regain his composure.

Billy appeared behind Joe. "This some kind ay sick joke Ah take it?"

"I've got a warrant in ma backtail. Now let us in will ye," said Dougie before barging his way through to the living room.

"So, what can Ah do fer ye's now that we've got aw that hilarity out the way?" Billy sat down, as Joe began nervously pulling on his trainers.

"Woah, woah, what's the bloody hurry Joe? It's both ay yous we wantae talk tae. Have a seat." said Dougie with a sternness that suggested the hilarity had ended. A nervous looking Joe sat down, his leg hammering itself against the floor like a pneumatic drill. He began gnawing at his fingernails as Dougie sat forward.

"Ah wis just curious as tae whether or no you could confirm these rumours Ah've been hearin recently," said Dougie.

"What rumours?" said Billy.

"That jewellery shop on St Stephen Street. Ah hear you boys turned it over a couple eh weeks back."

"Who told ye that like?"

"Doesnae matter who telt me son. Let's just say it wis a reliable source. Now you can sit here an speak oot yer arse an say it wisnae yous or ye can confirm what I already have on good source."

Billy sat back in his chair as he pondered Dougie's motives. "Awrite. It was us. Good fuckin job we done an aw," said Billy cockily as Joe stared at the ground. Gordon coughed away the last bit of laughter.

"So Ah hear. The thing is, Ah'm in charge round here. An when someone in this area starts gone aboot daein this an daein that waeout comin tae clear it wae me first, or offerin me a slice ay the pie ootae respect, it makes me edgy. Ye might think it's no ma business but Ah make everything that goes on around here ma business. Whether you young cunts like it or no."

"Even if Ah wanted tae come tae ye wae something like that how could Ah? Ye made it clear where we stood years ago."

"That still a sore spot is it son? Ye still feelin that sting of rejection after aw these years?"

Gordon sniggered as Billy tried to swallow an ever-rising anger.

"Ye've got yer father tae blame fer that son. If he hadn't tried tae be the cowboy in front of every cunt in The Gunner all those years ago then maybe there couldae been a future fer me an you. But that's the past an this is the present, an Ah'm no gonnae let a bunch of upstarts like you an aw yer pals like Joe here think that ye can walk aboot, dae whatever ye want an no have tae worry about answerin tae me. Yer auld enough tae ken better now. Joe!"

He looked up in an instant. "Aye Dougie?"

"Ah've known you since you were a bloody bairn an aw. You know how it works around here better than this cunt don't ye?"

"A-aye Dougie."

Billy flashed a wicked glare at his fearful pal.

"At the end ay the day it's me that runs the show round here, an it's about time Ah reminded ye's ay the fact. So what Ah'm wantin is a forty percent cut ay your take."

"What?"

"This job ye done oan the jewellers, forty percent goes tae me. An that goes fer any other jobs ye might dae in the future, everythin gets back tae me eventually, don't you ferget it. An don't forget either Ah'm responsible fer aw the hash ye smoke an aw the powder ye stick up yer nose. Ye can leave the area if ye dinnae like it."

"You havin a laugh?" said Billy.

"Dae Ah look like Ah'm laughin son? Ah'll give ye yer due, you've got some fuckin balls tae even think aboot questionin me on this. I could be a real bastard an just say Ah'm takin the whole shebang. Truth be telt, maist cunts speak tae me like that wouldnae walk outae here. But outae respect tae ma laddie George, who for some fuckin unknown reason thinks the sun shines out of your arsehole, Ah'll cap it at forty percent. And Ah'll let ye walk."

Billy leaned forward and put his head in his hands as he gritted his teeth even harder. The speed was rushing to his brain already. He had ingested so much of it his teeth felt like they were going to crumble under the increasing pressure of his gurning jaw.

"Are you gonnae make this a problem?"

Billy didn't answer.

"Ah says: dae you have a problem wae anythin I've just said?"

"Would it matter if Ah did?"

"Ah'm gonnae gie ye a few days grace then Gordon here comes round tae go over the particulars an collect our share. So I'd suggest ye get yer house in order in that time frame an work out who's due what."

As Billy sat back in his chair he locked eyes with Gordon who had been staring a hole right through his head. "Dougie Ah'm gonnae go through him the now if he doesnae look away, Ah swear it."

"Come oan Gordon, save it. Aw aye an dinnae ferget Ah've got a few acquaintances workin fer the Police Department, that would give their right arm tae ken who wis behind that job, if ye catch ma drift? So I'd advise ye come up wae our share in a timely fashion, gents."

Billy smoked away furiously at a large joint as he thundered towards the shopping centre later that day. He was still speeding out his tree from the three wraps he'd ingested earlier and he was chomping vigorously on several Wrigley's he'd stuffed inside his mouth, merging peculiarly with the taste of the joint. He was too furious to even notice. "Fuckin joke! Fuckin joke man. Forty percent he's wantin, forty fuckin percent! What right has he got tae demand that? Threatenin tae shop us tae the CI fuckin D! Greedy schemin bastard."

"Come oan Billy ye cannae say that aboot here man." Danny Walker looked about the shopping centre nervously.

"Ah'll say what Ah fuckin want."

"He says forty percent aye?" said Jimmy.

"Aye."

"Well who's tae say what forty percent is? Fuckin just bum them off wae any auld number. Stick in fifty quid each. How are they meant tae ken? Fuck it."

"Jimmy, chances are they've found out the cost ay what's gone missin. Specially If he has cunts on the inside, Dougie's no daft. He wouldnae make a move like this waeout havin planned it first. No be usin that wee prick again anyway. We'll be seein him at some point." He pointed at Joe accusingly. "Wernae half in a hurry tae get ootae there you, eh? Just leave me tae take the heat while you sit there starin at the groond?" Billy shook his head in disappointment and looked away.

"Fuck off. What am Ah meant tae dae? It's Dougie an Gordon we're talkin aboot here. Ah dinnae like this any mair than any other cunt, but at the same time Ah dinnae wantae end up getting cut up or nailed tae a fuckin wall. Cause that's the kindae things they dae."

"Aye the whole area's shit scared ay thum eh? That's how they get tae walk about an dae what they want, through fear and silence. Cause nae cunt's got the baws tae stand up tae thum. A whole area ay shitebags. Well Ah'm no feart ay thum."

"Well goan then Billy. Go through one ay their doors, take one ay thum oan an let's see how far ye git afterwards."

"Aye Joe cause you'd be backing me up right enough eh?" Billy rolled his eyes at Harrison before looking away as he blew hard at the end of the joint to try to stop it from sideburning.

"Billy you ken Ah've got yer back. You ken Ah'm in fer ye wae jist about anyone, but no wae these cunts. There's a reason they run this area. These cunts are serious, man. You ken that as well as Ah dae. We aw ken the stories, man."

"Well when are we gonnae get serious eh?" Billy looked around at the faces of his friends one by one. "We jist gonnae stay small time forever? Oan the steal, getting bullied aboot by auld men that should have had their day a long fuckin time ago?"

"Fuck that," said wee Jimmy as he spat harshly on the concrete.

"Exactly Jimmy, fuck that. In Dougie's own words we're no young laddies any mair. We're men, an it's aboot time we started actin like it. Bout time we started takin responsibility."

"What ye sayin Billy?" asked Danny Walker.

"Ah'm sayin let um have is forty percent. Let thum think they're in control. That they're the big shots. Then it's time fer a change. Where's the big money nowadays eh?" Billy held up his joint as a symbol of what he~~~~ ing. "Drugs. That's where the real cunts make their money, no fae stealin turn over a jewellery store ye've got a bit cash tae dae ye a few weeks, then it's gone, *kaput*. Then ye spend the next however many weeks searchin fer the next score, an scrapin by, while ye sign on an pick up yer dole check. What kindae an existence is that? Wae drugs on the other hand yer talkin steady cash flow, status, respect."

"Dougie's got this whole area sewn up Billy, who would we sell tae? Hate tae rain on yer parade like," said Danny cautiously.

"Who says we need tae sell it here? We start off small, elsewhere if need be, build our custom, then once we're makin good money we can sell it wherever the fuck we like. It's no fuckin rocket science laddies. What choice dae we have? Got enough bodies behind us, let's put something together an make some real fuckin dough."

"What about George?"

"If there's money tae be made George will be there, trust me. How much dae ye think he's makin fer is auld man? Fuckin pennies! Heard um moanin about it enough. Bottom line is, first things first, we need a supply, one not connected tae Dougie. So let's every cunt keep our ears tae the groond."

14

itter rain hammering against his helmet as he pulled it
bed off his motorbike on Glasgow's Sauchiehall street.
The streets ... y, dozens of folks out to try and scavenge what they
could from the last of the January Sales, braving the cold and the rain. Clearly
George's outburst of frustration had achieved the desired effect with Dougie.
All of a sudden he was being invited through to sit in on the arrangement of
a large scale drug deal, holding court with John Spencer, the guy that as far
as they were concerned was at the top of the chain. George felt calm and relaxed, eager to take another step up the ladder. He often heard the older generation remarking about how well his head was screwed on, and the fact he
carried a wisdom that went beyond his years. George didn't need to mouth
off or act the big shot, because everyone knew what he was capable of. This
was the reason why the Bull didn't and never had done blades, a fact he prided himself in. With hands like fucking sledgehammers, what was the need?
Violence aside, George was a good observer. He had learned plenty about the
business from a young age simply by keeping his gob shut and his ears open,
and now he felt it was time to start putting it into practice.

A wasted Willie Graham emerged from the back seat of Sean's BM, dragging himself out by his hands, his drawn in face and vacant eyes hidden beneath a Reebok cap, his light blue lacoste jumper looking too big for him
all of a sudden. He still had enough energy to aim a lazy feint at Georges
stomach, prompting George to throw a couple back, grinning as Willie acted
knocked out against the side of the car, his arms akimbo.

"Ye got me big boy. Sat oan me. Suffocated."

"Wouldnae take much, look at ye, aw skin an bone," joked George as
Willie flung an arm around his shoulder. They stopped there smiling and joking as a grim faced Dougie emerged from the passenger side.

"Enough ay the carryin on like bairns when we get tae the boozer you
two. An you." Dougie aimed a stiff finger at Willie. "Fuckin smarten up.
Driftin in an ootae consciousness aw journey."

"Heavy night Dougie, what can Ah say."

"Aye an it will be a much heavier night the night if you show me the fuck up the day. Should have bloody well left ye at Harthill service station."

"Am good. Dinnae worry aboot me."

"Better be."

As Willie walked off in front with Sean who was compulsively checking his watch every few seconds, Dougie leaned in close to George.

"Time tae make the intro then son, you ready? This is what ye've been pinin for after all. More responsibility an all that"

"Course I'm ready. Why wouldnt I be?"

"No reason." Said Dougie as he pulled his raincoat hood up over his head. "Jist be careful what ye wish for, eh." George stopped in his tracks, his father's words rankling.

"Whats that supposed tae mean?"

"Jist a figure of speech son. Mon, we're late."

They reached the pub within 5 minutes of negotiating Glasgow's grid like city centre streets, passing by two young girls with matching buns held up by multi-coloured scrunchies, fighting over a Walkman and its headphones as they went, trying their hardest to keep it sheltered from the downpour. The girls stopped their tussle as Sean passed by, as if lightning had struck right in front of them.

"You're tidy by the way!" shouted one of them before bursting into a fit of giggles as he passed by and into the Variety Bar, aiming a smirk over his shoulder at George as they went.

"Mair your age Georgie boy?"

"Aye, right ya cunt."

They were met by large, brown, marble pillars, a dusty bar, black leather seats that stretched round circular tables. A proper old man's joint George thought to himself. They made their way through the thick smoke and huddled circles of drinkers supping their pints of lager and bitter as *Elton John's "Don't let the sun go down"* played out from the juke-box. George had to take a second look when he saw him sitting at the end of the bar. He was perched on a bar stool, studying a paper through stern eyes as he puffed on a thin rollie, a whiskey on the rocks sitting in front of him. He had on a faded brown Corduroy coat. His thinning jet black hair was slicked backwards on top, with shades of grey coming through on the sides that extended into matted sideburns. He blended in effortlessly, just like a regular punter, someone's old man, popping in for a pint after finishing his shift at the steel mill, but this was anything but your average punter. This was a guy that ran a multi-million pound Heroin enterprise with tentacles that stretched through to Edinburgh. A guy that ran a slew of local businesses, car-washes, scrap-yards and more, one of the most feared and respected gangsters in the city. George had half expected silk shirts, Rolexes, flash and swagger, but he realised now that was just naive. That was films, this was real life. This was a guy that clearly wasn't interested in drawing attention to himself, and more at ease doing his business in murky corners and dark shadows. John Spencer stood up as Dougie approached and synched in a firm handshake before introducing him to a stocky, hard looking gentleman with a goatee beard and a tall wiry young guy in a grey hoodie and jogging bottoms with a baseball cap on probably not much older than George. He had a hawk nose, and small slits for eyes. Had the appearance of one of those English bull terriers with the long white faces, ugly fucking things. George clocked the unnerving expression on his old man's face as John Spencer embraced Sean in a hearty hug. He knew the deep insecurity his old man was feeling around the imminent release of his older brother David, George's uncle, Sean's Dad, after 14 years inside for armed robbery. He knew it was David who brokered the initial meet between Dougie and John Spencer from his jail cell a decade earlier, a move in the interest of both parties. For Dougie it was a chance to progress from "hard man" and serious robber, to hard drugs and kingpin status. A steady supply rolling along the M8, and with it a consolidated control of the northside of Edinburgh having seen off the threat of his main rivals the Mcdonalds from Pilton. For John Spencer it was a chance to expand his growing empire into new territories, having outgrown his north Glasgow stronghold. In the middle, of course, you had David, who had certainly earned throughout his time inside thanks to the move, however, George knew all too well that his father was a power hungry control freak who after 10 years of lording it over the streets of Muirhouse, *his* streets, had absolutely no intention of giving up half of his empire to his big brother upon release. The problem with this picture of course was Dougie and John was mainly business, David on the other hand? He and John had done time together, shared a cell, they were close. And George knew it was precisely this close relationship that was giving Dougie sleepless nights, as much as he would claim otherwise.

"This is my son, George," said Dougie. George nodded his head and shook his hand. He was struck by a winding scar that started behind John Spencer's ear and ended at the corner of his mouth, all the while wondering what the other guy looked like, and if he was still breathing. Spencer had eyes that could charm you one second before turning to stone the next. Might not have looked much on the surface, but George could see all he needed to in those eyes.

"Ye no sayin hi tae yer Uncle John, Willie son?"

"Pleasure as always John."

"Christ what's wae these baseball caps eh?" John pointed to the laddie next to him. Pasty faced, angry looking, like he had a massive chip on his shoulder he couldnt git rid of. "He can git awey wae it cause ay his age, but fer fuck's sake yer a man Willie, an ye come intae ma bar wearin a cap? Fuckin act like a man eh? No a kid."

A nervy silence descended as John Spencer aimed a cold, unrelenting stare at Willie, who reached for the cap with shaking hands.

"Ah'm sorry John Ah'll take it off eh. Didnae mean any disrespect."

"Hey Ah'm only playin wae ye! Wear a fuckin tea cosy fer all I care. Ye'll still look jist as ugly."

After Spencer ordered a round of drinks in, talk quickly turned to particulars regarding the next consignment of Heroin scheduled to make its way onto the streets of Muirhouse. Then, having hashed out all the details and put it to bed for the moment, talk turned to a new topic altogether.

"These junkies arnae gonnae be around forever," said Spencer. "Their a dyin breed. Ecstasy, now there's the future. Kids are gaun crazy fer it, aw that electronic shite? Nows the time tae get involved, while the markets wide open, nows the time tae create a presence, ye know? Move with the trends, diversify, somethin you've always had a dab hand fer Dougie let's face it." Spencer jerked a thumb towards the laddie, a relative of some kind perhaps, looked like he was being kept close, groomed for the business. "Young Alan here sells thousands ay thum, him an is pals oan the estates, movin in on all these raves and clubs tae, spreadin like wildfire in't it?"

"What does it do to you?" said Sean. "Out of curiosity."

"Fuckin dynamite by the way," replied Alan. "Like nothin ye've ever experienced. Just a half a wee tablet an yer pure melted aw night man. Dancin, talkin non stop, shaggin, whatever ye wantae use it fer, like the *ultimate* drug. Aw ye need is wan, or half a wan, an thats you till the sun comes up. It's that fuckin strong man. Everywans gaun pure mad fer it by the way. Jist makes ye feel like pure love."

"Awrite, you," said John awkwardly. "Dinnae be feelin too much love fer yer fellow man or we'll have a problem." Alan laughed nervously as he scratched his neck.

"Gettin big through in Edinburgh tae. Now's the time tae jump on, ride the swell of the wave," said John.

"A lot of money in it by the sounds of things Uncle Dougie," said Sean.

"Definitely. Sounds like the winds of change are blowing."

"Indeed," said John. "Biggest drug craze since the smack at the start ay the 80's. Difference is this comes without that stigma. The fuckin griminess, mucky fingernails, needles, junkies, goin intae yerself, detaching. This is a party drug, more accessible, brings folk out their shells ye know? Has the opposite effect."

"Sounds like another way ay escapin the fuckin rape of a Tory Government," remarked Dougie as he sipped his whiskey.

"Heroin helps thum escape. Ecstasy? Helps thum rebel, and stand up, so they think at least. Give the bastards a big old noisy fuckin headache, drivin thum mad. Tories would probably prefer they were on Heroin. Dyin slowly, quietly, fadin out," John replied. Dougie shrugged his shoulders.

"Rebel, escape, party, pass out, all equates tae the same thing where we're concerned doesn't it?" Dougie turned to Willie who was drifting again, his tired eyes closing in on themselves, spaced out on a cocktail of smack and downers that was rapidly getting the better of him. Like the symbol of that sleeping enemy, fading into obscurity George thought to himself. Sean shook his head as he fiddled with his cufflinks, clearly feeling deeply unimpressed himself at his best pals sliding descent, especially in existing company.

"Willie? Ye with us?" piped up Sean, losing patience as George kicked him subtly, knowing that if he didn't buck up his ideas he'd be getting dragged out the back by Dougie.

"W-What?"

"We were saying, it sounds like there's a lot of money in those pills?" Sean said slowly and deliberately as Dougie looked on with gritted teeth, clearly aggrieved at the poor showing.

"Aw aye, sounds good, aye."

"Heavy night kiddo?" said John.

"Somethin like that John. Am good though. All good." He wiped at his face.

"Maybe yer man could do wae a wee half? Bring um back tae the land of the livin," Alan said with a sneer.

"Aye, goan then. Test the goods. Let me stick it up Thatcher's farter fae all sides," Said Willie, rousing a barrage of laughter that seemed to ease the frustration at his poor showing. "See, I am listenin, dinnae worry aboot me."

"Sounds like somethin I could run?" said George, tired of taking a backseat, sensing the time was right to put himself out there. As all eyes turned on him, he put his pint down on the bar, lifting his head up above his shoulders, rising out of his own shell as he crossed his arms, striking a stance of power, eager to make a strong impression. "The ecstasy that is. Could put a mob together to run it, no bother. Move in on those events at Ingleston I've heard about, take over. If no-ones controllin the market yet who's gonnae stop us?"

"One step at a time," said Dougie before glaring at George. "Baby steps."

"Cannae fault these young ones fer their tenacity Dougie eh? Showin he's got ambition tae carry on the family name."

Dougie slowly nodded his head as he stared into the bottom of his whiskey in a ponderous fashion.

"True." He raised his head offering George the faintest of smiles. "Even if they need tae learn tae toe the line and exert a bit of obedience from time tae time. And patience at that."

"Speakin of the family name. No long till Davies out, eh?"

"Aye roughly 4 weeks tae be exact," said Dougie before throwing a casual glance at Sean, like he was measuring his reaction.

"Still through here fer the homecomin? Ah believe that's his wish seein as he's stuck in our own Bar L after all."

"Aye, makes sense tae do it through here. Feel free tae hang ontae um if ye wish?" Dougie laughed gruffly before tossing back the last of his whiskey. He signalled to the barman who rushed over.

"So, how you feelin about Daddio comin home after so long?" Asked John as he slapped Sean on the knee.

"Be fuckin weird. Been 14 year he's been inside know what Ah mean?"

"No long enough, the doss bastard," said Dougie as more laughter broke out.

"Any plans fer um Dougie? The Devil makes work for idle hands after all," said John before interlocking his fingers over his knee and sitting back intently. Looked to George like Davy had whispered a word in his ear.

"He's family. Course we'll work somethin out. Whether ma big brother can handle takin orders from me is another thing altogether of course. The natural order has changed after all." John smiled.

"Aye he's a bloody handful is our Davy. Can attest tae that. Just as long as he's looked after that's all that matters, which am sure he will be." John raised his hands. "Family eh? Ye's are big boys am sure ye's can work it out."

"Ah think its in the best interests of *all* involved that we maintain the current order of things as much as possible John. It's no broke is it?"

"Far from it. Anyway, enough business talk for one day."

George excused himself and headed for the toilets as talk turned to football. After taking a leak, he was greeted by Dougie standing there at the doorway waiting on him.

"I want you to go with the young boy, Alan."

"What fer?"

"Want you to pick up a sample of those ecstasy tablets tae bring back tae Edinburgh. Feed thum tae the bams fae the scheme. See what they dae, see if there any good or no. If they do as advertised well put an order in. The laddies waitin fer ye out front, awright?"

15

George wasn't keen on the fucker, just couldn't take to him. Scowling away with his bull terrier face as they exited the pub, ordering George to follow him, and then leading the way with an audacious swagger that suggested he was gangster number 1 and George was some wannabe from that posh place along the motorway. Still, George was happy to swallow his pride, and let the dafty think he was in charge for the sake of the greater good.

George sped underneath a massive railway bridge, leaving the River Clyde behind him, as the rain lashed against it's waters like one enormous puddle in the middle of a steadily enlarging shithole. He took a right, deeper into the spider's web of schemes and estates on the outskirts of Weegieland, as large menacing tenements crept into view, reminding him of home. And all the while he wondered why the fuck he had to travel a half hour out here just to pick up a few tablets. The occasional passer by stopped and stared as if he was a UFO. Bairns running rampant, trampling across what looked like an abandoned building site, a trashed building with tanned windows and CUMBIE YA BASS, spray-painted across it in large blue lettering. As they turned another corner they passed a clutch of youngsters with their trackie bottoms tucked into their socks and Berghaus jackets 2 sizes too big for them synched up around their faces as the rain increased in intensity. Alan pulled up at the side of the road in front of a lamp post, prompting George to do the same.

"Where the fuck ye takin me?" said George, feeling tense, the sweat seeping through the fibres of his thick Stone Island jersey as Alan climbed out of his Fiesta.

"Ye want this bag ay sweeties or no big yin?"

"Aye, but why we needin tae come away oot here tae git thum?" George looked around him at the stark wasteland. "Fuckin doesnae look much different tae the bomb sites in Kosovo." Alan laughed as he jingled his keys about in his hand, before jumping into the middle of the road with arms outstretched.

"Big man! Welcome tae the badlands ay the Gorbals! This is worse than fuckin Kosovo, or Bosnia or any ay that shite oan the news. Please believe me, this makes any ay your schemes look like fuckin Disneyland tae."

"Aye awright," said George, unimpressed, shifting on his toes restlessly. "Look just lead me tae these tablets an ah'm out of here." A grinning Alan aimed a finger wrapped in a massive sovereign toward the tall, grey high rises in the near distance.

"That's you jist down there pal, at the dampies."

"The dampies?"

"The dampies aye, the damp flats, big tall wans doon there. Go speak tae the boys standin at the bottom ay the stairwell, they'll see ye right."

"Eh?"

"Relax. They'll be expectin ye. Friendly bunch, so they are."

"Noones knows me out here. Dont Ah need someone tae vouch fer me?"

"Ye'll be brand new big yin!"

"It's George."

"Awright. Got places tae be an people tae see George. Hard work bein a drug dealer ye know?" He slapped George on the back as he passed him by.

"Stick in. Just tell thum John sent ye, ye'll be fine." Alan sniggered as he swaggered up the road, leaving George standing there, stranded in the middle of the fucking Gorbals.

He pulled up in front of the dampies, feeling the pounding heart of a man that was way out of his comfort zone as he stepped off his bike. The broken glass crunched under his feet on the wet concrete as he approached a team of young laddies that must have been at least 20 strong, guarding their stairwell, patrolling their territory like it could come under attack at any minute. Up above he could see a middle aged woman with bags under her eyes, elbows perched on a pillow as she gazed out of her window, surveying the scene down below. With the sloped white roofing dripping with green fungus and blue cladding that looked like darkened sponges it was clear where the handle "The dampies" came from. A young boy whistled, the chatter going into overdrive as one laddie after another stopped what they were doing, all sizing George up like a piece of meat they weren't particularly impressed with. Suddenly they were slipping tools from the back of trackie bottoms, and from behind socks, George raised a hand, eager to relay the message that he wasn't there to raise hell.

"Whit ye wantin bigman?" said a laddie that stood about 5 foot 4 odds, with a big navy cagoule on that went down past his knees, making him look ridiculous.

"Am here for the pills, John sent me. No trouble here, ye's can relax."

"Am very fuckin relaxed by the way. Who sent ye? John fuckin who."

"John Spencer." The laddie looked at him as if he was stupid then turned around and laughed out loud at his pals. Soon the whole gang was in fits of laughter, as George stood there, feeling like a complete bam.

"Some balls on you bigman, fuckin comin up in here oan yer ain an drappin names. Where ye fae an who dae ye run wae?" George felt boxed in as they circled. Suddenly, he was back in that gym class at Ferryhill. That dark place inside from which he'd never quite emerged. Rising from the deck, his top over his head and his belly spilling out, a bit of scrunched up blue tape stuck to his face as the rest of the class tried their hardest to hold back their own spillage of laughter. He had only went and fell sideways, and crashed awkwardly to the deck after a shocking attempt at vaulting the wooden horse. He felt idiotic, ashamed and embarrassed that day. Heavily conscious of his weight, and size difference in comparison to his peers. Felt like he was being inspected and laughed at like a weird looking animal on the yearly visit to Edinburgh Zoo. He'd never quite been able to shake that awkward feeling of self consciousness ever since.

"Muirhouse, Edinburgh."

"Fuckin Edinburgh!? Ha ha!" You're a long way fae home big man. A long fuckin way fae home by the way. People that get lost out in these parts don't always turn up by the way."

"Look Ah jist wantae get the pills an be outae here. Ah wis told you were the boys tae speak tae so here Ah Am. No lookin fer trouble, there's one ay me an about fuckin forty ay you's. Ah wis told ye's were expectin me."

The rising agitation was clear in the faces that were gathering behind the ringleader, as they scratched at their chins, and spat on the ground whilst whispering to one another in spiky tones.

"Were any ay yous expectin anyone? Naw? Didnae hink sae. But seein as yer here now, many pills ye after?"

"Supposed tae be pickin up a sample tae take back through. Then if ma old man thinks its the right move we'll..."

"Gies a hundred quid."

"Make it fuckin two hundred Gary!" shouted a boy from behind.

"Aye fair enough. Two hunner. Haun it over an we'll see what we can dae."

"Nice fuckin bike, by the way!" shouted someone from behind as George felt the heat cranking up underneath his skin. He was in over his head and he knew it. Felt like he'd been sent to the slaughter. His heart was booming now, his hands shaking, the hostile sounds and murmurs growing in amplification as the rain slowed its assault.

"Am no handin over nae cash, am no stupid. Just give me the fuckin pills, gettin tired ay this shite."

"Awrite, al take yer fuckin bike then. And yer money. An there's fuck all that you can dae..."

"Your no takin nae fuckin BIKE!" yelled George. He lifted his arm just in time as the flash of the razor caught his eye before tearing clean through his bomber jacket. The bottle bounced off the back of his head as he took toes before buckling to the deck as they swarmed around him like angry wee wasps. Within seconds he was crouched over, covering up as the kicks came flying in from all angles. He felt something hard being driven into his gut before a piece of wood came crashing over the back of his head. Then, just as quickly as the barrage began, a set of car-lights on full-beam brought it to a close. A car door opening and shutting and then.

"That's ENOUGH! SCATTER YA WEE BASTARDS HE'S WAE ME!"

He came up for air, feeling like he was about to pass out. He rose wearily to the sound of rapid footsteps and a torrent of shouts and screams behind.

"Ye awright? Least yer face is intact. Smoke?" George waved it away as he staggered towards the car and propped himself up on the bonnet by his hands. He checked his arm, somehow it had avoided a slashing.

"Here. Yer bag ay tablets as promised." As Alan dropped the bag in his hand it quickly sunk in.

"What the fuck wis that, somekindae TRAP!?" Alan raised his hands casually in response.

"Nothin tae dae wae me awright? You want answers? You ask closer tae hame." George turned his spinning head as another car pulled in, Sean's car, with Dougie in the passenger seat and Willie in the back.

"What the fuck?" He felt his insides boiling as Dougie emerged from Sean's motor. "You wantae explain what just fuckin happened!? I've just been set aboot by half the fuckin Gorbals!" Dougie walked calmly up to him, his hands in his pockets, his steely eyes that betrayed any shred of emotion or soul, staring right through him as if he wasn't there.

"That will teach you tae go against my orders. A wee wake up call shall we say. Next time I ask you tae go an have a word wae yer pals on my behalf, *maybe* ye'll be a wee bit more obedient. Ye want the world son, don't ye? An ye want it on your terms an your terms only, no prepared tae wait. No fuckin patience! Well you'll get it as an when *I* see fit. When Ah wis your age Ah wis still robbin fuckin hub caps off cars an sellin thum down the fuckin pub! Now you know as if there was any doubt before. That I call the fucking shots. And you do as *I* say. When I fucking say! Got it?"

George stood there, paralysed with rage, his chest heaving in and out as the condensation clouded up in the air between them that was scorched with violent tension.

"Fuckin CRYSTAL!" It echoed round the Gorbals, their noses now inches away from one another as George felt his whole frame wobble and shake with fury. He turned to the car as Sean and Willie sat there, switching their eyes about awkwardly. George knew this came from one man and one man only he turned his back on him. Now all that was left was that sickly feeling of self conscious humiliation and embarrassment, deep in the pit of his stomach, fortified and embedded even deeper.

He climbed onto his trusted companion and kicked the suspension with power as he cinched the helmet onto his head and strapped it tight. He flashed a middle finger at the defiant cross armed figure of his old man as he flew past, no doubt contented in the knowledge that the letter of his law had been laid down once again in such ruthless fashion. Now George had his mind set on blazing his own path, sick to death and suffocated by the Father's power trips and dictatorship.

16

"What the fuck are you playin at?" said Sean as he pulled up outside Willie's door later that day after dropping Dougie.

"Fuck ye talkin aboot?"

"What the fuck do you think Ah'm talkin about? You made us look like fuckin idiots the day. It's John Spencer we're talkin about here! Turnin up tae a meet like that an your fallin asleep standin up just about? Makes us look a shabby outfit Willie! Fucked on yer own product in the middle of a big drug deal."

"Sorry fer fuckin embarrasin ye eh." Willie fished about in his jeans pocket before pulling out a fag that was broken in half. He sighed before dropping it. "Got a smoke?"

"You knew we had this the day, an ye couldnae even stay straight! One day that's all Ah asked!"

"Why didn't ye jist fuckin leave me at hame then ya cunt!" spat Willie with contempt.

"What the fuck am Ah meant tae tell Dougie like? Aw Ah'd bring Willie but he's too out is face on junk. That shite that he's pumpin intae is veins an killin umsel wae! An ye dinnae seem tae give a fuck!"

"What? Ye mean the shit that he peddles all over the area? Through me?" said Willie with a smile, letting the irony settle in the air.

"Through *us* ye mean."

"Spare ees the fuckin lecture, eh? Fuckin good impressions, lookin professional, what a lot of pish. See the nick ay the cunt John hud wae him? In his fuckin joggers an that? Real fuckin classy."

"Spare ye the lecture? Does anythin actually process in that fucked-up skull of yours?"

"Ken what? Ah've had aboot as much ay your shit as Ah can take! Ye make oot like yer concerned aboot ma state. Fact am oan the smack an that. Ye make oot like yer a mate, but all you give a fuck about is you! An how you look! An how Ah fuckin make ye look! Well dinnae worry aboot me pal. Am just fuckin fine an dandy me. Ah handle ma business like I always have done." Willie reached for the door handle.

"That what ye think aye? That Ah only care about number one? That what ye think when Ah'm draggin ye tae hospital, tryin tae get ye tae sign up fer the methadone is it? Or helpin grind ye through cold turkey just tae come back around the way a few days later an find ye wae needles an burnt foil lyin in front of ye. Out yer biscuit on smack again. You think that's easy fer me after all we've been through? Mates fer what fifteen year!?"

"Ah'm the one that gits the fuckin monkey work!" Willie pointed his dirty fingernail at Sean. "Ah'm the cunt that's oot there in the front fuckin line, makin your life easier! Goin through cunts' doors! Daein this, daein that tae protect our firm, sittin wae fucking ounces upon ounces ay smack in ma gaff while Ah sort oot one safe house after another tae keep ahead ay the game. You barely go anywhere near the shit you! Naw, no the golden boy. Squeaky clean fuckin Preemo. Fuckin clean hands. Ye know what? The only reason you've ducked a jail cell is cause yer spared the shite that Ah git tasked wae. When wis the last time you hud tae pull some cunt oot their hoose in broad daylight, an scalp thum in the street? Eh!? Ah'm the evil cunt! Ah'm the one takin the fuckin risks! An you wonder why Ah need tae hit the fuckin gear now an then!"

"The reason Ah'm no in jail, is cause Ah use ma heid. An cause Ah'm careful, somethin you never were."

Willie pushed his face closer. "Ken what? You could take a few lessons fae yer auld man when he gets out. From what Ah've heard, at least he has fuckin balls."

Sean grabbed Willie by the face and shoved him up against the side window, snarling, "You ever compare me tae ma auld man like that again an I swear I'll fuckin do ye. He's the one stewin in the fuckin jail cell while Ah go about ma business, who do you think is on top?" Willie pushed his arm away, and prodded a finger at Sean's face again.

"Go on then. Do me! Dae it now! What's stoppin ye!? Always hidin behind Dougie. Dinnae huv the fuckin balls mate." Willie grabbed his crotch, sneering, as Sean shook his head in disbelief, wondering what was becoming of their friendship. A once tight knit bond ravaged by the skag.

"Ken what? Yer no even fuckin worth it Willie. Yer wasted. Ye dinnae ken what yer sayin. Jist get out ma fuckin sight. Away an do yer works ye'll be cluckin like fuck." Willie laughed callously.

"Cunt, Ah banged up in the toilet before we left the boozer. Lightenin quick, me. An Ah know exactly what am fuckin sayin." He flung open the door.

"Ye know all this bollocks aside, ye know the one thing that struck me the day?" Sean looked out his side window. Clenching his jaw as he tried his damnedest to maintain a modicum of composure.

"What?"

"If the bigman can dae that tae is own fuckin son. Settin him up fer a doin just tae prove a fuckin point, an put um in is place fer darin tae go against his orders. What in the fuck do you think he would do tae us if push came tae shove an he wanted tae make a point?"

17

The Telford Arms wasn't exactly the most romantic of spots for a first date, but then dates were unchartered territory for Billy. About as romantic as it had got was the summer he turned 16. Nighttime walks round Fettes with wee Kerry from D Mains that normally ended with an extended bag off, followed by a hand job in the bushes, or more if he was lucky. Sadly, the nighttime walks had been abruptly cut short when wee Kerry discovered Billy was two timing her with her pal Diane, a discovery that had sparked a hellish tear up in the middle of the centre the following day. As the two lassies went at it like scalded animals, Billy stood back against the railings, acting sheepish, trying to pretend his ego wasn't swelling, as his reputation as a "wee heart-breaker" soared before his very eyes.

Lyndsay was a different breed altogether from the usual foul mouthed sorts from the scheme with which he had enjoyed fleeting relationships and encounters over the years. Just a minute in her company, and one or two phone-calls had induced in him a different level of desire altogether from that of those impressionable young birds that found themselves drawn to angry young troublemakers like moths to a flame. Lyndsay was top of the league material.

As he approached her outside the Telford, feeling his insides whirling round like a rickety tumble dryer, he was overwhelmed again by the idea that a common thief like Billy Wright wasn't worthy of her.

"Someone's looking smart." She flashed that beaming smile that he feared might reduce him to a blithering bag of nerves if he locked onto it for too long. He glanced down at his skin tight white shirt and stonewash Levi's, drawing some confidence. She had a point after all.

"Cheers. Not looking too bad yerself," she chuckled.

Her hair was worn up in curls, her lips even more luscious looking than that that first time he'd seen them. She wore a red, tightly fitted top that exposed her slender shoulders, and a tight black leather zipper skirt that had Billy's pulse racing like it was fixed to a Scalextrics track. He found it hard to keep his eyes away the moment she turned her back on him. And then when she turned to face he was instantly sucked into those shining eyes that were like an ocean that hooked you, and dragged you in, promising the world amidst the underlying fear that they would end up delivering so little for someone like him.

"Shall we grab a drink?"

Lyndsay opted for a Southern comfort and lemonade, Billy took a pint of Tennents. He fought back the instinctive urge to snarl and ward off the three laddies crowded round the puggie, eyeing her up from behind with wagging tongues, yet there was no need. They just as quickly turned their attention back to the machine the second they clocked who she was with. They retreated to a small table at the front end of the pub, where you could see who was coming and going, a handy thing where Billy was concerned.

"Look am sorry fer takin ye here. Cursin masel fer no takin ye somewhere nice in town. A nice restaurant know what Ah mean? This is a bit of a dive, really."

"Dont be daft." She said, waving it away. "It's nice and cosy. Sometimes those other places are just full of folk lookin down their nose at you. That's the type of place I get dragged to for family meals. This? This is a nice change to be honest. Feels more real."

"Aw well. Sound then."

"At least you showed up, which is more than I can say for my last date."

"Well, Ah said it before, Ah'll say it again. Boy needs a good slap. Standin up someone as gorgeous as you?" She smiled, her face taking on a tinted glow.

"Ya wee charmer."

Two hours flew by as they chatted about everything from dinosaurs to school days, Neighbours and Home Away, to cartoons they loved when they were kids. From their favourite scary film to what they enjoyed having for breakfast, it was effortless, felt like he'd known her for years. For two people from such vastly different backgrounds, it shouldn't have been so easy but it was. Hanging on his every word, in fits of laughter at all his jokes, melting away his insecurity with her kind, honest eyes. It provided a welcome break from the constant necessity to hustle and steal just to stay afloat, and the memories of childhood brutality at the hands of a monster called Dad. None of it seemed to matter anymore in the face of Lyndsay showing an interest in him, and lighting up his tormented existence. Then, just like that, he was brought crashing down from the clouds, as he looked up to the dreaded sight of Gordon Trevor, standing there, staring down on them like a haunting spectre, his big ham like fists clenched as he towered over the table.

"Check oot the two love birds, eh?" Billy sighed as he watched Lyndsay squirm uncomfortably in her seat. "Well. Arent ye gaunnae introduce me then? How rude darlin, eh?"

"Lyndsay this is Goggs."

"Hey, hey. Gordon tae a beauty like this. Get it right son."

"Gordon."

"An tell me, what on earth is a stunner like you daein wae a reprobate like him, eh?" Billy turned to Lyndsay, eager to bring Goggs cheap little tirade to a close.

"Scuse us fer a minute will ye, Lyndse?"

"Okay."

Billy ushered the big pest across to the toilet area, eager to get him out of earshot before he fucked things up in some way shape or fashion. It was the first date, and he knew fine well Lyndsay wasn't ready to be introduced to his world. Not yet.

"How the fuck did a wee bam like you land a bird like that, eh? The rack oan her? Too good fer the likes ay you by the way, can tell that a mile off."

"What are ye wantin Goggs? Ye pick yer times awright."

Gordon moved in close and prodded a big finger into Billy's chest. "You know fine well what am fuckin wantin ya wee radge. Money. We've no seen a fuckin penny ay the haul you took fae that jewellery store. An you know what the fuckin deal wis. Dougie outlined it in no uncertain fuckin terms, ye hear me?"

"Look, nows no the time awright? As ye can very well see. Come by ma flat the morn an we'll work somethin oot."

"Naw! Times up, Ah want a taste. An Ah want it fuckin now. Tonight. That will do fer starters till you've had a chance tae round the money up off the rest ay those wee mugs. What ye got oan ye?"

"Look, what dae ye want me tae dae? Am oot fer a drink. Give me till the morn fer fuck sake."

"Empty yer pockets, cunt." Billy sighed through gritted teeth.

"Dae we huv tae dae this? Here? Right fuckin now?" Gordon unzipped his black barbour coat and dipped his hand in before brandishing a sharp hunting knife, ready for gutting.

"Dae Ah need tae say anymair? Now let's see what ye've fuckin got." Billy shook his head as he went into his pocket and pulled out his notes. He counted out 60 in 20s and handed it over.

"There. Ye can make do wae that the now, surely tae fuck."

"And the fuckin rest."

"Come on, eh?"

"Ye want me tae wander round there an tell hot stuff round there who her boyfriend *really* is? An what he's capable of? Robbin fuckin jewellers an that? Cause somethin tells me shes none the wiser at this stage." Billy's head dropped. He handed over the remaining 60 quid he had on him, knowing the evening was now over.

"Good lad. That will dae fer starters anyway. Tell yer pals they can chuck in the same if they want big Goggs off their backs at least fer the minute. An Ah dont think Ah need tae do any remindin that addresses are known."

"Are we done here?"

"Aye, beat it." Billy shook his head as he turned his back.

"Aw aye Billy?"

"What?"

"Tell yer wee sweetheart that once she's done foolin around wae wee boys. There's a whole 10 inches of Goggs here, ready an waitin. That's if she wants a real fuckin man."

18

Billy could hardly believe his eyes as he walked down Easter Drylaw Avenue on the way to Pick and Save with Jimmy close behind. Big Guiseppe's ice cream van, sitting there unattended, with the window wound half way down. They had just been up at big Bri Ketchen, a local Drylaw dealer's flat, picking up some acid tabs for them and the rest of the boys. Billy had sounded Bri out about the possibility of introducing him to his supplier in the hope of starting some business, but Bri wasn't interested. As he was an unstable, unpredictable maniac, practising strokes with his favourite samurai sword, sunglasses on at seven pm, melted on acid, Billy thought it sensible not to push the matter. Now however an opportunity had presented itself that was just too good to pass up.

"Ya fuckin Dancer. Keep shotty Jim," said Billy as he glanced about the street, before reaching in and winding the window all the way down. He was distracted by the sound of Jimmy's laughter, as he pointed to a flat window, where big Guiseppe's flabby arse was bouncing up and down as he forced himself into an even flabbier vagina. Billy grabbed Jimmy and motioned for him to keep the laughter down as he forced it back himself. There would be plenty time for recounting the scene and crying with laughter when they were in Joe's flat melted on acid themselves, but for now he wanted that cash register to ease the financial squeeze they were all feeling amidst increasing pressure from Dougie and Gordon. He climbed into the driver seat and checked the inside of the van for the goods, and there it was. It wasn't even a register it was a large metal tin, sitting there stuffed with notes and coins, too easy...

"HEY YOU YA THIEVIN BASTARDS!"

He snatched the tin and stuffed it underneath his coat as he heard the cry coming from the flat stair, and by the time he had pulled himself out of the van, big fat Guiseppe was tearing his way down the pathway at the pace of a milk float whilst trying to pull his trousers up at the same time.

"AH'LL PHONE THE POLIS OAN YE'S!"

"Away back in an ride they waves big boy!" shouted Jimmy as they legged it round the corner, pishing themselves laughing at what they had just witnessed.

The racket blaring its way down the flat stair was unbearable as they made their way up the steps to Joe's flat. There was a high pitched squealing noise that sounded like one of those nippy little bastards from that cartoon the Chipmunks, behind it a frantic beat that reminded Billy what it sounded like when you cranked up the tempo on a record player.

"What the fuck are they listenin tae?" said Billy as he thumped the door. Billy had seen Joe in some conditions but even by his standards it was an eye opener when the door opened revealing pupils like black holes, a twisted jaw and a stripped torso drenched in sweat.

The living room was in its usual chaotic state, *Mayfair* magazines lying everywhere, pinups stapled to the walls. In one corner there was a shelf stacked full of pirate videos, in the other a wardrobe jam-packed with counterfeit clothing. In the middle of the room was big George in a world of his own, eyes closed, hands outstretched, reaching for the ceiling. He jumped out of his trance the moment Billy placed a hand on his shoulder, wondering if his old mucker was alright or not.

"BILLY!" George embraced him in a sweaty hug that had him gasping for air. After pulling himself away he looked down to see a plastic bag in Georges hand within which there were five tablets.

"You dinnae wantae know what I've been through tae get ma hands on these hings but fuck me it wis worth it. Take one ay these, and I swear tae God that music will be the best thing you have ever heard!"

"What are they?" said Billy with curiosity as the rest of the room crowded round.

"Ecstasy. We both hud one at two o clock the day an we've been like this ever since they kicked in! MELTED!"

"Ah swear tae God this is the highest Ah've been in my life," said Joe "It's hard tae describe man, just feel this pure warmth right through me. It's like, spiritual. Just feel like Ah love every cunt! See this wee cunt here!" Joe flung a sweaty arm around Jimmy's neck forcing him to pull himself away, wiping his face with his sleeve as Billy looked on with amusement. "Ah've known this wee bastard since we were both three year auld, ye ken that? Three! Love um like he's ma brother."

"Dae those pills turn ye intae a bender?" said Billy, prompting an outburst of laughter.

"Here!" shouted George, opening the plastic bag and tipping the five remaining pills into his sweaty palm. "Fuck the acid. An fuck ma old man tae, these are on him!"

Once the pill had kicked in fully the music sounded heavenly. The thumping beats had everyone bouncing about Joe's living room with joyous abandon, Billy had never seen anything like it. For the first time in his life he felt nothing but pure, natural love and warmth for his fellow man, for his brothers. He didn't care that he was an unemployed bum that had to steal to get by. He didn't care that his dad was an evil drunk. He just didn't care. Just being alive felt beautiful all of a sudden, now that it had been freed of all the painstaking trappings that weighed it down. That little pill had turned the dark world around him full of threat and turmoil into a sea of warmth and happiness. He felt a deeper connection to everything. Big George bounced into him interrupting his euphoric daydream. "They things are amazin eh!?"

"Aye man," said Billy with a wide smile, as he sucked on the last part of his cigarette. He blew a stream of smoke into the air that rose like a great cloud in the sky. Then suddenly it hit him, like a bolt out of the same clear blue sky that was Joe's ceiling. All the answers to their money problems lay within the chemical that made up that small white pill that was going to change the world as they knew it.

Ya fuckin dancer...

19

Sean felt the nerves piercing him like little pins as he stood at the gates of the infamous Barlinnie flanked by Uncle Dougie and John Spencer, with the rest of the welcoming mob standing behind. His Dad's release had stirred up some painful shit inside, as much as his front suggested otherwise. There was still a small part of him, that bewildered thirteen-year-old boy that resented his father for getting sent down for all those years. It was a major life event that had effectively split up the whole family. Not only did Sean lose his dad, but his mum Cindy too, who upped sticks and emigrated to Canada with his two sisters shortly afterwards, having grown sick and tired of the life of crime she had married into so young. Cindy tried to take Sean with her but Dougie blocked the move, backed heavily by David from his jail cell. Sean had stayed in touch with them both for a few years by letter but somewhere along the line something deep inside of him said that holding onto that massive part of his past was far more painful than simply letting go. In burying that part of him Sean had in a sense buried the ability to feel deep affection or emotion on any level for anyone of the opposite sex, whether it be Kim his loyal partner of five years, or any of his many other conquests. Letting himself get too close was just too much of a risk to take. On the flip side, after burying the troubles of that sad, pitiful wee teenager, what had emerged was a clever, cunning young guy with wily street smarts and a flare for the drug business.

Aye he was a smart mother-fucker alright. Could have gone to any college or uni in the country and passed any number of degrees with flying colours if he'd so desired. Fact is he scored passes in most of his O levels without even breaking a sweat, with most teachers crying out for more application. Mr McDowell in particular had him marked down for a Masters in Economics or Business Management, but unfortunately for Mr McDowell, all Sean's application had gone into the family business, which just so happened to involve drugs.

Now, at the age of twenty-seven, most of Dougie's distribution lines ran through him. The problem with the current model was that his Dad was now up for release. Sean knew his father felt he had earned a hefty chunk of Dougie's business after taking fourteen long years in one of Scotland's most notorious prisons for the family, and rightly so. He also knew however that what his father saw as compensation and what his Uncle saw as compensation for all those years inside were two very different things. He drew in a deep breath as he looked up at those six Victorian chimneys sitting loftily atop the notorious Bar L and watched them chugging out thick smoke, as he subtly slipped the screw top coke container from his back pocket. He needed a pick-me-up to kill those nagging nerves, and it was preemo shit.

His father didn't look a great deal different than he had on Sean's last visit as he approached, with the heavy white gate clanking shut behind him. The thin greying hair now reached down to his shoulders, the face drawn in with an angular jaw much like his own, and stern squinting eyes. The difference was he now wore a look of triumph hiding the bitterness that was boiling angrily beneath the surface.

"Where's the fuckin women, eh!?" he screamed as he swaggered toward them, sparking laughter not just from the welcoming mob but from the screws standing at the gate.

"Dinnae worry, Ah've got that covered," said John, who winked and laughed as he approached. The two old jail buddies threw a few pretend jabs at one another before embracing in a hug.

"Been a long time, brother," said John.

"Aye a bit too long eh?" said Davy, as Dougie stood patiently in line in front of Sean.

Whilst the taller of the two, there was a fair difference in bulk between Sean's father and uncle. What the old man lacked in build however he made up for with a psychopathic temper and large bony hands capable of hellish violence. There was a firm handshake and a brief hug, devoid of the warmth you would expect. "Good tae see ye David," said Dougie as Davy pulled back, his eyes squinting suspiciously like he was trying to sniff out any falseness.

"Good tae be out Dougie, good tae be out, wee brother."

As they parted, Sean stood there, hands in his pockets, smiling awkwardly. His father pulled him close and flung an arm around his neck. "C'mere you. Too cool fer school this one eh?" Davy synched him into a tight hug and spoke quietly but firmly in his ear. "Yer old man's back fer good ye hear me son? It's me an you now, all the fuckin way. Ah'm no going nowhere again so help me God."

They retreated to John's associates strip joint for drinks. They were met by a hefty doorman standing against the wall, arms crossed, staring into space. He had a deformed nose with scars etched into his battle hardened face. A cheap tacky looking sign hung above the doorway. "The Dancer" was the name. After a brief, formal grunt he attempted to administer a pat down to check for weapons which John halted with one hand signal, clearly aggrieved that the bouncer would dare to administer such a check on one of his party. He sent them inside the club, his mug now flushed red as he stared down at the ground, a massive bag of nerves now as Spencer glared at him. Sean winked at a smoking hot redhead as they strolled across the red hexagonal dance floor, with blue and white neon lights above. It was still early doors and there were only a handful of punters inside, the volume soon rose when the sizeable organised crime contingent swallowed up the bar.

"What about big Tam Bryant John, eh?" said Davy as Sean sighed, having heard the story before. He took a sly bump of the preemo to prepare himself as his attention wandered across the room to the stripper.

"What a fuckin way tae announce masel that was by the way! I'd been in the joint what a few weeks at that point John eh?"

"Aboot that aye."

"So anyway, am an Edinburgh boy, an ye can imagine the talk when Ah touch down eh? That's that cunt fae Edinburgh that done the bank, swaggerin aboot thinkin he's a big shot, wae a fuckin target oan ma heed bigger than the one oan ma erse. An believe me that place was scary enough for a Glesgae guy that wisnae connected but Edinburgh born an bred? So there's this big bastard in there, name wis Tam Bryant. Tam was a very well known cunt in Glesgae in the Sixties an Seventies eh, used tae run wae the Tongs, well known street gang in Glesgae at that time, right violent bastards so they were. Tam wis daein a life sentence fer murder. Nae cunt al go near um eh, Ah'm tellin ye this cunt wis aboot six foot five and wide as a bus, wae a reputation fer pinnin folk doon by the throats an rapin thum in their cells, forcin thum tae watch is big gruesome face while he done it. Big ugly bastard, foul lookin. So, I've been in there a couple ay weeks, an this big cunt's been makin serious eyes at me, every opportunity he gets." Davy shrugged his shoulders before continuing.

"Ah mean who can blame um eh? Am a handsome man after all. So one efternoon there's a few ay us playin pool, an big Tam Bryant's sittin oan a bench wae these two wee arse bandits he wis always wae, an Ah comes swaggerin through. Now I've walked past um, stopped fer a couple ay seconds, looked right at Tam, an gave um a big smile eh. An jist tae hammer the point hame, Ah've blew a big kiss at um eh! Big bastard thinks is lucks right in! So, on Ah've go's, walkin roond the corner, fuckin shiftin ma erse fae side tae side an that, lookin over ma shoulder as Ah dae it, an he's in a trance followin me. Clocked John an his mob an their just starin on thinkin what the fucks gaun oan here? So in Ah go tae ma cell, leavin the door open behind me, an obviously he follows me right in. Next thing Ah've bent right over, an what dae Ah dae next?"

"Ye took it up the erse?" Said Dougie. Davy paused his story as he waited for the laughter to stop.

"Naw, wee bro. Thanks fer fuckin ma story when am in full flow by the way. Naw, Ah pulls oot a big screwdriver fae behind ma sock, turnt aroond an plugged um as hard as he could RIGHT IN THE FUCKIN SIDE! An believe me he's let out the loudest fuckin scream. Next thing ye know am pluggin um tae fuck in the heid, in his fuckin BACK! In is FUCKIN LEGS! Ah mean he's tryin tae escape this fuckin cell, an Am like a man possessed by now, full on black out. Big huge man wae a reputation ye wouldnae believe, reduced tae a bubblin bairn by a guy half is size! Aboot five screws come boltin along – dae ye think ah stops there? Dae ah FUCK! Am swingin at the screws man, full on tryin tae stab thum. Eventually they've got a hud ay me. An that's when John an is boys have got ower excited an came steamin roond the corner, all of us against the screws, while big Tam Bryant crawls off intae a corner bleedin like FUCK! Fuckin madness so it wis. Now Ah wisnae daft wae that move. *Every* cunt hated that bastard. An Ah took um out the game."

"We welcomed Davy like one of our own after that."

"Ah tell ye what, see this younger generation. Like ma son here. Wouldnae last five minutes in there let alone fourteen year! The 87 riots John eh? Fuck me. Too soft these young pups. Here's tae the future though boys eh! Raise yer bloody glasses! Ah'm a changed man. Reformed, strictly oan the straight and narrow, nae mair fuckin aboot. Need tae get masel a decent joab, mibbe become a postie who knows."

"You serious?" said Bob Callum.

"Aw aye, definitely." Davy smiled as he knocked back his nip. "April first is still well over a month away you doss, fat cunt! Ha, ha, ha!" He slammed the empty shot glass down on the bar as he wiped his lips, still laughing. "Trust Big Bobby the Bampot tae take the bait eh? Knew one ay you reprobates would!"

"First thing we'll need tae do is get ye a new wardrobe, faither, fuck. It's no the Seventies any mair," said Sean, pointing at Davy's shining grey suit.

"This is Saville Row, smart arse. And the Seventies will dae me just fine. Speakin of which, what's this shite?" Davy screwed up his face and pointed toward the speakers, as *Michael Hutchence* sang about *two worlds colliding*.

"No got any ay the *Kinks*, John? *The Who*? Even the Pistols are better than that shite."

"Bet you've dealt wae a few sex pistols the last few year right enough. Ah'm no buyin yer patter," said Dougie, grinning.

"Less ay it, little brother. Where are the women anyway, all jokin aside? Expected mair than that. Had nothin but bloody magazines tae keep me company aw these years, an no a hairy in sight fer fuck sake."

"All in good time David, all in good time. Anywey they're no aw hairies anymair Ah'll have ye know. Some ay thum like a good auld shave down there nowadays, no like your time," said John, smirking.

"Anywey, see this wee brother ay mine? Tubs Ah used tae call um. Used tae greet when Ah called ye that eh? Used tae greet yer fuckin eyes oot. Aw they years ago. Eh Tubs? Fuckin waste ay time playin hide an seek wae this cunt!"

Dougie glared at Davy. "Aye well, a lot's changed since they days eh."

"Aye you're no jokin. Ah've been stuck in a cell stewin away fer the last fourteen year while you've coined it in eh?"

An uncomfortable silence descended. Time for another bump, Sean thought to himself, slipping it slyly from his backtail, feeling the unease in the air. "Aye well that's no ma fuckin fault. Wasnae me that got caught."

"Never said it wis your fault. All Ah'm sayin little brother..."

"It's Dougie, call me Dougie, David eh? Ah know we're brothers but ye dinnae need tae say it in that sarcastic fuckin tone like its some sortae secret joke that Ah'm no in on."

"All Ah'm sayin, *Dougie*, is that maybe you're due me a favour or two eh. Ah've done a lot ay time fer this family, dinnae go fergettin that."

"Fuckin airin shite in front ay everyone. Have a bit dignity fer fuck sake. Has the joint robbed ye of it?"

"Come oan guys eh take it easy," said Bob.

"Hey, fat cunt! Keep yer fat nose ootae this! It's family business awright?"

"Cunt's gonnae find it hard tae keep is nose oot when ye go airin it in front of a room full ay people," said Dougie, pouring himself another nip.

"Awright, awright, keep yer hair oan. Jist noisin ye up anyway. This is a special occasion after all. Ma HOMECOMING!"

The conversation slowly resumed and Sean felt his nerves settling as the coke took a hold of him again. He tried to engage his Dad in some banter to take his mind off things, but it was a lost cause. He could see the muscles continually tightening and releasing in his face and knew he would hold on-to this beef like a dog with a bone until Dougie had done right by him in his eyes.

Sean went into his back pocket for the umpteenth time that day, but as he did so a pint glass came flying off the bar, shattering across the dance floor. His Dad was now screaming his lungs out like a man possessed, trying to muscle his way through the cluster of bodies to Dougie.

"Ah've been earnin favours fer fourteen fuckin year you fuckin ungrateful BASTARD!! Who helped set ye up fae his jail cell!? ME! Half that business is mine an you FUCKIN KNOW IT."

Dougie smiled and shook his head as he dropped a smoking cigarette butt on the floor. "What did Ah say? Where's the fuckin dignity eh? Rantin an ravin like a fuckin loony tune. Ken what? Let um fuckin go boys. Ah'll fuckin slap some fuckin dignity intae um! We're no wee laddies anymair. Ah'm the one that hands oot the spankins now! If you'd been mair careful back in the day ye wouldnae huv ended up in that mess!"

Davy pointed a long finger back at Dougie through the crowd as he at-tempted to regain some composure. "Least Ah was there! Mannin the job while you sat at hame countin yer fuckin money, ya greedy, power hungry bastard! We shouldae both gone down ya bastard!"

"It's aw comin oot now eh? Been holdin ontae this aw they years? It's me who's kept our firm strong the last ten fuckin year, through thick an thin! You would've run it intae the fuckin ground!"

John had seen enough. He stepped in between the warring family members, as Sean felt his heart beating at an unhealthy pace, and shouted with a booming tone, "ENOUGH! It ends here! Whatever family issues you two have ye can deal wae thum out in the car park if ye need tae. Ah'm no havin it in this place. If ye wantae scrap, take it tae the fuckin street!"

As Dougie made for the door, Sean attempted to stand in his way. "Uncle Dougie, come on, eh? Dad!"

Sean turned just as Davy bumped into a curly blonde haired dancer who was headed inside the club. She couldn't have been older than twenty-three, stunning, with a tight ass that poked out beneath a black skirt that was almost as small as a belt, revealing a leopard print thong that had Sean gaping. God only knew what she looked like to his Dad after fourteen years inside. Within seconds Davy was speechless, all bluster and bravado gone as his eyes began wandering slowly downward toward the v neck collar of a white T-shirt that hid what looked like the most petite and perfect pair of breasts. Sean felt his jangling nerves calming again as his father just stood there, staring.

Meanwhile, Dougie had already wandered back toward the bar. "Away an blow off some steam, ya crazy old bastard ye."

20

Billy could feel the grin planted on his face like concrete as he lay back in his bed and accepted the joint back from Lyndsay. He had managed to get a nice rare bit of quality grass through Joe. A refreshing change from solid, and night and day compared to the usual home grown shite that periodically did the rounds, full of sticks and seeds that snapped crackled and popped when you smoked them.

"Nice stuff." She said in between giggles.

"How would you know? This no your first time? Wis surprised ye were so keen." He said smirking.

"Och, Billy. I'm not a complete straight peg. I have had it before you know. On a *number* of occasions."

"*Ooooooh*!" He said poking her in the side feeding off her giggles. The revelation that she was into a smoke had taken him by surprise after weeks of going steady. He hadn't been aware posh birds took drugs even if it was just a smoke. What's more he had been at such pains to conceal his criminal nature that it hadn't exactly been at the forefront of conversation up till now.

"Wouldn't touch anything else."

"Aw naw. Me neither," said Billy, bullshitting through his teeth as he took another long drag and passed it back. "Just a smoke an that's it, eh."

"Some of the girls at Mary Erskines are going on about trying ecstasy."

Billy coughed and spluttered before scrambling to regain his composure.

"Must have gone doon the wrong hole, eh." She continued.

"One of them can kill you, you know."

"One wee pill?"

"Aye. Swells your brain, you pass out, go into a coma, then die. Not a nice way to go."

"Fuck me! Can we change the subject please darlin? Talk about heavy," Billy said before leaning over her and turning the volume up on the ghetto-blaster that was blaring out *Bob Marley, I wanna love you.*

The music whisked him up to his feet, and before he knew it he was dancing around his bedroom to *Bob Marley* in a pair of Y fronts. Within seconds the gruesome prospect of dying after taking an eccie evaporated, as Lyndsay ended herself in tears of laughter whilst Billy swayed to the rhythm, occasionally thrusting his crotch in her direction, a maneuver that was sending her laughter into the realms of the uncontrollable.

Is this...

Was it love? Billy asked himself the question as he danced around the room idiotically for Lyndsay's amusement. It was something he had never really experienced, not this kind anyway. Sure, he felt a level of brotherly love for his muckers that would occasionally bear its head when they were off their tits. He was pretty sure he loved his Mum to some degree, even if it was diminished considerably by the way in which she had turned a blind eye on so many occasions to Jack's brutality growing up, but love for a lassy? Hadn't felt anything close until now. For him to be making an absolute cunt of himself in this fashion for the sole purpose of bringing enjoyment to another person, certainly suggested strong feelings were at play. It all felt such a welcome break. It was tiresome having to keep up that hard front all the time, it was a strain just on the facial muscles having to bear that anger 24 7. Felt like such a release to just let it all drop. To act and feel normal, and content, even if there was still a certain level of deception involved.

Suddenly there was a banging on the flat door.

Fuck sake...

He snatched the joint from Lyndsay and stubbed it out in the ashtray, catching a look of alarm on her face as he did. He dragged a t shirt over his head and pulled on his trackie bottoms, as Lyndsay pulled on her jumper.

"Are you alright?"

"Am fine. Jist gonnae go an check who it is darlin, awright?" He said, trying to keep his cool, conscious of how much he was unsettling her.

"Who is it?" said Billy at the door, thinking once again that he needed to get that spyhole sorted.

"I have came to repossess your grass." Billy shook his head before opening up the door to the sight of Joe doubled over in the stairway.

"Fuck sake Joe, ye ken no tae just come bangin on the door like that. Phone ahead first, how many times dae Ah huv tae say it?"

"Awright, awright ya cunt," he said wiping the tears away from his red eyes.

"Look Ah've got company. What ye wantin?"

"Company aye? You got a wee birdie in there? Sly bastard! Kept that quiet likes!"

"Aye, aye. What ye wantin Joe?"

"Got some good news mate. Had tae come an tell ye in person."

"What?"

"Boy fae ma college class Ah got the grass fae. Ah had a word wae um like ye asked, an guess what? He's got a line on some pure bangin ecstasy mate! Loads of it comin up fae down south, best stuff goin…"

"Fuckin keep it doon ya cunt! Wee bit discreteness eh?"

"Awright, awright. Gonnae meet um after is college class the morn, ye free?"

"Aye. Aye al be there. Anythin else?" said Billy as Joe crossed his arms and offered his best hurt wee boy look, his mouth gaping open beneath that massive beak.

"Am Ah no gettin introduced, nut? Look, the main reason Ah came roond is am all oot mate. Any chance ay a toke? Yer flats stinkin." Billy sighed.

"In ye git then. But 5 minutes that's it."

Joe snatched the last part of the joint from the ashtray and lit it before collapsing back into a chair as Lyndsay sat up on the edge of the bed.

"I was beginning to wonder if he had any friends," joked Lyndsay.

"Ye ashamed ay us or somethin mate? Haha."

"This is Joe. Joe, Lyndsay."

"Hi Joe."

"What attracted ye tae this nutball then?"

"His dashing looks and great sense of humour probably had something to do with it." Billy felt his face tinge as she flung an arm around his neck. "Aww. He's all embarrassed, look."

"Billy, embarrassed? No chance, ha. Never known Billy "Curtains" Wright tae be embarrassed. Wait till ye get tae ken um hen."

"That right? Go on, dish the dirt then."

Billy's face began to burn as his heart raced. Joe grinned, looking like he was tempted before one raised eyebrow and a searing glare from Billy clearly forced some second thoughts.

"Ma lips are sealed. Gees the stuff fer skinnin up then an I'll make a stick."

To Billy's relief Joe departed as soon as the roach was stubbed out. The moment he closed the door, he turned to the sight of Lyndsay standing there in the hallway, her arms crossed, fixing a determined stare on him that made him sweat again.

"Why do I get the feeling there's things you're hiding from me?"

"Donno, why would you get that feeling?" He edged past her, ignoring her stare, and then fell back onto his bed.

"Wantae watch a video?"

"Come on Billy don't change the subject. You got really uncomfortable when he made that comment about dishing the dirt, and before that I could hear some kind of shady dealings going on at the door. Every time I try to talk about you, what you do, your background, you clam up and start changing the subject. Why?"

"Yer imaginin things Lyndse. Honestly. Nowt tae hide here..."

"Okay. Well, you say you work in construction. What kind of construction I have no idea, you never go into details."

"Why would Ah? It's borin shit, why would Ah wantae talk about work? Dae you go intae details about what ye dae at Jenners? Naw, cause it's pointless shit that neither of us wantae talk about."

"Fair enough. But then why would you need this?" His heart sank as she lifted the giro slip in the air. Mortification turned to rage.

"What the fuck!? Snoopin round ma room now?"

"It was lying on the floor Billy..."

"Am no carin! Still lookin fer stuff! Fuckin investigatin me!"

"Okay, fine! I've found it. Care to explain why you've been lying to me?"

"Look. Ah don't need this shit. Ah was just fine on ma own. Knew deep down this wis a bad move." Billy jumped to his feet and flung the bedroom door open. "On ye go."

"Is that what you want? Really? Is it?" He shrugged his shoulders.

"What Ah dont want is someone pryin intae ma life! After what a month?"

"It's called a relationship Billy! Honesty! Sharing. Shouldn't be any secrets."

"Awrite. You want fuckin honesty? I'll give ye mair honesty than you can handle. And trust me. You'll be runnin through that door by the end of it screamin fer mummy an daddy. Am a scumbag Lyndsay awright? A low life. An unemployed bum that signs on. That hasnae worked a day in his life at that! That has to steal and scam just to get by. I have committed unspeakable acts of violence over the years, and the chances are?" He raised his hands in the air. "I'll commit more. That enough honesty fer ye? I'm fae the fuckin streets! Believe me, you don't want any ay this. Bad to the fucking bone! So why don't ye get yer shit together, an go find a proper, decent guy. Someone wae a career Lyndse. Someone that's goin places! Cause believe me you're in the wrong part of town. Wae the wrong fuckin boy."

Lyndsay looked down at the floor, despondent.

"I probably should. Go that is." She sighed and then looked up at Billy. "But I'm very, very stoned." The statement shattered the tension sending them into more fits of laughter that took at least a minute to let up. Billy sat down on the edge of the bed.

"You sure you want this? You deserve better Lyndsay. You went tae Mary Erskines, ye live in Morningside. Got a nice family around ye, a good up-bringing. Fuck, the last place in Edinburgh you should be right now is sitting here wae the likes ay me. Could have *anyone* ye wanted. Look at ye!"

"Maybe so. And if I'd found this out after the first week or Two, I would have ran a mile, no question. The problem is, I love you now, you prick. And yeah I probably need my head examined for saying it, but if I'm honest I always did find nice boys a little boring. And on top of all that? You're not bad to the bone, you're a product of your environment, that's all." She looked him deep in the eyes. "There's good in you. I can see it, even if you can't, or don't want to."

21

Billy had to look twice as he sat in the motor with George outside Telford College, watching Joe's newfound drug buddy Andy Riley approach, closely followed by Joe himself. He looked like he was coming off a three-day bender, with a pasty white face covered in spots and dark bags under his eyes. He wore a striped beanie hat, a white T-shirt with a yellow smiley face on it over his skinny frame and baggy jeans that looked like they were about to drop any minute. Surely this phantom wasn't the poster boy for this new ecstasy scene, Billy thought to himself as he jumped in the back followed by Joe.

"Andy aye?" said Billy as he turned around, trying his hardest not to catch George's eye. He knew it would set him off, and the two of them would be pishing themselves laughing all the way to Cramond.

"Aye man, nice ta meet ya."

A flock of seagulls scattered away from the grass verge that led down to Cramond beach. Ever since he had set foot in his first motor, fifteen years old, barely able to see over the wheel, Billy had visited Cramond. Staring out at the cold blue sea, mind drifting off into the distance felt magic, peaceful, if that was at all possible. He used to come down as a kid with the rest of the young team, exploring all the nooks and crannies of the River Almond further on, dive-bombing off the waterfall on a cracking summer day, as disapproving old cows stood and scowled, skelping their bairns round the ear for trying to jump in themselves. Wandering to Cramond Island in the distance across a bed of murky wet sand, now that was the real adventure. One time the tide came back in, leaving them stranded there for hours. Didn't matter a fuck to Billy, he loved being stranded out there, felt like freedom.

"So Andy. These pills,"

"They're fuckin sweet man." he replied, in an accent Billy wasn't quite able to place.

"Where are you fae mate?" said George, his eyebrow raised with confusion, clearly wondering the same thing.

"I'm from Gala originally, Galashiels like. Moved up last year to go to college, staying up at Liberton now."

Billy could tell he was trying to talk rough but it was painfully obvious he was anything but. An oddball, a geek, kicked about and bullied, trying to find a place in life, a place that ecstasy had suddenly provided. It wasn't surprising given the way Billy had felt after that first pill hit him. That drug would make anyone feel like they belonged. Not just like they were part of *something*, like they were part of everything.

"Can ye roll joints Andy boy?"

"Aye, maaan." He said drawing out the "man" part in a strange fashion, like it was supposed to sound cool. Billy flung him a polythene bag containing a half ounce of soap bar, a packet of green Rizla and ten Regals. "So these tablets always that good? Cause the ones we had were fuckin dynamite."

"Oh aye. Get all kinds too, from a mate of a mate, They come up from Manchester. Doves, dollars, supermen, but doves are the best. You guys were lucky to have them fer yer first time, man." He grinned, as he licked a skin.

"Much dae they sell fer? On average like," said George.

"Bout ten, fifteen, sometimes twenty quid."

"Fuckin twenty quid, aye?"

"How much fer a thousand, Andy?" said Billy. The skins stopped rustling, Joe sat forward, and George turned with two raised eyebrows this time.

"Ah. Ah'm not sure. I only get say fifty to a hundred a time, sell to friends, folk from college, folk at the raves."

"Well it's no gonnae be ten to twenty a pop with those kindae numbers anyway," said George, clearly trying to do the maths in his head as to the potential profit at stake.

"Exactly. Think about it, we buy a load, right fae the get-go. We've already got Andy an all his pals tae sell tae, that's what, fifty tae a hundred a week you says?"

"Aye."

"Then between the lot eh us, we split the rest week in week out, go wherever the demand is. Cunt we awready know how strong they are, we'll no be able tae sell thum quick enough. We could do a thousand in a month no bother when ye take intae consideration personal as well."

"See anyone else sellin their ain, just tell thum straight, from now on ye get yer goods fae us. If they dinnae like it they get filled in," said George.

Billy caught a look of raw fear on Andy as he nervously crumbled the hash. Billy smiled, wary that George's approach might just scare him back down to Galashiels. "No need fer you tae worry Andy san, you're wae us. Naebody will fuck wae you pal." Billy glanced down at Andy's half-rolled joint. "By the way is that a carpet you're rollin us? Fuckin how many skins you usin?"

Joe laughed as he had a look himself. "He's usin the fuckin Evenin News!" said Joe as Andy joined in the laughter nervously at first and then with enthusiasm.

"Long as it smokes, eh."

22

Sean looked down at the steaming mug of coffee in front of him and sighed as he endured poor old Bob Callum's woes. Dad had been at it again, stirring up trouble, this time in the bookies. In the weeks since his release Sean had been at pains to keep him under control. He was bitter, that much was blatantly obvious to everyone, and it was a difficult one for Sean because every time he tried to reason with him he got his head bitten off, accused of taking his uncle's side.

Problem was, his Dad wasn't interested in compromise or patience, or seeing sense or reason. He just wanted his demands for half the business met, or else. Just as stubborn and hard nosed as Dougie, neither-side prepared to budge an inch. What made matters worse was every time Sean turned up at his Dad's flat there was a different escort on the go. Sean could barely go fourteen days without a ride let alone fourteen years, so yeah, he was making up for a lot of lost time. Sean got that. Still, it wasn't an image he wanted in his head as he tried to get to bed at night, the old man all bare arsed and rampant, hammering away at a quarter of a century of frustration, while some skanky whore howled with excitement.

Though at least when he was getting laid he wasn't stewing away, aggrieved that Dougie had given him the cold shoulder.

Davy had struck an easy target in Bob Callum no doubt, but it was what could only be construed as a thinly veiled warning shot at Uncle Dougie, for the bookies was his joint. Sean knew he was going to have to broker some kind of agreement between father and uncle, or shit was going to go off the deep end, and soon.

"So he's waltzed in like he owns the joint, swaggered straight up tae the counter, right? He's layin bets left right an centre, refusin tae pay. Ken what he keeps sayin? It's on Dougie, take it out of my settlement fund. So eventually I've put the foot down, or tried to at least. Ah've says tae um, no more bets till ye've paid what ye owe, a wee bit give an take, ye know? Ken what his answer is tae that? *You* give and *I* take! So I've tried tae stand ma ground ken? Customers lookin over, getting wary an that. Next thing ye know he's started howlin with fuckin laughter, like it's all a big joke, like he's havin me on, right? So I've eased up a wee bit. He's pattin me on the back, tellin me tae relax an that. Next thing, he's gripped me in a hug, but a long lingerin one, ye know what Ah mean? Like a scary, fuckin deeply uncomfortable one. An all the customers huv stopped what they're doin, lookin over, wonderin if he's fer real, probably wonderin when he's gonnae turn. Then he's kissed me on the cheek. So by this point, as ye can imagine, Ah'm just a wee bit uncomfortable. And he's honkin of the bevy too, stinkin ay it. So Ah'm tryin tae back away at this point but he's pulled me back intae another hug an by this point he's squeezin me as hard as he can, an Ah'm sweatin like, shitin it! Then it happens. He goes tae kiss me on the other cheek, except he doesnae kiss me this time, he sinks is dirty fuckin teeth, right intae ma cheek, Ah mean takes a fuckin chunk ootae it. Pulls away wae this sick grin on is face, an spits a mouthful of ma blood on the ground!"

Bob's plump face had turned scarlet.

"Then he swaggers toward the door. Ye know what he shouts as he's leavin? Ah'll be back same time the morn. And you better have ma coupon ready ya fat bastard!"

Bob pulled the top of the plaster down exposing a nasty hole that looked in danger of infection.

"Look at that. Now Sean, Ah don't want tae speak outae turn. Ah know Davy's yer old man, an Ah know you're doin yer best tae keep the peace an all that, but he's outae control man. Talk about an occupational fuckin hazard. Ah'm fuckin scared fer ma life! Ah'm gonnae need tae get a tetanus shot fer this shit. Biggest mistake Ah made wis tryin tae step in between him an Dougie at the homecomin. Big fuckin mistake, cause he's had his targets set on me ever since."

Dougie sat forward, staring through the coffee table with a dark brooding look. "He's goadin me Sean. Ye know this eh?"

"Aye. Aye, Ah get it."

Dougie shook his head. "An what's more, he's gonnae be back there the morn, raisin more hell, callin me out again. Sean ye need tae go back tae him. Tonight. You're the only person he'll listen to right now. If I get within a hundred yards of him right now I'll take his fucking head off." Dougie pushed an authoritative finger against the coffee table. "Give him my terms. An tell um they're non negotiable. And if he shows up at the bookies the morn demanding money again, fuckin scarin off customers and makin threats, Bob here will be pickin up that phone and the time for talkin will be over. And brother or no brother he'll be dealt with." Dougie pounded a fist into his palm as he growled. "Fuckin family!"

Sean pulled up outside his old man's flat. It had been a wee homecoming present, son to dad. A no bad wee flat, three months rent covered. Little did he know his old man would effectively turn it into a nightly whorehouse.

The lights were on and the music was up loud, above which he could hear his Dad shouting the lyrics at the top of his voice. At least he wasn't shagging, or at least Sean hoped he wasn't. Sean went into the back pocket for his wee vial. Time for a pop star. He racked it out on the dashboard before hoovering it up the right nostril, for the left one was getting a wee bit worn. Boom. Good to go.

The old man was yelling a distinctive chorus at the top of his voice as Sean rattled on the door as hard as he could. *The Who, The Kinks, The Stones.* Three bands his Dad had listened to nonstop since his release on the three cassettes that from all accounts he had been rocking all the way through his sentence. Sean didn't mind the older acts, he had a thing for Sinatra especially. Any guy who could croon like that, birds falling at his feet left right and centre, whilst the Mob did his dirty work, had Sean's respect. The door swung open to reveal his bare-chested old man grinning away whilst gripping onto a half-drunk bottle of vodka.

"There he is! The handsomest devil in town. Come in an have a drink wae yer auld man, eh?"

"Christ Dad, stick some claes on will ye?"

Sean took in the sight of the latest hooker sitting on the couch puffing away on a massive coned joint. She had bobbed red hair. Her pursed lips did little to hide yellowing teeth, and she kept pulling at a tight red pvc skirt that was hugging her freckly thighs.

"Son, meet Carol."

"Hiya pal."

"Bloody hell he's even mair handsome than you, doll."

"Hey!" said Davy, clearly eager to keep his ego on an even footing. "Yer right, though. Ah have reared an absolute cracker of a laddie though eh?" He grabbed Sean by the shoulders, pulled him close and kissed him on the cheek, prompting Sean to back away.

"No gonnae bite me are ye?"

His father turned to Carol. "You wantae make yersel scarce fer a wee bit hen? Father an son stuff, that's all." She passed Davy the cone and threw her nimble hands up in the air before heading for the living room doorway. Davy sat down on the couch and took a large puff of the smouldering joint before aiming his hand toward the armchair. He threw on a top and picked up a glass from the floor before dusting it off some and pouring Sean a vodka.

"What dae ye think of Carol then?"

Sean looked at his father, trying to sense if he was having a laugh or not.

"She's awright, ah suppose."

"She's a bit rough around the edges Ah know. An Ah know she couldnae hud a candle tae yer mother in the looks stakes, but she shoots straight. Tells ye when yer shit stinks, know what Ah mean? A man needs that. A strong woman like."

"Wait a minute Dad. She's a whore is she no?"

His father looked him straight between the eyes. "I met her at the Telford Arms yesterday afternoon son."

Davy grinned as he took another puff on the joint. "Keeps me occupied, eh."

Sean nodded his head awkwardly.

"So. Ye've been talkin tae the pieman Ah see?"

"Dad, Bob's harmless. Couldnae fight sleep."

"Aye well, it got yer uncle's attention at least. Knew he'd go running tae Dougie, he always has been his fuckin lap dug. Ever since we were young. An what's he sayin tae it anywey?"

"He's willin tae work somethin out."

"Ah'm listenin."

"Ye get the deeds tae The Gunner, signed an handed over, it's yours. And ye take over the loans in the area, for which, all the vig goes directly intae your pocket on a weekly basis."

"And? That's it? So he's gonnae leave me tae stick ma neck oot chasin after loan payments, an run a pub, *his* fuckin pub, while he sits there rakin in aw the drug profit? He can ram it sideways. If you think what happened the day was bad that's only the tip of the fuckin iceberg son. Ah'm gonnae bring him and his business tae its knees..."

"Ah thought ye'd say that. So that's why I've worked out a Plan B. It's no ideal, but as long as we can keep it discreet hopefully it can keep us all happy an prevent all out fuckin war between family."

Davy sat up.

"Guy that runs this hotel up the town. Tony Parker's his name. Always lookin fer charlie, always gantin on it. Thing is it's no just him. He's got a line on a whole bunch of privileged motherfuckers that were born with a silver spoon in their mouths an a mummy an daddy tae tend tae their every need. Ah'm talkin footballers, lawyers, real wealthy clientele. An they're payin way over the odds, an I mean *way* over the fuckin odds for their coke."

"Go on." Davy leaned forward.

"I figured things would go the way they have with you and Uncle Dougie. So I had a wee word with John at the homecoming about the possibility of getting some coke. An ounce at first but at the strength he gets it we could make that two ounces. Tony will bag it up and do all the legwork. He's got the network know what a mean? We split the lion's share fifty fifty. If it goes well an they keep comin back for more, next time we could get two ounces which then becomes four and more again the more the custom builds. These cunts will pay a hundred quid a gram for this stuff no bother, that's what they're payin the now an I've tried it, it's shite. Gave Tony one line of the stuff I get on personal an he was climbin the walls."

Davy couldn't stop the grin on his face growing wider by the second.

"An it gets better. As part of the deal he's gonna let us clean our money through his hotel. Fuckin perfect. Saves having to put more cash through The Gunner an get him suspicious know what Ah mean? He even says we can use different rooms on a weekly basis tae stash and cut the coke. It's fucking perfect, Dougie has no control. If we do this though, I have one condition Dad."

"Which is?"

"That ye let things settle wae Uncle Dougie. Keep the peace, accept his offer. Make like everything is fine and dandy. And ye don't under any circumstances tell anyone about this deal, cause if it gets back tae Dougie that we've set this up right under his nose without cutting him in it will kick off an that's exactly what Ah'm tryin tae avoid. He'll come round in time Dad, just play the game wae um."

"Ma lips are sealed son. And there will be no meddlin in Dougie's affairs fae me. Ye've got ma word."

23

Billy and George muscled in at the front of the queue for the Venue, as the powerful beats made the rain soaked ground beneath them shake. Billy had copped half before the car ride up and he could already feel the early signs rising in his stomach as the rest of the team barged their way into the queue behind them. Dollars were on the menu now, and as always Billy had been assured by Andy Riley that they were dynamite.

Riley had proven the ticket into all kinds of raves and parties in the weeks since the first batch had been purchased and they had taken full advantage of his network of E-heads. Now, however, ecstasy was pushing its way into the city's nightclubs, with The Venue on Calton Road at the forefront of the scene. The place looked like a stony sweat-soaked hole, filled with dirty techno and probably at least a couple of hundred folk looking for sweeties. The only problem with that picture was that the word on the street was Dale Alscott had the place sewn up, using Hibs casuals to push his product.

A well known gangster around Edinburgh, and an all-round sadistic bastard, Alscott was also a trained Thai boxer with a reputation for using swords on his enemies.

With hundreds of eccies between them, Billy knew that he and George may well be leading their mob into a world of danger, but they had managed to punt so many in the first few weeks of custom that they were already onto their second thousand and looking for anywhere and everywhere that they could push them. The danger was part of the excitement. The raves were a cakewalk, far too wide open for anyone to fully control. It was a breeze. The Venue on the other hand presented a challenge, and that challenge was providing a buzz similar to the feeling he had felt inside when they took to the Astroturf at Pilton all those years ago to exact revenge upon the unfortunate Kevin MacDonald, who now lived with a daily reminder on his face as to why you shouldn't fuck with the Muirhousers.

The bouncers didn't look familiar; that was a relief, at least. Chances were, they belonged to Dale Alscott. One of them who was grinning childishly wore an Ellesse tracksuit, a hefty beer belly and a nasty tan down his cheek. The other smaller built one was a little smarter looking with a white suit and tie and pinstripe trousers. He was stone faced, well chiselled. Looked like one of those wee cunts that could fight like fuck with folk far bigger.

"Ye sorted, boyos?" said the tracksuit wearing bouncer as Billy and George arrived at the door. This was a new breed of bouncer altogether, that was for sure. Billy and George looked at one another and back at the wired wideboy.

"What a shitehole, man," declared George as they made their way up the slippery stone staircase. Billy had brand new Nike Air Huaraches that would surely be mocket by the time they left. Still, he couldn't stop his body jerking to the beat as they made their way to the bar. The hard, menacing techno was deafening. The place was full of smoke, billowing from machines at the side of the dance floor. There were three guys on the dance floor, complete stormers, all with their tops off, waving glow sticks about, eyes popping out of their heads. Another boy was bouncing up and down close to them with a boiler suit and goggles on, thrusting his hands in the air like he was able to touch the moon, whilst a girl in a tie-dye dress danced lazily behind. It was basically an indoor rave and Billy liked it. Felt like a dark, dingy box, full of menace and euphoria in equal measures. As he turned and accepted a bottle of water from Joe he felt that grin stretching across his face again.

"You're melted ya cunt," said Joe.

"Who me? No quite yet." Billy waded through the team and found George at the bar, bobbing his head, arms crossed. If there was one thing about the big man, he very rarely let rip on the dance floor, no matter how fucked he got. He would just stand there, sweating like a rapist in his big bomber jacket, arms crossed, bobbing his head whilst looking about for custom to direct the young team toward. By the end of the night he might have progressed to lifting those big hulking arms in the air, able to relax, as most of the business had been done.

"Might be a shitehole Georgie Boy, but just wait till that half hits ye an it'll take on a whole new fuckin look."

George smiled as Billy slapped him on the back before taking his place at the bar next to him. "Ah was thinkin," said George. "Should wait till it's filled up before we start askin aboot. Dinnae wantae blow our cover too early."

"Bang on." Billy turned to George, unable to control the grin that had taken over his face. "Let's hope we get tae cut loose an enjoy oursels a bit before we go tae town in here, eh?"

Some time later, Billy pulled himself away from the dance floor to check how many eccies had been punted. It was clear that most folk had already purchased their goods from one of the head-cases doing the rounds, decked out in attire that screamed football casual.

It was becoming pretty obvious that they had their work cut out for them in this establishment. Billy caught sight of the doorman in the Ellesse tracksuit making for the toilets, closely followed by an associate who had on a cream Ted Baker polo top. He turned and nodded at George, who nodded back. It was time to introduce themselves, so they pushed their way through the clouds of smoke and wasted strangers bouncing to the beat, and made their way to the WC.

George started splashing water on his hands as Billy checked himself out in the mirror whilst sizing up the competition. The bouncer pulled a wad of notes from his tracksuit bottoms and began openly counting the night's takings as they shared a joke. These cunts were blatant. Clearly Dale Alscott had the owner in his pocket.

"Fuckin murder fer business the night George eh? Cannae sell shit in here man."

The two casuals began eyeballing Billy in the mirror as he turned to George with a smirk on his face. Within seconds he could feel the breath of the bouncer against the back of his neck. He looked up to see he now had his fists clenched, staring through the back of Billy's head, as George turned to face the other one.

"You tryin tae sell gear on our patch ya cunt?" The boy took a step closer as Billy continued checking himself out, whistling a catchy tune he had heard the DJ rocking moments earlier. He was so close now that if he'd had a hard-on, Billy would be able to feel it.

The bouncer turned to his friend. "These wee cunts obviously don't know who they're fuckin wae, eh Simon?"

"Naw. CCS, Capital City Service. We run this club. We run this fuckin town!" As Billy wiped his hands on his jeans, he clocked the boy pulling something from his backtail but barely had the chance to act before George wiped him out with one punch. As he lay there trailing out of a cubicle, knocked spark out, workie's arse spilling out the back of his trackie bottoms, Billy noticed the Stanley scuttle along the toilet floor. He picked it up and extended the blade, still whistling away at that catchy little tune as George flung the other casual up against the toilet wall like a rag doll. Billy wandered up to him and pressed the Stanley against his cheek as he felt the fear ringing out of his watering eyes.

"Tell yer boss we're taking over this fucking club, an won't stop until every fucking E that's popped in here comes directly fae us. And just so ye know we're serious..." Billy calmly ripped a line down his face, and watched as the blood gushed onto the cream Teddy Baker top.

The message had been delivered. Shame, as the music was getting good and Billy was starting to feel the full effect of that half E, but for now it was time to get out of dodge before the cavalry arrived.

24

"Eat this ya cunts!" was the cry from an eager youngster as he hurled a brick at the Venue doorway, sending an enraged Dale Alscott and his entourage diving inside for cover.

Billy ground his teeth as he stepped out of the motor, took a couple of steps run up and lobbed a large boulder of his own, which clattered against the white sign above the doorway. Within seconds there were boulders, bottles and bricks flying at the doorway as everyone poured out of the three cars and joined in the barrage. Billy stuck two fingers in either side of his mouth the second the onslaught came to an end and whistled at young Ricky Bowden, who ran up to the door and yelled "MON THEN!" as loud as they could.

Within seconds a wild-eyed Dale Alscott was out in the street waving a samurai above his head. As the two young laddies hightailed it up the street closely pursued by six Hibs boys, Billy made a rapid retreat to Jimmy's motor. As Billy went to yank the door open he noticed the trench coat clad, sword wielding psycho coming up from the rear, forcing him to turn and face. Alscott took a wild lunge, forcing Billy to arch himself backwards, the blade whistling dangerously past his Adam's apple. George emerged from the rear, tackling him to the floor.

Billy collected himself in a frenzy and jumped as high as he could, coming down two footed on Dale Alscott who managed to cover his face just in time to let his arms take the weight of the blow.

"Mon Billy, let's fuckin go!" screamed Joe from behind them, hanging halfway out of his car.

"Dale, there's two ay thum ran up the street. Let's fucking do thum!" yelled a burly Hibs boy, as Billy flung himself in the passenger side and pulled the door shut.

"You'll see me again! I'll fuckin remember your face ya little CUNT!" screamed Alscott, pointing his finger squarely at Billy from outside the car as he gripped onto his sword, his piercing eyes bulging out of their sockets.

Billy pushed his lips against the glass and blew him a kiss as the Volvo kicked into gear.

As they pulled away from the stone wall that divided Waverley Station from Calton Road, the sirens began ringing out loud and clear. Billy felt his heart hammering against the walls of his chest at a frightening pace as they drove past three meat wagons that were coming the other way. The plan had worked a treat. An anonymous phone call about serious trouble at the club had ensured the polis were there in a heartbeat, and the only thing they would find now was a tooled up madman and his CCS entourage chasing two young laddies down the street.

The other anonymous call had circled Dale Alscott's name as the number one ecstasy distributor inside the Venue.

25

Sean and Willie had barely exchanged more than pleasantries since their spat outside Willie's flat. And now he was walking down there with a request that wasn't likely to improve things between them, but nonetheless Sean was willing to use the opportunity to at least try. The shit was getting tiresome. The one word answers. The frosty welcomes. The sly looks. Their friendship had been through a lot since high school. The birds, the drugs, the crimes had all taken their toll from time to time, but since Willie had introduced himself to his own product in such a big way, they had become two very different people.

Sean now embodied everything that Willie had once loved. Willie's once rampant libido was disintegrating underneath the weight of the smack and Sean could see and feel the envy staring back at him every time he looked into his friend's eyes. Problem was, he now seemed beyond help. Willie had ounces of smack around him all the time and with the likes of Simon Lockhart and all the other junky hangers on that he mixed with these days, Sean felt like he was wasting his time despite his best efforts.

The dark bags were hanging twice as low beneath those disdainful eyes and his ribs were even more prominent than the last time Sean had seen him as he stood at the doorway, bare-chested with chains dripping from his neck. Sean entered the living room behind his pal, stepping over charred pieces of foil and fag stubs. A neglected Nintendo console lay on the floor in front of a television set stuck on an episode of *Eastenders*. A dim table lamp was barely lighting up a room that was shielded from the outside world by thick dark curtains.

The Clash poster was still there though, a symbol of Willie's glory days – the young nutter that passed the birds back and forth like a rolled-up note, that angry, witty maniac, that walking hard-on, brash as fuck. There it was, peeling at the corners, tattered and worn, but still clinging to that otherwise bare wall, stuck there like a constant reminder of the real Willie, not the crumbling junky he had become.

One thing that hadn't crumbled though was Willie's capacity for violence. He was still an asset in that regard. That was why when Davy needed a debt collected but was too proud to ask Dougie to handle it, they had agreed on Willie.

"Fuck sake Willie. Look at the state of this place. If the polis bust doon that door. Ye ken how dodgy it is sittin aboot here out yer faces, could be watchin this place as it is."

"Aye well, Ah'm the cunt that takes the rap eh. Stuff''s always gone within days anyway, jist personal here eh."

"Aye still man, think about it eh?"

Sean shrugged his shoulders knowing he was wasting his time. He twisted up a one skinner with tobacco and coke in rapid fashion, lit it, and released a puff of sickly sweet fumes into the air, feeling his head steadily lighten. He turned and edged the curtain open, exposing a beam of light that forced Willie to coil into his couch like a scalded vampire.

"You need tae get out mair, Willie. It's nae good fer ye sittin in here aw the time. Ye dae yer business then ye retreat tae yer hole tae pump aw yer profit intae they veins. It's nae way tae live man. You're probably daein twice as much of that shite as half the cunts on the streets man. You've got money, unlike any of them. Problem is all yer profit just goes straight back intae yer arms."

"Aw dinnae start eh. Standin there smokin coke."

"Aye yer right. Ah'm only wastin ma time after aw. There's somethin else Ah need tae talk tae ye aboot anyway. Asian boy fae Telford. Name's Rasheed. Took a loan off ma old boy a few weeks back and he's yet tae make any payments. It's three grand an ma dad's getting antsy tae say the least."

"An what's that got tae dae wae me like?"

"He wants you tae go through the cunt's door an make um pay up. If he's no got it, give um a doing, tell him he's got another week or him and his family are in danger."

"Yer kiddin aren't ye? Ah'm spent the now, no fuckin way. Tell um tae dae it umsel."

"Dae you wantae go an tell um like?"

Willie looked at Sean for a second with strained eyes before looking away.

"Thought so. It's too dodgy for him anyway, just out the jail."

"What, an it's no too dodgy fer me? One false move an Ah'm stuck away fer years. Cunts are after me twenty-four seven, chokin tae bust me so they are."

"Look, he's asked specifically fer you, ye know how proud he is. Doesnae want tae go askin Dougie's muscle, so he asked me tae come tae you."

"An what's in it fer me like?"

"Look, it's no me givin the order awright? If you wantae head up tae The Gunner an bargain wae ma auld boy then on ye go, but all Ah can say is good luck."

Willie knelt forward as he peered up at Sean with searching eyes. "Does Dougie ken yer auld man's dishin oot orders tae cunts on his payroll?"

"Naw, an he's no gonnae. No his business is it?"

"Aye Ah'm sure he'd see it that way right enough. If Ah didn't know any better I'd think he was lookin tae make a play against Dougie, wae you tae back um up, gatherin the troops, rock the boat an that."

Sean pondered Willie's words as he held in the hit from the joint, feeling his head grow light as he let the smoke drift from his mouth up his nostrils. Was that his dad's plan? Use Sean to get Willie on side, gradually growing their own firm underneath Dougie's nose? "Dinnae talk stupid. Dougie knows he's loan sharkin anyway."

"When's he want it done?"

"Might as well get yerself up there the night. He runs a corner shop. Wee hole next tae the flats. That's where ye'll find um."

"A fuckin shop! Ye havin a laugh? Plenty opportunity fer witnesses."

"It's a shed mate, nae cameras or that."

"Here, gies a blow ay that."

Sean flung him the last of the coke joint. "Mair where that came fae here." He pulled a wrap out of his back pocket and dropped it on the table. "There's over a gram in there. It's the good shit an aw, completely unjumped on. Git that up yer snout before ye head up there, ma treat. That'll give ye all the energy ye need, fuckin marching powder. In fact bosh that out now an do us a couple of big ones before I shoot off."

Willie shrank back into the couch, zoned out, clearly struggling to move a muscle.

"Looks like I'll have tae do it then, eh?" Sean emptied the wrap out onto the table and chopped out two thick lines. "Willie mate, this thing with the smack is getting old. Dae ye wantae end up like Ryan Lockhart, or Derek Rennie? In yer forties, nae bird, skagged oot yer brain twenty-four-seven? Use this shit tae get ye back on yer game man. Used tae be a fuckin ladykiller, man. Ye can be again."

Sean's false hopes felt even more genuine after he emptied the line up his nostril and stood up straight, brain focused. He thrust his hands downwards at the used needles on the floor. "This shit's killin ye man. The coke's all ye need tae keep ye on point. Let all the other mugs shoot up." He looked down and watched his friend follow suit, before watching as it breathed life back into that frail body. Willie wiped vigorously at his nose before sitting up straight.

"When's he wantin it done then? The night?"

There it was, that violent urge raging out of him, an urge that no manner of smack could drain. Sean reckoned it was the only other hit that Willie lived for now. What was even more dangerous was that urge had now been fuelled by preemo cocaine.

Willie powered his way along the railway toward Telford later that night as the *Happy Mondays* blared into his ear drums. Sean was right, in his own superior and sanctimonious way. Willie needed to kick the smack. Hadn't had a ride that he hadn't paid for in close to two years. His flat was a doss house occupied by cunts. Cunts the lot of them, all hangers on, looking for a spare bit of gear like fucking vultures. Get in line and pay like the rest of the sorry cunts in the scheme.

Willie knew the only way he would ever stop the gear was if he stopped selling it, but that wasn't going to happen anytime soon, was it? He was responsible for supplying most of the jakie cunts in Muirhouse, and the best of it was he was a jakie now too just like the rest of them. Only difference was he had a bit more cash to throw around, that was all. He felt an angry itch beginning to burn underneath his skin. Pretty soon it would be too hard to ignore. That was the problem with ching, it didn't last long enough. He'd arsed the whole gram after Sean left but once that buzz wore off all that would be left was that burning urge for the skag brought on tenfold. He slapped at his face a few times and growled at the dark path in front of him, as he tried to focus on the sawn-off that was stuffed down the front of his Levi's. Still gave him that sense of power that he had felt when he first held a piece. At least that feeling hadn't died, strong as ever. Even felt it giving him a bit of a hard on as the cold hard steel rubbed against his tadger. What the fuck was wrong with him? A shotgun could bring it to attention in a heartbeat but a naked bird could barely muster a thing these days. Willie Graham. Fucking mental, of that there was no doubt. Pure crazy. No drug could take that away from him.

As he approached the graffiti covered walls, from the muddy slope at the edge of Telford Park, a grey hoodie pulled over his head and a scarf wrapped round his face covering everything but his black coked up pupils, he wondered what the fuck he was doing turning up all barrels blazing without a getaway. Had Sean and his coke to blame for that though, the cunt. It was marching powder all right. He'd marched from Muirhouse to Telford in what felt like seconds.

There were two of them, great. One behind the counter, who was obviously Willie's man, and another smaller man leaning on it from the other side scanning the pages of a newspaper. He could just make them out through the sliver of doorway as he snaked his way along the side of the offie and peered round the corner before looking all around him for unwanted witnesses.

He felt the sweat pouring from his face and soaking into the fabric of the scarf, and pulled it down so he could wipe it away with his sleeve. He was beginning to feel that agitated way, how you sometimes got when you'd had a load of ching but it was starting to wear off. Worse for him he would be clucking like fuck very soon, his brain, and body desperately aching to replace one high for that other more cosy and familiar one. The thing that was adding to his agitation was he had been here before loads of times. It was one of those off licences, popular amongst cunts who liked their bevy at unusual times. Such as the times when you were at a house party full of folk speeding out of their nuts, and that last glass of vodka and coke had been tanned. Certain places wouldn't bat an eyelid at dishing you bevy even at half five in the morning if need be and this was one of them. He was knee deep in Telford after all. Who gave a fuck about a licence? The important part of this angle was that he had been one of those raging speed freaks turning up demanding bevy at an ungodly hour, and he hoped to fuck the cunt wouldn't be able to finger him. Lucky that sweat drenched scarf was pulled tight around half his face. Best he kept it there, as irritating as it was becoming. He looked down at his shaking. What was wrong with him? All he needed to do was charge in and take as much money as they had in there. If it wasn't enough, tough, Davy could go chasing after the rest.

Without letting another thought push its way into his head he barged the door open and whipped the sawn-off out of his jeans, raising it to head height, and walking toward the counter where the two men hadn't even looked up yet.

"HEY!" He dragged the shotgun handle along a shelf, knocking dozens of chocolate bars to the floor. He had their attention now, as they stood up straight with their hands in the air. The first guy, stood there, frozen, looking straight at Willie through his spectacles, clearly too petrified to turn away as he stalked toward him.

"You! Look at the fuckin groond awright!?" He slammed the shotgun handle into his face, knocking him to the floor as several teeth spilled from his mouth and danced along the deck like tiny skittles. He aimed the sawn-off firmly at Rasheed, who was breathing heavy.

"Jist calm down man eh!? Ah'll get you everything I have in the till. Just give me two secs!"

"Aye fuckin right ye will. This is what ye get fer fallin behind oan yer payments ya cunt."

"My payments?"

"Yer payments aye! It's no a robbery, it's a fuckin collection! Now get the money out pronto before Ah lose ma fuckin patience ya pakki bastard!"

He rammed the shotgun handle into the front of the till, sending it crashing to the ground on the other side of the counter. "Jist hurry the fuck up will ye! An pick it back up so Ah can see what yer daein. Nae tryin any funny business behind there, or yer pal here gets a bullet in um."

The specky wee gadgy on the floor peered up at Willie again before catching a heavy boot that clattered his glasses sideways.

As Rasheed frantically pulled a stack of notes from the till, Willie heard the door open.

Fuck Fuck Fuck...

It was a wee woman standing about five foot tall, also of Asian descent. The whole fucking family was there now. Willie cursed himself for agreeing to this mental job. "Hands where Ah can fuckin see thum you!"

She began muttering her native words under her breath, as she threw her nimble wee hands in the air. Sounded like she was praying. Nippy as fuck.

"Shut up!"

She continued muttering, prompting Willie to thrust the sawn-off at her.

"Ah says shut yer fuckin noise!!"

The words had barely come out his mouth before he felt the blade go into his shoulder.

"YOU CUNT!" Next thing you know he heard the scream of a banshee and the crazy little dyke was clinging onto his back with her little arm tight around his neck, trying to choke the life out of him.

He backed hard into the sweet shelf, knocking enough wind out of her so he could loosen her grip enough for him to ram an elbow against her jaw, forcing her to fall to the deck next to Specky. Willie turned his attention back to the counter, puffing and panting, trying to block out the sound of the irritating muttering coming from down below.

Shut up shut up shut up...

Sounded like little insects crawling underneath the sweaty scarf that was now clinging to his chin. He wrapped it firmly back around his mug.

"Money. NOW!"

She sprung up at him like a relentless little ball of fury, the momentum forcing them to collapse into a stand full of car air fresheners, the wee felt trees spilling everywhere as they wrestled for control of the sawn-off.

Willie pulled the trigger in a panic and watched as she collapsed under the force of the point-blank gunshot that tore right through her arm. Her face was now white with shock as she lay there in a bloody heap. Her prayers were now tiny murmurs and all fight had left her.

"AISHA!! YOU EVIL BASTARD I'LL KILL YOU!!"

There was no time to stand and stare as he now had a knife wielding shopkeeper tearing his way round the counter looking for revenge. Willie fired off another three shots as he came at him, the last one hitting its target, a short shrill scream as he dropped like a sack of tatties. Willie scarpered out the door and back up towards the railway, before frantically wiping down the sawn-off and chucking it in the bushes.

What an amateur, turning up with a shooter and no getaway. The longing for that sweet skag engulfed his mind like a dirty cloud as he bombed it down the railway to the sound of distant sirens.

26

Sean pressed his fingers into his temples, his elbows resting on the edge of the bar in The Gunner as the paper lay open in front of him. This was very bad shit.

ASIAN WOMAN SHOT AND LEFT FOR DEAD IN OFF LI-CENCE.

Aisha Ahmed (44) was shot at point-blank range in a newsagents on Telford Drive at around 9pm last night. Her husband, 46-year-old shopkeeper Rasheed Ahmed, managed to escape the attack unscathed despite a further four gunshots heard around the area. The Police have detained their main suspect in what is looking like a possible race attack. Whilst currently in critical condition, Aisha Ahmed has been lauded by officers who have praised her heroic actions in trying to wrestle the shotgun from the attacker.

Davy appeared cutting an image of dark turmoil, setting a bottle of whisky and two glasses in front of them, before scrunching up the paper and dumping it in the bin behind the bar.

"I cannot believe he took a fucking shotgun with him. Fuckin idiot. If he talks, we're fucked, you and me, ye know that eh?"

"Willie's solid Dad, he'll no grass."

"You sure about that son? Even if they tag this as a fucking race attack and he's facin what fifteen to twenty years? Who knows how much if she fuckin crokes it!"

"Look, I'll speak tae him. We'll work it out."

"Work it out? Sean, Ah know he's yer best pal, but Ah'm no goin back inside fer nae cunt!"

There was a rapid banging at the front door. Sean's arse fell out for fear of the worst. If Willie had buckled under the pressure, they were fucked, Dad was right. He felt the dread rising up in his chest like a sickness, his heart started thumping like a hip hop beat, this was it, either a heart attack or a collaring, with both scenarios looking pretty grim to say the least. They both looked at one another as the banging continued.

Davy put a finger to his lips. "Out the fuckin back door. We need tae get our stories straight before we face those cunts."

Sean felt his knees trembling as Davy unbolted the door at the back of The Gunner. This was it. The heading was clear in his mind.

SEAN DONALDSON – RACIST MURDERER.

The door had barely opened an inch before an irate Uncle Dougie bulldozed his way through it, sending Davy tumbling under the force of a heavy right hand. Soon they were all over each other, sending Sean tumbling himself under the weight of the struggle. He sat there trying to catch his breath as father and uncle rolled around the floor like laddies on the playground, both trying to gain the upper hand so they could smack the shit out of the other.

After a minute or so of struggling Sean stepped in having seen enough, helping them separate. Dougie dragged himself to his feet, still raging, his shirt ripped open exposing a red, heaving chest.

"Been ootae jail five fuckin minutes and already yer hell bent on fuckin everything up in't ye!?"

Davy spat a mouthful of blood from his busted lip, as Sean stood in between with arms outstretched, determined to stop them from going at it again.

"I've had Willie on the phone fae the fuckin jail, cause he couldnae get a hold ay you Sean! Cluckin like fuck, freakin out. The heat this brings down on everyone, dae you have any idea?" He jabbed his finger at Sean. "I expected mair fae you. You gonnae let this fuckin idiot drag ye doon with um are ye? So keen tae follow in Daddy's footsteps wae a nice hefty prison sentence!?"

"ENOUGH!" yelled Davy. "We sent him tae pick up a debt! How were we tae know he'd end up blastin the cunt's wife!?"

"Ye should've came tae me! I could've got Gordon or George tae handle it properly! Not Willie when he's roasted on fuckin smack! But ye were too proud weren't ye? Had tae try an deal wae it yersel! Well look where it's got ye. Bravo. Well this is your mess, both ay yous, so you can clean it up, better no fall in my fucking lap! You better make fucking certain he keeps his mooth shut! Oh and another thing. Thanks tae you, big brother, I've now lost one of my main dealers. He's caught red handed. They've got the shooter and two witnesses, so he's no gonnae see the light of day in a very long time. That means I lose a lot ay money while I rearrange things. That's money you're gonnae cover. You're responsible so it comes outae your pocket!"

Davy laughed. "So what – ye gonnae put a tax on me now are ye? Like ye've no got enough money ya greedy fuckin bottom feeder!"

"Fuckin right! Until further fucking notice!"

"Steady Uncle Dougie, I can manage the full distribution in the meantime. It's workable."

"What and cut him in on the sly? No likely! Am cuttin you outtae the smack Sean. Until such time as Ah feel Ah can trust ye again."

Sean shuddered at the impact of the back door slamming shut behind Dougie.

"If Willie can spill the beans tae that bastard what dae ye think he's capable of sayin tae the polis when they press him? Eh?"

Davy stepped closer to Sean, who was feeling the strain, stuck in an increasingly tough spot between Father, Uncle and best friend.

Before he could answer back, there was another loud banging at the front door.

By the time they made their way through and noticed the flashing lights outside, it was too late, they had the place surrounded.

27

Davy sneered at the two detectives as he stubbed a cigarette out firmly on the table in front of him, willing one of them to object to it. On the outside he was keeping up a cold, hard, defiant front that betrayed the fact he was flapping like a flag in the wind on the inside. He had been out barely two months after a stretch of fourteen long, hard years and there was no danger he was going back for seconds. He sat there enduring the onslaught, lighting fag after fag, with the occasional break to utter the words, "No comment". All the while the cogs were turning in his mind. Had that little scumbag smack-head Willie Graham dared give him up? And why was it they were only interested in him and not Sean? And as if all this wasn't enough, he now had Dougie, his ungrateful bastard of a younger brother, trying to use the situation to exert his self assumed superiority, demanding a cut of his takings to make up for the money Davy had supposedly cost him, but that was all bull shit and Davy knew it. Just another excuse for Dougie to try and keep him in his place. No danger, Tubsy. This was the older brother's time. Sooner or later, Dougie would have to step aside and allow him to assume control. If Davy was able to stay out of prison long enough that was.

"So much for keepin yer nose clean, David. Fourteen years in Bar L Didn't think ye'd be in such a hurry to go back. Ye homesick?"

"Ah dinnae ken what yer talkin about. Ah'm no sayin a thing until ma lawyer's here."

"An how ye gonnae pay fer a lawyer? Wae yer loan sharkin money?"

"Ah dinnae ken what yer talkin aboot, pal."

"Aw come on David, we've been keepin tabs on you since ye got out. Did ye think we were gonnae let ye outae our sights?"

"Look boys, Ah'm awfy flattered by aw the attention, but seriously, stop wastin ma time an let me outae here. Ah've kept ma heid doon an steyed ootae trouble since Ah got oot. Ah collect glasses an serve pints, fer fuck's sake just let a man get on wae his life eh?"

The detective moved over to the table and clamped his hands down on it before looking squarely at Davy. "Stop talkin shite, an start talkin! We know you're behind this!"

He looked the detective square in the eye with defiance. "Ah'm no sayin a word until ma fuckin lawyer's here." Davy took the last draw of his cigarette before stubbing it out on the table. He took another cigarette out and lit it up as he locked eyes with the other detective who had been keeping a back seat till now. His blonde hair was slicked into a quaff, with boyish looks. Looked like he was barely out of high school. "You'd get eaten alive in the jail you."

"Ye got the photos Sam? Gettin a bit tired of this merry go round."

"Aw dinnae tell me ye's have been takin photaes an aw? Nothin too explicit Ah hope?"

"Better than that." He pulled a set of photos out of a folder and dropped them on the table, a smug smile stretching across his pretty face. They showed Davy handing Rasheed a wad of cash outside The Gunner.

Davy sat back in his chair, his brain hard at work trying to decide which card to play next. The good thing was this meant all they had was a hunch that he was behind the shooting, based on a few photos. The bad thing was all they needed to do was press Willie a little harder and they might just connect the dots that led to Davy heading back in for another ten stretch at the very least. He didn't like those odds.

"What's the matter Davy? Cat got your tongue?"

The detective pressed his finger against the worried looking figure of Rasheed in the photo.

"This man was shot in his off licence last night. His wife is currently in a critical condition in the Western. Better hope that condition doesn't get worse."

"We've got the shooter and it's only a matter of time till he fingers you. He'd probably give you up for a score bag right now the way he's itching for it. Might as well make it easier on yerself and come clean now Davy pal. Only a matter of time till we fill in the blanks."

Davy could feel a vein throbbing away at his temple as he drove back to Muirhouse from the station, every now and then smacking his large bony hands against the top of the steering wheel and screaming out of the window as the stark reality set in. The pressure was unbearable. Fourteen years was a bloody long time, too long. It had cost him a wife and two daughters, a big part of fatherhood, not to mention a big part of his life, and he would stop at absolutely nothing to stay out. Whether it be a desperate smack-head facing a twenty stretch, or a money dodging chancer ducking payments, not a soul who posed a threat to his newfound freedom was safe.

As he swerved round the corner into Pennywell Road, forcing another motorist to slam on the brakes, he noticed a familiar sight plodding its way down the pavement. Bob fucking Callum, the perfect target for him to deflect his fury.

"BASTAAAAAARD!!"

He spun the steering wheel to the right, forcing the car onto the pavement and made a beeline for the panicked bookie owner whose fish supper was now scattered across the road. He took him out by his trailing leg, before slamming the car into reverse, hoping that his body was underneath the wheels.

After screeching to a halt at the side of the road Davy lurched out of the car, grabbed him by the ankles and dragged him into the middle of the pavement before snatching hold of his collar as he glowered over him with fist clenched.

"That your idea eh? Fuckin taxin me because ay what happened wae Willie!? Ah ken your fuckin game ya fat bastard ye, always feedin him wae ideas!"

"Ah dinnae ken what yer talkin about Davy!"

"Dinnae gimme me yer shite! Ah bet you've put him up tae this! Think Ah'm fuckin well stupid? Ah see ye havin yer little quiet words in his ear. Clingin tae his side like a fat fuckin lap dog!"

"Ye've lost yer bloody mind man!"

Davy rammed a fist hard into Bob's jaw, sending him sprawling as he tried to drag himself out of harm's way. "Well here's what's gonnae happen. Whatever figure that greedy bastard comes up wae, you're gonnae double it! Fer as long as he wants tae keep up this fuckin power trip! Ah know the majority of his drug money goes intae that lock-up you've got in that back room. So every week when Ah come knockin you're gonnae remove as much as Ah feel like takin. That way he's the one gettin fuckin taxed!"

"Ye cannae dae this tae me David! Yer gonnae bury me!"

"An if any of this gets back tae Dougie this time around that will be the last fuckin fish supper you ever eat ya FAT BASTARD!"

28

Billy slowly lifted his head and rose from his pit, wondering for a second or two where he was and what day it was. He rolled over, attempting to clear the cobwebs, straining his mind to try and retrieve some memories from the previous few days of blurry oblivion. He walked across the room, standing on an empty can of Tennent's and knocking over a full ashtray as he went. He looked back for a few seconds, wondering where Lyndsay was before slowly making his way into the kitchen, using the wall to prop up his shaky frame as he went.

As he filled up the kettle and switched it on, small details began creeping into his fried brain. Making a moronic attempt at mixing a pair of turntables in Joe's flat, a running battle with a bunch of angry Leithers on Lothian Road. Snapshots, bits and pieces, but from Saturday night onwards nothing but black space. As the kettle came to the boil he fished around in his fridge for a half empty pint of milk that was a week past its sell by date.

Bastard...

After braving the walk to the shops for a pint of milk, an *Evening News* and a chippy, he picked up the receiver pondering who to call. He considered Lyndsay but he had a feeling in his gut that would be a bad move. They had only been seeing each other a few months and already in that short time frame he had pissed her off more times than he could count. He knew he had promised to meet her on Sunday and yet he had no recollection whatsoever of that entire day so either they had met and he had made a complete cunt of things or he had blanked her. Either way she would be pissed off and he wasn't in the right head space to deal with that. Billy and girlfriends, not a good combination. Maybe he was destined to be a cunt to women. Bravo Billy, finally taking after the old man. He picked up a half smoked joint from the night before, lit it up and fell back onto his mattress.

He picked up the *Evening News* as he released a cloud of smoke from his mouth and scanned the front page. What he read made him jerk forward, spilling several hotrocks onto the bed sheet.

A bad batch of the dance drug ecstasy has been blamed for two collapses in an Edinburgh nightclub. Two youths collapsed in the Venue on Calton Road in the early hours of Sunday morning. The collapses were blamed on a suspect batch of ecstasy tablets that have entered Edinburgh. The tablets, known as Snowballs, are said to contain high levels of the horse tranquiliser ketamine, as opposed to the usual levels of the substance MDMA which is said to create the loved-up ecstasy feeling.

Billy snatched up the receiver and jammed in George's digits.

The following morning Billy pulled up outside Telford College, George in the passenger seat and Joe and Jimmy in the back.

"Fuckin horse tranquiliser, explains a lot. Fuckin blackout material," grumbled Billy as he searched the crowds for Andy Riley, trying his hardest not to let the tidy fanny on all sides distract him. It was a cracking day but his head was still burst from the weekend. This was why he had a pair of jet black Ray-Bans wrapped around his dome. Not for the sun, but to disguise his bloodshot eyes. "Ah can barely remember a thing since Saturday." Billy shook his head sadly.

"Last Ah remember is bein bent over a fuckin bin spewin ma load, no kennin where Ah wis. Ended up wanderin aboot toon fer hours tryin tae get ma bearings. Felt like Ah wis walkin aboot in slow motion man," said Jimmy as he pressed his freckled forehead against the window.

"Nae ride again then?" said Joe, prompting laughter from Billy and George in the front.

"Aye you can talk ya lanky bastard."

"There he is!" shouted Billy, watching as George flung the car door open and bounced out. He grabbed the pale faced figure of Andy Riley by the scruff of his collar and dragged him across the pavement like a rag doll, his Reebok pumps trailing behind him as several startled students stopped in their tracks and looked on with concern, clutching their books and folders. It was clear they weren't used to seeing other students manhandled into cars and abducted from the campus in broad daylight. As George flung him in the back next to Jimmy and Joe, Billy leaned forward and addressed the gathering audience outside.

"Show's over, people. Nowt tae see here! We'll have um back in one piece dinnae you worry!"

"Guys what's goin on? I've a class to go to!"

"Change of plan, Andy pal." As Billy stepped on the accelerator Andy let out a high pitched yelp, punctuated only by the clunk of steel against knee cap.

Jimmy flung an arm around Andy's neck. "Do you wantae explain the story in yesterday's paper, Andy?"

"Look, it was a dodgy batch, it happens! Aaaaaahhhh!" Again that sound of steel against knee cap.

"No tae us it fuckin doesnae!"

By the time Billy had reached the roundabout at the Shell Garage, both Joe and Jimmy were taking pot shots at will, giving poor Andy's legs a hammering. Billy slammed a Rez tape in the player and cranked up the volume to drown out the screams. It was a shame, because Billy kind of liked Andy in spite of all his geekiness. But they had to make a statement that shit drugs were a serious no no. Since Dale Alscott's arrest, they had moved swiftly and with force to occupy the void left within the Venue, giving them a regular base with which to operate and push their custom. They were making good cash with plenty to go around for everyone. Even the young team at the bottom of the ladder were getting a taste. Add to this the raves, legal and illegal, the house parties, the widening customer base it was all kicking off.

Billy increased the speed up to fourth gear as he swerved round the roundabout past the Shell Garage and off in the direction of Silverknowes. "Jist goin fer a wee drive doon the beach Andy boy!" he shouted as he stepped harder on the accelerator.

Billy pulled up at the very same spot where they had first brokered their arrangement a couple of months previously. The place was choc-a-block with families, dog walkers and groups of teenagers. It was early May with a bit of sun ranging above ten degrees and everyone was out basking in it. Tops off like they were in the Med.

Billy pushed stop on the tape player, leaving nothing but the sound of Andy's whimpering in the back. A couple of seconds later and he was screaming again as Jimmy began pushing the metal bar into his windpipe.

"Right guys, leave um be," said Billy before turning around and flinging a copy of the *Evening News* at Andy's face.

"So what's the deal wae the shite eccies then Andy? Now we look like right cunts."

"It was a b-bad batch, n-n-nothing I could do. This makes me and my crew look bad as well man."

"It's no fuckin good enough," said Billy.

Joe skelped him round the head before pointing in his face. "Ye hear that? No good enough!"

"Ah'm s-sorry Billy! Ah donno what ye want me tae say?"

"Ah want assurances it's no gonnae happen again is what Ah want."

Joe cracked him again this time in the shin, followed by another one from Jimmy.

"Please make them stop! Please!" Tears were now streaming down his face.

"Well we're gonnae give ye a chance tae redeem yersel awright? See we're sick of havin tae go through you an yer faggot arse pals fer our gear. Fae now on we deal directly wae the supply."

"That's gonnae be difficult. They only deal with a handful of folk. They're funny that way, folk they can trust. They're big-time."

George turned around, having stayed silent until now, casting a stare that clearly had Andy shitting bricks, as if he wasn't already. "What and we're no like?"

"You callin us small-time? Eh!" screamed Jimmy, before throttling him with the bar again.

"Right Jimmy, let the cunt breathe," said Billy with a smirk. "Things are gonnae change awright? End of fuckin story. We're the cunts wae egg oan our faces an we want proper assurances. So you're gonnae talk tae your pal, who's gonnae talk tae his pals pals an me an George are gonnae go meet thum, have a drink and talk business. An they're gonnae have tae trust us cause we're shiftin a lot ay gear fer thum. An if ye don't do what were askin ye tae dae, Ah'll cut you up personally. An then we'll come after yer pals. Ye got it?"

"A-aye."

"Clever laddie."

After dropping a shaken and limping Andy Riley back at Telford College, Billy headed for The Gunner. As he pulled up outside however something was nagging at him. It was a weird feeling. He wasn't used to giving two fucks about anyone other than himself, his mates and his mum, certainly not some bird, but the fact he was concerned he may have messed things up altogether this time either by standing her up, or worse, meant he clearly gave a shit. He stared at the front of The Gunner whilst the lads got out the car, weighing up whether to sack it and go for a pint or go and speak to Lyndsay.

"Ye comin or what?" said George.

"Ah better go an sort things oot wae her guys eh."

The response was predictable, especially with this crowd. Within seconds they were falling over one another with laughter, and he couldn't say a thing because if it had been one of them he would have been exactly the same.

"Aw aye, hear that boys? Goin crawlin back tae the bird are ye?" said Joe.

"Aye aye, get it oot yer systems. Least Ah've got one tae crawl back tae ya cunt."

"Ah can dae waeoot the heidache mate." said Joe.

"Jist let her come tae you Billy. Fuck her," said Jimmy.

"Nah, fuck it. Ah might as well go an find oot the damage while her battleaxe ay a mother isnae aboot."

George smiled. "Just dinnae let her get her claws in too deep mate or next thing ye know ye'll be spendin yer Saturday nights sittin in watchin Easties."

"No chance," smiled Billy.

As he walked up the path to Lyndsay's front door, closing the gate behind him, he was knocked off guard by the piercing yapping of her Jack Russell Stanley.

"And what exactly do you want? We're over, period."

"What ye talkin aboot?"

She laughed out loud. "What am I talking about? I'm talking about you turning up at Fraser's an hour late on Sunday afternoon, stinking of bevy, shouting and swearing your head off. Going fighting with folk in the street. And then falling asleep in a restaurant. Just as we were about to order. Then as if that's not bad enough, after we were politely asked to leave the restaurant you started on the waiter, collapsed on your arse, then when I tried to help you up you shoved me away and left! Looks like you were right to begin with. You are bad to the stinking bone! I'm worth more than this so you can go and find some other mug!"

"Fuck sakes, at least Ah turned up!?"

She threw him a look of disbelief before slamming the door hard in his face.

He spent the next five minutes ringing the doorbell, tapping her living room window and throwing stones up at her bedroom window but to no avail, as the sound of Stanley's barking tore away at his thumping head.

All the while he wondered what the hell he was playing at. The guys were right. This was mental, relationships weren't for him. The thought of ending up like his mum and dad was his biggest nightmare anyway. As he stormed back down the pathway with the image of an ice cold pint in his mind, suddenly the door opened.

"Five minutes."

The scent of her house reminded him of bubble baths when he was a bairn, one of his few happy childhood memories. In the living room there were two enormous fluffy beige couches that were the comfiest things he had ever sat on. Wished he had one as a bed, he would never leave the fucker. That was Morningside for you, folk with serious money, the other side of society. Made him feel awkward, out of place. He was probably about the only Muirhouser who had set foot in a house on that street or even that area without the intention of robbing it.

"Shall Ah take ma shoes off?"

She sniffed at him. "No. Yer not staying."

He pulled the *Evening News* out from his back tail and dropped it on the glass table in front of her. "Page four, read it."

"What's this, my star sign?"

"Just read it eh. An dae me a favour an get rid ay that dug. What a racket, man."

"Stanley! Out!" She picked up the paper and began reading.

"Snowballs, bad E's. Picked up a load ay thum oan Saturday. Nae wonder Ah wis in such a state."

"You were out of your mind on speed and vallies. Couple of dodgy tablets aren't gonna make much of a difference are they?"

"Ah cannae remember a thing fae Saturday night Ah swear it. Tryin tae tell me ye've ever seen me in a state like that before?"

"Not far off anyway."

"Come on eh."

"You're out yer brain all the time Billy. What kind of a life is that?"

"I've no touched anythin since Sunday."

"It's now what, Tuesday? Two days!"

"Talk about the pot callin the kettle black. You've dabbled now, after aw that pish that ye never would. You an yer wee pals fae Mary Erskines days."

"Aye once, for a rave. Not every bloody weekend!"

"What, an that makes it awright does it? So it's awright fer you but no fer me?"

"I'll not be touchin thum again after reading that, as if I didnt already know. Don't know what you're taking; it's too dangerous."

"Dinnae worry, there'll no be any more bad ones. We've made sure ay that."

"You an George flex yer big muscles did you?"

"Ah'm jist makin a livin awright? What dae ye expect me tae dae, live off ma dole cheque?"

"Get a normal job! Like normal people!"

"Wae a record like mine? Come on eh! Ah make anywhere up tae a few grand a week, untaxed." Billy puffed out his chest. "Ma money paid fer that watch oan yer wrist, an Ah didnae hear ye complainin aboot ma choice of career when ye got that did Ah?"

"Aye well that money won't count fer much when yer sitting in a prison cell or dead will it?"

"Ah'm careful eh."

"So! It'll catch up with you eventually."

"Aye, well it beats slavin away oan a buildin site an endin up wae a broken back by the time Ah'm forty. Look at ma auld man. Sorry cunt's practically a fuckin cripple."

"What a lovely way tae speak about yer own father."

"HEY! He's no said one good word tae me since the day Ah wis born awright? Only time he opened his mouth tae me was tae drum it intae ma wee heed how worthless Ah wis! An how Ah'd never amount tae fuck all!"

"Ah'm sorry."

"It's awright." Billy turned and walked towards the window. He pulled the curtain to the side and looked out onto the street. "Sorry fer bein a fuckin idiot, an lettin ye doon. Ah sometimes get jealous, ye ken that?"

"Jealous of what?"

"You've got a nice home. Parents who get on well. That look after ye. Want the best fer ye. Granted they think Ah'm the scum of the earth. Well yer auld dear anyway. But it's only because they want the best fer ye. Dinnae blame her fer thinkin that. Ye wantae ken what used tae happen tae me if Ah stepped ootae line when Ah wis a laddie? Ah used tae get hit wae a stick. Had this long thin piece of wood, that he'd hit me wae again and again. If he wis in a good mood he'd maybe use a belt." He shook his head. "That wis light treatment, ken? Ma auld dear didnae huv his tea ready fer um when he got back fae his work, or made um somethin he wisnae happy wae, she'd get slapped aw ower the kitchen. What gave um the right? Should've been locked up."

"I'm so sorry, Billy. I had no idea."

"Dinnae be. It's the past eh. If Ah ever caught um at it now Ah'd murder um. Last time Ah wis at the hoose Ah walked in an ma auld dear wis wipin the tears away. Ah knew somethin had gone on. Fuckin knew it. Seen um sittin there in the livin room wae that screwed up guilty look oan is face. Made me sick. Tried tae speak tae ma auld dear, but she wisnae sayin a word. Made some half ersed excuse fer um eh, same old, same old. Ah went an sat in ma room an Ah jist felt this anger man, like fuckin fire burnin in ma stomach. Hud this vision ay walkin straight intae the livin room an murderin um right there in cauld blood. Only thing that stopped me wis the fact that Ah knew ma auld dear would never speak tae me again. That's the only thing that stopped me Ah swear it. Anyway Ah shouldnae be tellin ye this shit."

"It's alright."

"It's like see when Ah take eccies? It feels like nowt matters anymair. Aw that shite fae the past melts away. Aw that anger an everythin that goes wae it just vanishes, an jist fer a wee while Ah'm happy. Actually happy, ken? The only other thing in this world that can mae me feel that way is you. Ah love ye Lyndse. Ah've no had a lot ay good things in ma life, ye ken that. Ah jist, Ah jist dinnae wantae lose ye. Ah know Ah can be a bastard tae ye when am oot ma face, an Ah know Ah'm a bad person, but you're the only pure thing Ah've got goin in ma life right now."

"You're not a bad person. Deep down you're not."

Billy felt her arms wrap themselves around him from behind. Felt that warmth once again. He turned around so that he was cradling her head against his chest.

"Come oan. Dinnae cry. Dae ye see me cryin eh? Ah dinnae want you or anyone else feelin sorry fer me, awright?"

"I'm not."

"Well wipe away they tears then."

"Ok. Can I jist ask you to do one thing for me? Just calm down a wee bit. Slow down, Billy."

29

George chuckled away as Joe rattled on about his latest conquest later that afternoon in The Gunner, every now and then subtly pawing at his biceps, chuffed at how they were coming along. George had made a conscious effort to increase the intensity of his weekly gym regime in order to cope with his increasing party habits at the weekend. He enjoyed putting his body through hell on a Monday and Tuesday. There was something about the process of grinding his body through a heavy session and sweating all that shite out of his system that he found satisfying, almost therapeutic. As an added bonus he had started punting eccies to a number of the guys in the gym who between them took a good hundred on a weekly basis.

On this particular week, however, there was no chance he was going anywhere near that place. He was still rough as fuck from those snowballs. He had gubbed three in the space of two hours in the Venue on the Saturday night, convinced they weren't doing a thing, and what had followed was surreal. He had found himself floating homeward where he had stuck the telly on in his room. Next thing he knew he was gripping onto the sides of his seat trying to stop himself from getting sucked into the screen, convinced that on the other side was another dimension. He didn't like the feeling of not being in control of what he was taking. That was why back when the rest of the boys first started getting tanked in about the acid George would stick stubbornly to the speed. That way he knew where he stood, no freaky surprises. One seriously bad trip when he was sixteen had been more than enough to convince him that acid just wasn't his thing. Ecstasy was another thing altogether however, and the big man had been swept along like the rest of the mob.

Anyway, the snowballs were a small hiccup that had been dealt with. Happened again and he'd be panelling Andy's puny wee heid into the concrete right outside college, while the rest of his class watched. That aside, George was happy he had taken John Spencer's advice and delved into the ecstasy market with or without his old man to oversee it. Him and Billy had a good thing going and he was proving he was more than just hired muscle like big Uncle Goggs. He emptied the rest of the beer down his throat before tuning back into Joe's story.

"So Ah've gone tae shag ur eh. Three fuckin weeks Ah'd been waitin. Ah've got her aw spread oot oan the couch an that. An Ah've gone tae bury ma mooth in it, eh. She's like, wait, wait! Ah'm oan ma dabs! Ah'm oan ma dabs! So Ah've looked doon an right enough she's no jokin!"

George spat a mouthful of bevy out as he pictured the scene and cringed.

"Ah'm like, lucky ye fuckin telt ees before Ah went tae go doon oan ye! What am Ah, a fuckin vampire?"

"What did ye dae then, pump er up the erse?" said Jimmy sniggering.

"Ye ken what they say, when the rivers are red just ride the dirt track eh," said George. They erupted into laughter, laughter that was abruptly cut short as Dougie appeared behind them.

"Sorry tae interrupt the party, girls. What ye's wantin tae drink?"

"We're good," said George, before turning his back on the old man as Jimmy and Joe looked at one another awkwardly.

"Naw, yer no." Dougie clicked his fingers at the young barman, who dropped his magazine and offered him his undivided attention. "A whisky fer me and three pints fer the youngsters. Speakin ay youngsters, is that you tellin mair stories aboot yer wee rendezvous wae the primary school lassies, Joe?"

Joe let out a nervous laugh.

"Better no catch ye at the school gates or Ah'll chop yer baws oaf. Anyway, if yer girlfriends will spare ye fer five minutes Ah could do wae a word in private, son."

"Am busy."

"George. A word. Five bloody minutes awright? Then ye can rejoin the fun."

George rolled his eyes as he took the pint.

"Five minutes, that's it."

George took a seat at a table next to the window as his dad followed suit. They had barely spoken more than a handful of times in the months since that ill fated trip through to Glasgow when he was set up for a mugging in the middle of the Gorbals to teach him a lesson. It was still a huge sore point, and one that George hadn't forgotten. The atmosphere between them was still so raw with ill feeling and bitterness that George couldn't even bring himself to sit at the dinner table on the odd occasions that they were both home at the same time. Lorraine had tried to mend bridges countless times but to no avail.

"What ye wantin?" said George as he inspected his fingernails, unable to look Dougie in the eye.

"Come on son. This has gone on long enough. You know it. And I know it. Need's tae end. Let's get it all out there an be done with it." George brushed some ash away from the scratched wooden table surface and looked into the distance as he crossed his big arms defensively. Dougie sat forward.

"Look, Ah get it. Awright? Yer pissed off. Still, after all these months. An okay, Ah hold ma hands up awright? Maybe Ah went a bit too far tae make an example of ye. There ye go." George shook his head.

"Ye think? That fuckin close." George pinched his thumb and finger together. "That close Ah wis tae gettin a razor right doon ma fuckin face! Set up fer a doin team handed, nae back up. An ye come tae me now, months down the line sayin ye went too far?"

"Ah made sure Spencer's boy knew tae jump in before it got out of hand." George laughed as he sipped his pint.

"Look you have tae understand that when you started goin against me in front of Gordon the way you did that day, it's like a ripple effect. People see that, see you goin against ma orders an gettin away wae it? Then suddenly Gordon thinks he can start pushin the boat a bit. Then Sean, then Willie, an before ye know it, big Dougie's seen as a soft touch. Dougie's losin his grip, Dougie's past it. Then Dougie's got a fuckin target on his head that every nut job within a five mile radius is takin shots at. Dont ye see son? Ah had tae make an example. Call it tough love, call it whatever ye want, it had tae be done. How dae ye think it is I've kept a grip on these streets fer so many year? By no givin a bloody inch, whoever it may be, family, friend. foe. Tough, sure. Some might call it worse than that. Me? I call it necessary."

"Awright, so then why didn't ye show ye had the bottle tae gie me a spankin yersel tae make yer point? Naw. Ye set me up fer a doin at the hands ay a bunch of wee weegie tramps armed tae the fuckin teeth. Al tell ye why. It's cause ye were scared if ye done it yersel it might backfire on ye. No such a wee laddy anymair am Ah?" Dougie shrugged his shoulders.

"Maybe so son. Maybe so. But look what's happened off the back of it. Ye've gone off, ye've done yer own thing. Ye've had a chance tae grow out of the shadow of yer old man. Tae prove ye can be yer own man."

"Aw aye so this was all fer ma own good was it?" George shook his head.

"Ah do think it's been fer yer ain good, aye. But things have changed. An yer wee period of findin yerself or whatever, It's over." Dougie looked George square in the eye. "Tae put it frankly, Ah need ye back on side, pronto. Yer Uncle is becomin a fuckin headache. If he progresses tae mair than just an annoyin headache then it could be a problem. Fer all of us."

"What, so you think after all that's happened, you can just summon me, an like that I'll jump tae yer beat? An drop everythin I've got goin on? Ive got ma own thing now Dad."

"You think Ah dont know? Ah need ye son. An besides, I've been busy the last few days. Buildin new connections up the town. A guy Ah know has just taken over the Vaults, a club on Niddrie Street. The problem he's experiencin is that due to the style of music, ecstasy's rife, an he's not getting his cut fae the dealers. He's asked me tae come in as a silent partner, instill a new order. Not only dae Ah get a piece of the club, but I also take control of all the ecstasy that gets sold in there so long as he gets a piece, but tae have full control of the ecstasy means Ah need tae take full control of the door. There will be one or two qualified bouncers on there, but the head doorman will be the guy that takes charge ay the real dough, the guy that the dealers in that place report to for their orders, the guy that makes sure the only tablets gettin sold in that place are ones he supplies. That head doorman will effectively be the fuckin Gov'nor in that place. He'll be representin me." Dougie looked his son in the eye and grinned. "Ah want you tae run this son. You'll be ma man in the Vaults. Ma eyes and ears, ma fists. Ye said ye wanted more responsibility, more cash, well here's yer shot. This is *exactly* what ye've been lookin for."

Dougie squinted his eyes at George.

"Well?"

30

"George. George."

George was miles away, staring into space, mulling the huge crossroads in front of him as the repetition of his name pulled him back into the present moment. He subtly checked his silver Tag Heuer for the umpteenth time that night before answering Billy back.

"Aye?"

"Ye with us big man?"

"Eh? Aye. Aye. Course, what were ye's sayin?" He sunk some of his pint.

"Was just saying that I understand there's been some misgivings about the most recent product."

The small frame, the specs, the thinning strawberry blonde hair, the shirt and tie, Brian "Specky" Clark, was the guy responsible for a large percentage of the ecstasy pouring into the capital, and it wasn't surprising that a character like this would be able to fly underneath the radar. He looked like a smaller version of one of the Proclaimers, albeit with one of Manchester's most prolific drug firms behind him.

"Aye. Aye that's right, they were fuckin pish," said George, eager to appear wholeheartedly invested in the situation.

"It's embarrassing, makes us look bad, and it's bad press we could do without."

"Makes us look bad tae," said Billy.

"We've had to move over the last few days to provide some reassurances, not just to yourselves. You asked for a face to face and with the amount of weight you boys shift it was only fair, so here I am." Clark slyly glanced toward the bar area where a massive lump lumbered over it with his back to them. His neck was so big it had what looked like arse flaps at the back. George bit his lip and forced back a laugh.

"And what reassurance are ye able tae provide?" said Billy.

"Well for a start it's been dealt with at source. We're not used to getting punted shite like that. Good, strong pills full of MDMA, straight from the heart of Europe where we're concerned, only the best and purest. Myself and the people behind me are firm believers in giving people what they pay for, keep them coming back. Course when there's delays moving the stuff across the Channel, or a shipment gets busted, what can you do? If you sit on your arse waiting for the wheels to start turning again you risk letting others cut you out of the equation, so we took a chance on an alternative supply rather than our usual, a move that was to our detriment on this occasion. You see in some quarters folk are starting to get greedy. Manufacturing their own pills full of anything from smack to the ketamine that was in those snowballs. Cheaper ingredients, higher profit that kind of thing. It was a wake up call, we got complacent. So, to make up for it, we're happy to set our next batch at a knock-down rate of four quid a pill, across the board to compensate." Clark smiled as he mopped the edge of his lip with a napkin, before sipping a little of his gin and tonic.

"It's no just that though," said Billy. "We're sick of havin tae go through middle men. Bampots. We wantae deal directly wae you. Means if we have any issues we can speak direct to the supply rather than having tae go through a bunch of students that dinnae huv a clue, know what Ah mean?"

"Don't worry, I'll make sure you've got a contact for me as and when needed should you have any queries about consignments etc. And from now on? No middlemen, direct deliveries, less fucking about. Sound fair."

"That us done, then?"

"Oh, there was one other thing."

"Aye?"

"Dale Alscott, the guy you ran out of the Venue a few weeks back. Impressive by the way, very tenacious."

"What about um?"

"He's lost a lot of face, boys. He wants your blood."

"Wants whose blood?" growled George. "Let um come, we're no hard tae find. Anyway, Ah thought he was facin a sentence fer dealin?"

"He is. But he's planning on putting a number of Hibs boys on your tail. Guys that don't fuck about..."

"An ye think we do?" snapped Billy.

Clark raised his hands. "All I'm saying is he has it in for you, and he won't stop till he's got his wish. The thing is that we happen to be their main drug supply as well. So all it would take is one word from Big Joe there to the guys at the top of the CCS chain and those same radges would be looking down at the ground when they passed you in the street."

"Ah appreciate the offer but we handle our own business eh. Dinnae need any cunt fightin our battles or steppin in fer us," said Billy.

Clark smiled. "Look, it's in our interest to make sure wars don't break out between our customers. Before you know it arrests come down, supply lines are disrupted, it's very bad for business."

Billy looked round at George, shrugged his shoulders and looked back at Brian Clark. "Fair enough. Do what ye have tae dae, but we're no hidin anywhere, an ye can pass that on."

As Billy stood up and pulled his yellow Ralph Lauren Harrington from behind the seat, Clark sat forward. "Oh and one more thing. We might need help with something in the future. A favour for a favour and all that. I'll be in touch."

"Eh? Ah didnae ask fer that favour," said Billy, puzzled looking.

"Point taken. Good evening gents, speak soon."

"A favour for a favour: What the fuck does he mean by that?" said Billy as they bounded down Lothian Road. George didn't respond. "Right, dae you wantae tell me where your biscuit's at the day, mate? Yer no with me mate yer somewhere else."

George stopped in his tracks just shy of the stone clock that stood in front of the Playhouse and let out a heavy groan.

"Ma old man needs me back on side, mate. This shit wae ma uncle, he's got a bad feelin about it, needs me close. The downside is he's asked me tae pull away fae yous. Says Ah cannae dae both. It's one or the other."

"Efter all that shit that went down in Glasgow?"

"Akno mate, but it's ma old man. Cannae hud it against um forever."

"Mate, yer twenty year auld. He cannae tell ye what tae dae anymair. An besides, you dinnae have *anythin* tae prove tae him. Trust me. Ah gave up that ghost a long time ago."

"It's family, man. What can Ah dae? Look, Ah told um straight if he wants me on side he keeps his nose ootae ma pals' business. Nae mair taxin, askin fer cuts, nae mair stupid power trips, it ends. He's got a fair old inkling about what we've been up tae. Doesnae Ken the details cause he's been so pre-occupied wae other stuff he hasnae stuck his nose in up tae now. Ah made um agree tae keep outae it, leave ye's be. Says as long as ye don't sell anythin in Muirhouse, or step on his toes he'll steer clear. Gave me his word."

"How nice of um. So yer wantin out?"

"He's set me up wae the door at the Vaults."

"Bouncer?"

"Aye. Ah'll take control ay the gear too obviously."

Billy smiled. "Sounds like he's got it aw worked oot fer ye."

"It'll hopefully only be till things blow over wae ma uncle. Or go South. Either way."

31

Sean felt an uneasy tension deep in his gut as he observed Willie gnawing at his knuckles on the other side of the table. He glanced around at the assortment of jakies, wannabe hard men and broken old fools resigned to their fate. This was the institution that had torn his family apart. That bewildered young lad, playing I Spy with his sisters on the ominous visit to Bar L. Trying his hardest to block out the sound of Mum and Dad raging at one another over her plans to emigrate to Canada and take all three of them with her. Scared, worried and helpless beneath the weight of it all, torn between the mother who had carried him, and the father that was determined not to lose him.

He gave his head a shake and tried to focus.

"So, how they treatin ye in here, mate?"

Willie shook his head, as he let out a snigger.

"Just makin small talk, Christ."

"Well how about, how are you daein out there eh? While Ah take the fuckin heat fer ye in here? How about that?"

Sean pinched the bridge of his nose as he tried his hardest to endure Willie's shite, all the while knowing that at least three screws had their eyes fixed on the pair of them.

"Ye'll know she's close tae crokin it, eh?" Willie pressed his fingertips together. "That fuckin close. If she doesnae pull through Ah'm a fuckin dead man."

"How come?"

"Ah'll tell ye how come. Because there's a bunch ay pakkis in here that are ready tae put ma lights out. That's how come. Only fuckin back-up Ah've got are fannies that cannae fight fer shit. An on top ay that, the smack in here isnae even fuckin smack! Shite!"

"Keep it fuckin cool."

"Fuckin desperate here, Sean. Ah'm cluckin like fuck."

"What dae ye want me tae dae?"

"Ah want fucking heroin. Ah'm carryin a lot ay fuckin weight fer yous here, dinnae ferget that."

"We know. And we appreciate it."

"That right aye? No so much that ye'd stick a scorebag up yer erse tae help a mucker out eh?"

"Willie Ah got fuckin strip searched on the way in. There's no way they'll let a Donaldson come intae this prison waeout makin sure we've got no gear, ye mad?"

Willie's head dropped into his hands. "Ah'm starin at a life sentence here. All over a wee bit money for your auld man. Couple ay fuckin grand."

"Well Willie Ah hate tae say it but Ah never recommended takin a shotgun along and opening fire like it's bloody Sunday."

"Ye came doon tae ma flat an filled me up wae fuckin preemo ching. What dae ye expect? Ah went stormin ootae there thinkin Ah wis fuckin Tony Montana, man."

Sean laughed, but it was clear Willie wasn't seeing the funny side as he stared back at him.

"This fuckin amusin tae you is it?"

"Not at all, mate. Look, fuck, what dae ye want me tae say? We've tried our hardest tae get tae the husband but it's fuckin impossible. He's under police protection, cannae get near the cunt, the case is too high profile what with the race thing."

Sean sat forward, searching for something, anything, he could give Willie in the way of hope. "Look, Ah know you're in a really tight spot here mate. If there was somethin, anythin Ah could dae..."

"Aye but there's somethin Ah could dae in't there?" Willie sat back in his chair and flung a leg up on the table, his demeanour calming some.

"What ye talkin about?"

"You ken fine well what Ah'm talkin about. They've been pressin me hard an Ah've no given thum shit. But desperate times call fer desperate measures—"

"—Don't talk fuckin crazy, Willie."

"If Ah give up your auld man Ah could be out eh here in a lot less time. And they'll make sure Ah'm comfy tae."

"Willie, you listen tae me..."

"Naw, you listen tae me! Right? Ah'm the one that's callin the shots this time. It's cause ay yous that Ah'm in this fuckin mess. You see tae it that I have heroin flowin intae this prison like a fuckin fountain, or Ah'm takin ye's both down with me. You and yer fuckin auld man. That clear enough fer ye? *Mate*?"

"Aye. Mate." Sean locked eyes with Willie for a surreal moment, not knowing who or what he was looking at anymore. It wasn't Willie that was for sure, or maybe it was. Sean had heard it said in some film at some point that a man only showed his true colours when all hope was lost and desperation set in. "You'll get yer gear, mate."

32

Willie woke in a panicked sweat to the sound of a tapping on his cell door. Who the fuck was it? One of The Asians? Felt like the walls were closing in around him, the stomach cramps were unbearable, and the dreams. When he was able to get any sleep that was. Everyone he had ever stabbed, slashed, shot, or scalped haunted him day and night. Most of all that crazy wee Asian woman. She didn't even need a dream; she appeared all the time. The previous night he could swear he had seen her crawling along the ceiling like a little rat, with claws for fingers. Then she just sat there in the corner, staring at him, that nasty little rodent. Muttering those prayers or whatever the fuck they were under her breath.

Fuck knows what would happen if she croaked.

The only thing that could make her go away was smack. He needed it. Felt like he could scratch the skin and flesh from his face in yearning for it.

There it was again, that fucking tapping at the door. It was probably just his terrors.

"FUCK OFF!"

He pulled the thin little quilt over his head and squeezed it tight, feeling the sweat drench it within seconds. He tightened his grip on that little tool he had sharpened for himself as he heard that noise again. That muttering, getting closer and closer, he wished he could rid it from his ear drums. He was petrified to remove the quilt just in case she'd be sitting there in front of him, ready to pounce.

"FUCK!!"

The door opened. He flung the quilt from his face and jumped off the bed clutching his tool, ready to stab the life out of whoever was there.

"Woah! Woah! Fuckin hell!"

The screw cowered in the corner as Willie glowered over him, ready to plunge him right in his fat, fucking face.

"Settle down or Ah'll need tae sound the alarm!"

"What the fuck dae ye want!?" said Willie, puffing and panting, his chest pounding.

"Ah've got somethin fer ye."

146

"Eh?"

"From Sean Donaldson."

Willie lowered his balled-up fist, as the screw slowly pulled himself backwards and extended a hand. There it was. A wrap of that precious brown.

He had wondered in his darker moments whether he had been too hard on his old pal, but clearly it had done the trick because there it was, his ticket to a few hours of rest from the terrors that were surrounding him on all sides. He didn't even notice the screw leaving the cell before he scurried underneath the mattress and collected his works. Finally, some proper gear.

"Oh ya beauty! Fuckin choking, man."

He frantically wrapped the rope around his arm and punctured that big inviting vein that was screaming out at him, injecting a large helping into his arm. He shook and quivered as he fell backward onto the floor, his eyes flickered upward, his pupils appearing completely white. It hit him like a breezeblock, at a hundred miles an hour, and pulled him downward and away from reality.

33

Sean stared at himself long and hard in the mirror as he sat there in his bedroom. The suit looked good, but he looked like shit. His eyes were bloodshot from tears, his nerves were on end, he couldn't get his hand to stop shaking. But Willie had become a liability. Threatening to bring down his old man after all these years of separation and even worse, Sean himself, after everything he'd been through. He had tried his hardest to hold onto this thought in the hope that it would make the burden easier to bear, but his head was so strung out he couldn't hold onto it long enough to stop the guilt from pushing through.

He picked up the white rock and crumbled some of it into the pipe with his trembling hand. It felt a necessary elevation in his drug usage. The powder just wasn't doing enough to blot shit out, and heroin was unthinkable.

One of John's henchmen had schooled him on freebasing a while back on a bender in Glasgow and now he had begun requesting a small order of crack on the regular along with the consignments of normal coke.

He flicked open the zippo and lit the pipe. The harsh fumes hit the back of his throat hard, forcing him to throw his head forward, coughing uncontrollably, spitting on the floor. Once he'd regained some composure he stood up and straightened his tie with his steadying hands, his head feeling light as a feather, as the hit grew in intensity.

The funeral was in an hour at Warriston Crematorium.

34

After several attempts Billy managed to guide the key into the hole and get the door open. As it opened he collapsed to the hallway floor, letting out what had descended from singing into drunken chanting. He burst into the living room, lifting his hands above his head in all his wasted glory. A mangled pair of sunglasses rested on his face.

"There she is, eh! Ma wee doll face! How ye daein?"

"Not good."

"Why the long face?" he replied, speech slurred.

"Don't rile me, Billy."

"Aw chill oot darlin eh." Billy weaved his way across the floor and fell down on the couch next to her. "Aw come on, darlin gies a cuddle eh."

"In that state? Yer stinkin Billy. I dunno how much more of this I can take. I was cooking you a meal tonight, or don't you remember?"

"S-sorry."

She turned away and shook her head.

"Aw come oan. Here." He went into his coat pocket, pulling out a pile of crumpled ten and twenty pound notes and throwing them onto the floor. "Order us a takeaway eh. This me gettin the silent treatment?"

"What do you think?"

"Och, gies a break. Ah've been workin aw weekend."

"Partying more like."

"When did you turn intae ma auld dear eh?"

"Look I don't need to listen to this shite, can you phone me a taxi to Morningside please?"

"Fuckin hell, you're nae fun anymair. Dinnae even huv a drink anymair." Billy sank back into the couch with his hands in the air, before letting them slowly drop to his sides.

"Ye wantae know why? You really want to know why I've not had a drink recently?"

Billy lay back on the couch and flung his feet up, too wasted to take his trainers off.

Lyndsay shook her head, looking out of the window as the tears welled up in her tired eyes. She sighed as she made her way across the room. She moved his hand away from his face and carefully removed the twisted, broken pair of sunglasses that had managed to get tangled in his blonde curtains. He was out cold and breathing heavily in a deep comatose sleep. She knew that dropping the heavy television in the corner of the room on his head probably wouldn't lift him out of it. As she tried to turn him over onto his side, he instinctively pushed her away in his sleep, knocking her off balance and onto the living room floor.

"Prick!"

35

The following day as Billy stood, eyes shut, with the shower on full blast, he reflected on another insane weekend. He stood, basking in it, not giving two fucks how long it was taking to warm up, just revelling in the cool spray as it eased his weary bones. Then, it dawned on him.

The meal. Bastard...

There simply was no space in this crazy existence for a female, so what had he gone and done? Given her a key to the flat. He still loved her like nothing on earth, but the rapid surge in his drug usage *and* distribution, was keeping him out all weekend, every weekend, squeezing her out and reducing her to an afterthought at worst, and an inconvenience at best. His initial analysis had been bang on the money. She was far too good for the likes of him. Luckily, he had still been out for the count when she had left for Jenners. He wasn't sure if he could have coped with the onslaught in such a fragile condition. He turned the shower off, climbed out and wrapped a towel around himself as he pondered what the day would hold. He was due money from a number of sources, so no doubt Jimmy would be getting a phone call for back-up now George was out of the picture.

He dried himself off and threw on a pair of jeans before grabbing his red Ralph Lauren jumper from the wardrobe, contemplating whether it would be too heavy with the July sun battering down. One thing he knew was he needed to get rid of the splitting headache that was sheer torture, so he went into his top drawer, snatched a lump of bass, crumbled some off onto the dresser and tipped some bicarb out next to it. He boshed it up into a big line and arsed it in one go. The perfect way to shake away the cobwebs on a Monday afternoon, get back on it.

The time was worrying him. Lindsay would be finished in a couple of hours and she would be fixing to terrorise his landline till he picked up, so it was time to head to the shops and see who was kicking about. As he ditched the red jumper and swooped in for his white Calvin Klein v-neck T-shirt, the phone rang.

As Billy marched up Lothian Road that evening, closely followed by Joe, Jimmy and Danny, his mind raced as to why he had been asked for.

He entered Lord Tom's, bobbing his head to the sound of the *Stereo MC's* shouting about getting themselves connected. Several heavy looking boys dominated the bar, glued to the Rangers re-run playing on the TV above it.

Clark appeared, leading them to a table at the back next to a stone pillar that was tattooed with flyers. Two stunners were sat there, instantly kindling an urge in Billy that once again put that speed cock pish out the window. One had long curly blonde hair, dark red lips and a slinky black Versace dress. The other was Spanish looking with long bronze thighs, cropped brunette hair, a shiny white D & G top and a frayed red skirt.

"Do you two wantae make yersels scarce for a bit?" said Clark, as Billy nodded his head at him.

"Dinnae tell me you're intae baith ay thaim?" said Billy, a respectable moment later.

Clark smiled as he took a sip of his gin and tonic. "The brunette."

"Fuckin tidy mate. The erse oan that by the way," said Joe as he ogled them from behind.

"Ye mind if we talk about this little something in private?" said Clark. Billy signalled to a slightly aggrieved looking Joe.

"What's the crack then?" said Billy as a pint arrived in front of him.

"Well first of all, big dues on the output. The way you've run the Venue, very impressive," said Clark as he adjusted his specs. "Said I might need a favour last time we spoke. It's a biggie, though."

"Aye?" said Billy as he lit a fag.

Clark casually looked around the pub before discreetly producing a small photo from the pocket of his long black coat. He placed it down on the table in front of Billy. "I need this greedy fat chappy to disappear."

Billy took a deep breath as he sat back in his chair.

"I know it's a bit of a bombshell. And trust me it's a last resort. Paul Goddard. He's had a big presence in Fife and South Queensferry for a number of years, heroin and hash mainly. Launders his money through a chain of chip shops. Now that ecstasy's got such a big presence in the Capital he's trying to make inroads, cut off supplies. Needs to be nipped in the bud before it's too much of a problem, if you catch my drift."

"An what's in it fer me exactly?"

"Thirty grand. Fifteen before, fifteen after."

"It's a tidy earner but it's a big fuckin ask. This is fuckin murder. An how do I know this cunt's family isnae gonnae come after us if we do this? Got enough fuckin enemies, me. Fuckin sleep wae one eye open every night."

"They don't know you from Adam. They'll have no idea who's hit and why. This guy has a ton of enemies too, a known grass with a penchant for underage laddies."

Billy squinted his eyes at Clark as he stroked his chin.

"I can give you his route to work, where he goes on shopping runs, the whole shebang. His routines are like clockwork, obviously thinks he can't be touched. Look Billy, I know it's a big one this. But I need to get the wheels in motion before this bastard really starts hurting my business. It's on a need to know basis. If you're taking any accomplices, they're the ones you fill in on the details, no-one else. This is a delicate matter, needs to be discreet..."

"Wait a minute. Just slow down a sec. You've got a bunch ay heavy hitters up at the bar there. Why me?"

Clark shrugged his shoulders as he took another sip of his gin. "Joe's got a lot of heat on him the now from police down South, and locals now too. Got eyes on him all the time, just waiting for him to make a wrong move. And he's trying to set up a security firm."

"I take all the risks so your hands are clean, eh?"

"Billy, you're an opportunist. And this is a big opportunity. If you do this for me I can guarantee you full uninterrupted access to some of the biggest events in the city once Joe takes over the security. Full access, no looking over your shoulder." Clark sat forward. "If you take this on you'll be one of the biggest ecstasy dealers in the city by the end of the year, mark my words. Isn't that what you've wanted? To step out of the shadow of the Muirhouse old school. The way you tackled Dale Alscott proves you've got ambition. I'm offering you everything you've been striving for on a silver fucking platter."

Billy smiled. "I've dished oot mair tans than Ah can shake a stick at, but murder? That's a whole other kettle of fish. Ken what Ah mean? No sure Ah need that in ma life."

He stubbed out the last of his fag, smoke seeping from his lips. "Let's see the photae again?"

Clark placed it down on the table. Goddard had shifty looking eyes, thick sideburns, with a grandad cap on and a massive stomach. Wouldn't be hard to take down if he was on his own.

"How dae ye know he's a beast? An how dae Ah know you're no jist feedin me that line tae get me tae sign up?"

"It's a rumour. Where there's smoke there's fire and all that. And I have it on good source, but, take it for what it is."

Billy took a large swig of his pint. "Ye'll have ma answer within a couple ay days."

As Billy slipped the photo into his backtail and stood, Clark produced a card from his pocket. "A wee token of my appreciation fer the numbers you's have been shifting. Blair Street Sauna. Whatever you and your pals need will be on the house. Blonde, brunette, black, whatever."

"Nice one. Ah'll be in touch."

36

Billy took in the comfy looking detached and semi-detached houses in Grigor and up towards Crewe Toll later that night from the passenger seat of Danny's car. He pondered the gulf between what he was moving past and the graffiti covered ghettos of Muirhouse just up the road. The thoughts raced through his mind faster than the car itself, like speeding lights, as he gazed out of the window at the other cars passing by, feeling the warmth of the ecstasy radiating throughout his body.

"Turn it up, Danny!" he screamed, yanking at the volume knob as he tried in vain to force a louder noise out of the speakers.

"Yer gonnae make ees crash ya fuckin lunatic!"

"Mind an stop at Vicky Wine Danny boy!" shouted Joe as he perched his gurning jaw against the top of the driver seat, drumming his sweaty hand against the outside of the car door. "Ah'll huv they decks blarin when we git back!"

Billy wound the window down as they drove past the garage. He stuck his head out, feeling the euphoria overtaking him. His vision started shaking, leaving tracing shapes all around. It was fast becoming too hard to hold on to any thought for longer than seconds as they descended into a wild blur of image and emotion.

The following day Billy sat there in that same passenger seat as a plane roared overhead, pounding his senses. The eccies were slowly but surely wearing off, leaving the after-effects of the amphetamine that had run like a constant strain underneath the MDMA for several days. Grinding teeth, a thumping heartbeat, a film of pasty sweat across the surface of his skin that wouldn't budge. His body had run like a steam train from Friday right through to Tuesday fuelled by chemical after chemical, and now the comedown was kicking in with force, halting the train in its tracks.

No amount of soap bar would halt the comedown, Billy thought to himself as he accepted another smouldering joint from Danny, winding the top of the window down to let some smoke billow out. He sucked that bad boy with ferocity, desperate to escape the impending doom that would soon be squeezing his head in its vice like grip.

As Billy looked out the window through the fence that separated them from the landing strip at the airport, straining his eyes through his Ray-Bans with the sun beating down, he reflected. Eccies, escorts, contracts, all on a fucking Monday night. Felt like his life was starting to race at a speed he was struggling to keep up with.

Slow down. Just slow down. Yer movin too fast.

That's what Lyndsay had said to him a couple of months earlier in her house. Problem was, he didn't know how. And as he observed each of his friends gazing into space in their own zombie-like states he suddenly felt alone. Felt like the tight brotherhood that had existed just a few hours earlier, that chemical unity, was a sham. He needed some sleep. "Danny. Take me hame."

Danny dropped Billy off at the shops, so he could grab four Tennent's before heading back to his flat.

As he walked in he could feel the last effects of the drugs rapidly draining away, leaving an empty, hollow feeling in the pit of his shrunken stomach. He flung a fiver down on the counter, unable to look the shopkeeper in the eyes as he picked up his messages, and barely able to muster more than a grunt in acknowledgement.

He could feel the sweat dripping from his neck as he pulled his T-shirt up over his head and wedged it down the back of his jeans. He was just barely coping with the short walk home, hoping he wouldn't bump into anyone he knew and have to engage in conversation or small talk of any kind.

Reality was kicking in and it was biting hard. The fact that he had blanked Lyndsay for days and slept with an escort behind her back had left a nagging feeling of guilt that was gnawing away at him. He was going to end it, it was decided. He was better off sticking with someone who expected to be trodden on as she had never known any different.

And then of course there was Brian Clark's proposition. Murder. Taking out a significant underworld figure, and all the dark ifs and buts that came with it.

The paranoia was ripping right through him; all the negatives in his life dark looming clouds following his every move.

As he walked through his gate and took the weary steps up to the service door he envisaged that beautiful little blue tablet and all its friends. His ticket to a day of rest from the world. To wake up refreshed, revitalised, free from this mental hell. His body was completely fucked, yet his brain was still very much awake and he desperately needed that sweet unconsciousness. He opened his top drawer and began sifting through a stramash of flyers, skins, fag ends, and empty lighters for his vallies. After going through the drawer a couple of times, he began emptying the contents out, determined to find them. He started to panic, dreading the thought of having to deal with his comedown for the rest of the day. In a flash it came back to him. He had swallowed the lot after getting back the previous weekend.

"Fuck! Fuck! Fuck!!"

He stood up and kicked the drawer as hard as he could, stubbing his toes on the hard wood. "Aaaaaagh!"

He limped through to the living room and fell down on the couch, head in hands, wondering how he was going to cope. He pulled the hash bucket across to his feet, and began crumbling big bits of soap bar onto the charred foil. He pulled the plastic bottle up out of the water, the thick green smoke gushing in, and then sucked it down in one go, feeling it hit the back of his throat harshly. After coughing the smoke out he sat back, his head feeling more and more hazy as the deep stone took effect.

As he turned he noticed the red light beeping on his landline with three voicemail messages waiting. He pushed the button.

Beep. "Hi Billy it's me. I came round for you earlier but you never answered the door. Not sure if you're there and avoiding me or fast asleep. Either way please call me back. We need to talk. It's serious. Bye."

Beep. "Hi it's me again, don't wanna nag you, I know you don't like it, but we really really need to talk Billy. Can you please call me? I'm off work at the moment so just call me any time at my house. If you're avoiding me cause you think I'll be angry then don't because this is more important. Not gonnae go into it over the phone, just please call me."

Beep. "Look, I've been round for you twice and you *know* I don't like coming into Muirhouse on my own in the dark. I've gathered by now that you're not in, don't know where you are or what you're doing, but we need to speak urgently. It's serious. Involves the two of us, just pick up the phone and call. I'm not going to keep leaving messages. If you don't call me back by tomorrow then don't bother calling at all as I'll assume you don't care enough to bother your arse."

Billy picked up the receiver and stared at it for several minutes, wondering what was so urgent. The calm, controlled tone in her voice was unsettling. He needed to know what she was talking about.

"Hello." There was a pause for a few seconds as he drifted into a trance.

"Is that you?"

"Aye. Look Ah'm sorry, Ah..."

"Save it, Billy. I don't want your excuses. Are you in the house?"

"Aye."

"Are you staying put or are you just gonna fuck off again?"

"Ah'm stayin put eh. Look, what's wae aw the seriousness man, what's the crack?"

"I'd rather wait till we're together."

"Dinnae leave me hangin Lyndsay, yer freakin me oot man. Has someone died?"

"No. I'll phone a taxi, and we can talk when I get there."

"But Lyndsay Ah..."

"Bye Billy."

37

Billy slowly came to, to the sight of a grim faced Lyndsay. She had a long red round-necked sweater on and a long black skirt that covered her completely.

"Billy, you look terrible."

"Thanks a lot. Fuckin love you too, eh. Look, if you're gonnae start lecturing me then..."

"I'm not."

"Well, what then? What's goin on? If yer gonnae finish with me, then fuck sake just dae it eh."

"Probably wouldn't be a bad idea."

"Look ye knew the package when ye started seein me. Ah'm no a saint awright? Far from it, ye knew this fae a few weeks in. So what is it Lyndsay? What is this big fuckin mystery secret ye've gottae tell me?"

"I'm pregnant."

The words stunned Billy like he'd taken a hard hook to the temple. Suddenly his aching insides and ravaged brain seemed insignificant.

"Please say something, Billy."

"How far gone?"

"Six weeks."

"Six weeks an ye've only telt ees now?"

"I've been trying, but I haven't been able to find the right moment. Only known for two weeks."

Billy leaned forward, putting his head in his hands. "What a fuckin bombshell, man."

"Well, what are you feeling? Are you happy? Sad? Angry? I need to know."

He stood and walked into the kitchen, grabbed the vodka from the top of the cupboard and poured a large nip into a shot glass before downing it straight.

"Well?"

"Well what?"

"How do you feel?"

"Gies a chance tae take it in fer fuck's sake. What are ye daein wae it?"

"I'm keeping it, Billy. I've thought long and hard about it believe me, but I can't kill something that's living inside of me. It's up to you whether you stand by me."

"Don't I get a say then nah? It's mine tae."

"I was hoping you'd want me to keep it. Don't you?"

"It's just that, it's a big responsibility ken? Ah'm only twenty-one. You're only 20! We could get rid ay this one, and huv another one in a couple ay years when were mair settled nah?"

"Ye talk about it like it's a possession. It's a little life form Billy. I can't get rid of it. I just can't."

"So that's you decided it then? Made up yer mind, just like that?"

"Wasn't easy, believe me."

Billy shook his head in disbelief. "That's all Ah fuckin need. On top ay aw the other fucked-up shite that's goin on in ma life. I've gottae worry aboot fuckin Dougie Donaldson sendin some cunt through ma door. Dale fuckin Alscott, whenever he gets ootae prison. Hibs boys. Getting lifted, jailed, fuckin killed. Whatever the fuck's goin on in ma Mum and Dad's hoose. An now oan top ay aw that shite, Ah'm gonnae have a screamin bairn pissin an shittin aw ower the place."

"Ah'm sorry but I've made up my mind. If you want out I'll understand."

"It's ma ain fuckin flesh an blood. What am Ah meant tae fuckin dae?"

"I was hoping this wouldn't happen."

"What did ye expect?"

"It takes two to tango! We both knew the risks when you have sex without a condom!"

He stormed through to the kitchen and slammed his glass down before pouring another vodka twice as big as the last one. Guilt over that escort was now stabbing him in the gut, whilst the thought of a baby tore at his fried brain.

"Stop it! You know what you're like on vodka!"

He turned and smashed the glass against the wall as hard as he could. "Ah'll do what Ah fuckin want! You're the one that's ruined ma life! Ah knew Ah should never have got involved wae a bird! Now Ah'm fuckin ruined!"

"I've ruined your life?"

"Ye might as well put a fuckin gun tae ma heid! Bang! Why couldn't ye huv just found some other joker tae tie down? Why me! Could've picked any cunt, someone wae an education, a normal fuckin joab. What am I some kin-dae project? Take a bad cunt and try and turn um good?!"

Lyndsay stood up. "I chose you because I wanted you! And for some fucked up reason I still do!"

Billy turned his back and fixed his hands to the work surface. Pressing his palms into them with all his weight behind it.

"Do you think I planned this? Don't you think there's sacrifices I have to make? No Uni for me Billy! Not anymore." She edged closer and placed a hand on his back.

"Don't touch me right now."

"So that's it. Can't even bear to have me touch you? Do you have any idea how that makes me feel? Do you even care?"

He grabbed the bottle and took another long swig before slamming it down. "You're getting an abortion. It's in both our best interests."

"Don't you dare bark orders at me about what to do with my baby!"

He turned round and pointed at her. "You're getting a fuckin abortion!"

"No!"

"Aye ye fuckin are!"

"Or what? Or you'll slap me around like your Dad does your Mum?"

Billy's arm came up in an instant. The back of his hand went stiff. He stopped himself just in time. "You ever fuckin use that against me again and I swear I will fuckin hit you. Now, get out ma flat. Get through that room, gather yer stuff, an get out!"

She left the room sniffing and sobbing. Billy sat on the couch, staring at the vodka bottle. He'd already drunk half of it and he was contemplating necking the other half in one go. The only thing stopping him was the thought of what he might do if he did. As he sat there with his head in his hands, he heard Lyndsay crying in the other room.

He pondered over what he would do if she left and didn't come back. How he would function. Moments of danger from his life began flashing through his mind. Jack wielding that stick as he cowered on the floor. Dale Alscott's sword whizzing past his face. The dealer in the Calton coming at him with the Stanley. How many more chances would he get?

He began thinking about the baby. The responsibility, the noise, the feeding, the nappies. The games of football. The walks to the park. The sitting on the swings, buying the clothes, watching TV together. The first steps, the first words.

Could it be a good thing? Was this what he needed to get his life in order, and establish some stability?

His attention was drawn back to the sound of Lyndsay's heavy sobbing, it sobered him. Suddenly the thought of throwing her out seemed insane. She looked up at him through tear-stained eyes as he appeared at the doorway, a half packed bag in front of her, he realised he couldn't do it. He felt the fury waning.

"Stop packing Lyndse."

"Why?" She sniffed whilst wiping the tears from her cheek as he sat on the bed.

"Cause Ah don't want ye to go."

"Maybe it's for the best."

"Maybe aye. But Ah donno what I'd dae waeoot ye."

"Ah'm sorry fer bringin yer Mum an Dad up."

"It's awright. Ah'm sorry fer bein a cunt."

"What about the baby?"

"Might turn out to be a good thing eh?"

"Really?"

"Aye. Ma life's been pretty fuckin mental the last few years. Come an lie wae ees, Ah'll roll a joint."

"Ah'll come and lie with you, but I can't smoke the joint." She pointed at her stomach.

"Aw fuck aye, forgot. Come an lie wae me anyway."

"Ok."

A strange sense of peace descended as they lay for hours in each other's arms, talking about the baby. About the kind of stuff they would buy for it, about the places they would go, about the type of life they could have just the three of them. They pondered the possibility of moving far away from the ghetto, away from all the chaos.

The comedown lost its power over Billy's thoughts as the possibility of being a dad began to excite him.

But, amidst it all, he knew, a bairn didn't come cheap. He excused him-self, headed through to the living room and picked up the receiver. It was time to stop dwelling on the dangers involved. He'd been surrounded by dan-ger his whole life. It was normal. This baby was a game changer, and the cash injection on offer was too good to ignore.

After several seconds of dialing tone there was a voice at the other end.

"Yeah."

"Call it 50 and im in."

"40?"

38

George batted the cubicle door open with his left paw while he wiped his nose with the right as he emerged sulkily from the Rutland Casino toilet. It was his fifth line of coke in rapid succession, shite gear. It was just making him feel moody and agitated and he knew where that was likely to lead.

The gambling had started off as a nice easy way of laundering his ecstasy money, but it was no longer just about concealment. It was about a habit that was growing with every passing day.

He felt the sweat dripping from his forehead and the tension building around his temples as he walked back out to the table. Eleanor, whom he had been dating for a month or so, stood at the table waiting for him with a full pint at the ready, looking fed up. Eleanor was a petite thing with bobbed black hair. The black fishnets that clung to her tight, milky white thighs along with the other black garments she often wore gave her a cheeky little hint of Goth. Even her lipstick was black from time to time. It was this twist, along with her tidy little frame and come-to-bed face that had grabbed George's attention in the Vaults weeks earlier. The discovery that she was up for anything in the bedroom later that night had sealed the deal. They were an item within days.

He pulled off his bomber jacket and tossed it on the metal stool as he took the pint from her hand, feeling the strain.

"Ah'm bored, George."

He blanked her as he checked how many chips were in his pocket.

"George?" She said his name again, clearly frustrated at the lack of attention.

"What?"

"Ah said Ah'm bored."

"Aye." He casually dropped a pile of chips down on the table as he re-took his seat, a new hand dropping in front of him.

"Haven't ye gambled enough?"

"Ah'm doon big time. Need tae at least break even, then we can leave eh."

"Aw fuck this."

"Language please," the stone-faced dealer replied through gritted teeth.

"*Sorry*," she said as she took a harsh draw on the last of her fag before squashing it beneath her high heel.

"Here." George grabbed her hand and placed the wrap in it, desperate to get rid of her for a few minutes so he could concentrate on the job at hand. "Away an liven yersel up, eh."

"Cheeky cunt." She stormed off, swinging her hips in an exaggerated fashion as George focused on his game. After managing to win back two hundred at the blackjack table he decided to head across to his old bread and butter, the roulette wheel, driving Eleanor across to the bar area.

After making a good start, his luck began to falter again. He noticed a tipsy looking Eleanor standing at the bar, knocking back a Jack Daniels whilst chatting to the foreign bartender. He shrugged off the nagging jealousy and fixed his concentration back on the roulette. His stock continued to fall, however, as he carelessly threw away several bundles of chips, feeling the pressure, anxious to make some cash back.

Just as he began to feel his groove again, he found himself distracted by the sight of Eleanor leaning over the bar, fixated on the suave-looking foreigner, clearly oblivious to him now. It was seeping underneath George's skin, the fucking nerve. She had his attention now, that was for sure. He observed the barman's athletic build, and tanned skin, and then looked down at the heavy-looking beer belly spilling over the top of his own belt. Those distant insecurities, still raw in the psyche, pulled at his nerves. He'd finally tied down a bird that made others envious. He'd be damned if he was going to lose her to some suave, sharp-tongued greaseball behind a bar.

"Sir?" said the croupier, bringing his attention back to the game.

He sized up his options in a matter of seconds before deciding it was time to go for broke. All on red, lose and he would cut his losses and go home, win and he was laughing. What the fuck was he thinking? He was so desperate to whisk Eleanor away that he was dumping all his eggs in one basket. She had him rattled, that was for sure. Should have known bringing her along was a bad move. He was starting to wonder if that tidy little piece of snatch that had the ability to raise him to attention in an instant was a bad luck omen. A fucking curse.

Fuck it...

He flung the pile down and watched as the ball tottered agonisingly round the wheel, teasing at the slots, as the sweat poured down George's beetroot face which was glowing as red as the red he had gambled on.

"Black 33."

"FUCK! FUCK!" George snapped. He banged a fist heavily against the table, causing several piles of chips to topple over to gasps from all around, as the other players jumped in their seats.

"Now come on sir, I'm going to have to ask you to calm down or..."

"Or WHAT!?"

He turned to a slick-haired high roller in a horrible Hawaiian shirt who had been puffing clouds of smoke all night.

"You an yer fucking cigar smoke putting me off! Stinkin man!"

"Steady on big chap."

"Big chap, aye?" A hefty shove was enough to send the man tumbling off his stool, landing with a thump on his side, the air gushing out of him as the cigar bounced along the faded red carpet. George stamped on it angrily as he heard the croupier frantically radioing for back up.

All surrounding noise and fuss was instantly drowned out by the sight of Eleanor leaning over the bar exposing her cleavage to the barman as he flexed his muscles. He made a furious beeline towards them with clenched fists, having built up a head of steam now that no-one was going to stop in its tracks.

"Hey Ah'm jist havin a laugh wae um!" she said as he picked her up with ease and dumped her down several feet away, before turning his attention to the barman.

"You wae the silver fucking tongue, Ah'll rip it oot yer throat an make ye swallow it if you dinnae wind those fucking beady eyes back in yer heid!"

"Hey what's the problem man? We're just talking," he replied with a smirk on his face.

"You're ma fuckin problem. Cunt! Look at her one mair fuckin time, Ah dare ye! You chose the wrong fuckin night and the wrong fuckin lassy pal!"

Two doormen arrived behind him. One of the men put his hand on George's arm. He shoved him away and pointed a finger in his face. "Step off, ya fuckin bam."

"George, calm it. Ye'll get yersel lifted!" shouted Eleanor in vain.

"Why don't you listen to your girlfriend. Do yourself a favour and calm down!"

George turned toward Jody, a young doorman who had previously done a couple of shifts at the Vaults. "Jody, why don't you tell that cunt who he's dealin wae."

Jody moved towards his colleague and whispered in his ear, causing him to back away.

"Aye, fuckin thought so. Just try an chuck me out, we'll see what happens." He turned his attention back to the barman who was now pressed against the back of the bar area, forcing the bottles to shake. "You, Spaniard. Fuckin El Matador. Ootside, NOW!"

"Leave it, George!" yelled Eleanor, but it was pointless.

"No so fuckin smug now are ye?"

"George, please man. Take it easy. Come back another day will ye?" said Jody.

"Ah'm no goin naewhere till that cunt behind the bar comes outside fer a square go."

As George smacked a hand against the bar, fast losing patience, he sensed bodies behind him. He turned to face, unable to conceal the grin.

Here we fucking go...

"Looks like the cavalry's arrived then eh?"

One of the bouncers stepped towards him with open hands. "I'm going to have to ask you to leave. You're threatening staff and making people feel uncomfortable."

Eleanor tugged at his arm. "Come on George, let's leave. There's six of them."

"How about Ah take you outside fer a square go instead?" He nodded his head at the head doorman. "In fact Ah'll fucking take yous all on right here."

George snatched a heavy glass ashtray from the bar, ready to mow down anything in his path before lunging for the head bouncer's face.

The next in line moved hesitantly towards him, catching a heavy left hand for his troubles, followed by a dull blow in the back of the head with the ashtray. He smashed the third aggressor clean in the mouth with the rim and watched on with twisted glee as his head snapped backwards, before taking a quick breath as he steadied himself.

After he let out a raging war cry, they all charged at the same time, backing him up against the bar, and just managing to hold him there kicking and screaming. The ashtray bounced to the floor as all six of the doormen forced him with great difficulty towards the doorway at the top of the stairs. As he felt the oxygen getting slowly squeezed out of him from a tight headlock, he tried his hardest to muscle out of their grip, but there were six of them, and the more he struggled the tighter the headlock became.

As they tried to force him down the stairwell, he bit down as hard as he could into the arm around his neck, forcing the bouncer to yell at the top of his voice before releasing his grip. George broke free, planting a hard headbutt right on his nose, watching him crumble backwards as his colleagues scrambled to get further up the stairs and out of harm's way.

"MON THEN?! WHO'S FUCKIN NEXT?!"

They looked at one another as George stood there at the entrance puffing and panting, itching for more.

"Boy's a fuckin maniac!" said one of the bouncers as Eleanor appeared at the top of the stairs screaming to be let through.

The two bouncers at the top of the steps parted as she bounded down the stairs, and tossed him his bomber jacket.

"George, let's go! Ye've made yer point. None of them want any piece of it."

He felt that explosive burst of rage slowly cooling. He looked up the stairwell, grinning at the fear in each of their eyes. These moments gave George a sense of power that no drug could rival. Hardest cunt in Edinburgh, who dared prove otherwise? The Bull had just bored a hole right through six bouncers single handed and Eleanor was right, they didn't want any part of it now.

He calmly pulled the coat over his heavy frame and brushed it down. He broke out laughing before thundering out onto Shandwick Place to the sound of the door being slammed shut and bolted behind him.

A rampant hen party dolled up like nurses came bustling past. The fat hen reminded George of most of his exploits pre-Eleanor. They obscured his view just enough for him to lose sight of the new standard. He could have sworn she'd been right by his side when he'd left.

"Eleanor!" he shouted, feeling that dreaded burst of panic in his chest, before catching sight of her stomping up Princes Street. He took after her, nearly upending a trailing hen in the process, as a car screamed to a halt in his path.

"Fuck off George! Fucking screwball," she snapped as he caught up.

"Hud on just a minute, ye were chattin up the barman right in front of me!"

"Had tae get yer attention somehow! Didn't know you were gonnae try and panel the guy and then take on all the bouncers! I don't need a jealous nut job in my life, I'm sorry."

George stopped in his tracks. "Well ken what? Ah dinnae need you either. Catch ye."

He heard her calling out his name as he marched in the other direction back down Princes Street with the wind whistling at his ears through the black railings of the Gardens, but his pride was too dented for him to stop. She could do the chasing and grovelling. He wasn't going to play the mug. For now, it was out of sight out of mind.

Besides, he had money to win back.

39

He could hear Davy's loud piercing cackle as he approached the back of The Gunner after bouncing out of the taxi. Dougie had warned him against going to his uncle's card games, said it was just a way for him to get people in his pocket. As he rammed the rest of that shite, council ching up his beak and tossed the wrap in the dirt however, Dougie's warnings weren't having any effect. All sense had left him. Still smarting from a hefty loss in the Rutland, he was eager to end the night on a high.

The door swung open after several knocks to reveal a paranoid Sean, looking jumpy and erratic.

"Fuck sake George, that was a fucking polis knock was it no? In ye come, man." Sean's eyes were pinned, darting all over the place. He looked edgy, unable to rest in his own skin. His normally sharp appearance had deteriorated in the months since Willie's death and he looked rough and dishevelled. His shirt was covered in deep creases with the collar twisted inside out. Looked like he was seeping sweat from every pore.

He led George through to the pub where Davy was cracking jokes with big Al Godfrey the Ferryboat owner, who studied his hand.

Davy stopped what he was doing as George approached. "Dougie junior, ma wee nephew. Tae what do we owe this pleasure?"

"Was wondering if Ah could get in on the action? Took a hefty loss at the casino, wantae try an make some back."

Davy stroked the grey jagged stubble on his pointed chin. George felt as if he was being sized up. He could see the plotting in his uncle's eyes.

"Two hundred buy in. If ye can cover that then pull up a chair, George. Join the party."

Davy began shuffling the cards in a rapid yet neat fashion as George took a seat, feeling the urge to cough as the thick layer of passive smoke caught the back of his throat. Felt strange seeing The Gunner so empty and dark, with just a lamp lighting up the table where the poker was taking place. Sean was standing at the end of the bar, oblivious to the game, muttering quietly under his breath as he obsessively counted the same pile of notes over and over.

"Texas Davy. That's what they used tae call me in the joint, George," he said proudly. "Ye'll be familiar wae Texas hold em bein the gambler that ye are eh?"

"We're no in Texas though are we? Can we no just play normal poker?"

Davy stopped shuffling for a second and looked up at George with a grin sneaking across his face. It was clear he thought George was out of his depth. Maybe he was; time would tell. "That's what they played in the joint an that's what we play here. Two card poker, simple, easy tae pick up fer beginners like."

George grabbed the whisky bottle from the table and glugged some back, growing tired of his uncle's patronising tones. It had been a long night and he wasn't in the mood. "Dinnae worry about me, Uncle Davy. Just deal the cards, eh."

"Oooohh, no nonsense here Al, eh? Jist like his old man. Dougie never was one fer small talk. Ma wee nephew's a chip off the auld block eh."

An hour in and George was floundering. He was now into Davy for five hundred and most of his profits had been gambled away, including Dougie's cut. He wiped at his eyes as he felt the strain, brought on ten fold by Davy's endless Barlinnie stories, big Al Godfrey hanging on his every word like a fucking vulture on his shoulder, nodding constantly, feeding his ego.

"What's the matter Georgie boy, tough night?"

The sound of that high-pitched cackle pierced at George's worn and irritable senses. He knew he should call it a day, the only thing stopping him being the thought of facing the old man empty handed. Worse still the fact half of it had gone in his uncle's fucking pocket. He noticed Sean disappearing to the toilet again. George felt sluggish from the whisky. He needed some gear to sharpen himself up for one last run, and John's was the best.

As he entered the toilet he heard a lighter striking several times. Two seconds later he could hear Sean coughing his lungs out, spitting on the floor.

"Sean?"

The toilet flushed, the door opened, Sean stood there looking white as a sheet, as the fumes gathered around him. That handsome face had been replaced by a twisted, gaunt looking wild-eyed stranger. It was more obvious now that they were standing nose to nose.

"What you up tae?"

"What ye daein through here?" said Sean as his eyes began darting all over the place again. George looked over Sean's shoulder to see what he was trying to hide in the cubicle. The fumes were pungent.

"Right George, come on eh, nowt tae see here. Let's get back through."

Now he looked seriously rattled. Like he was desperate to cover up whatever it was. The curiosity was too much. George barged past, looked down and there it was stashed under the toilet seat. A glass pipe with charred foil through which the smoke was seeping out.

"What the fuck, Sean. Crack?"

"Ye cannae tell any cunt George Ah swear it, right?"

"How long ye been daein this shit?"

"Since Willie. Ah jist, Ah jist, fuck knows man, Ah jist need it tae escape, eh. Ah'll get off it Ah will."

"Escape what Sean? Cunt died ay an overdose. Got naeone tae blame but himself. He fucked it all up, now what, you jist gonnae go doon the same route aye? Get a grip man, look at the nick eh ye. Fuckin smokin crack."

"Ah could have stopped it man. Ah could've."

"Stopped what?"

"There was nothin Ah could dae, had tae happen, had tae dae it."

"Sean yer ramblin man. What the fuck ye talkin aboot? What could've been stopped? What did you have tae dae?"

George grabbed him by the shoulders and gave him a shake. As Sean looked back at him with a look of brokenness that no drug could mask, the door opened to reveal Davy standing there stony-faced.

"Fuck's goin on here?"

"Just talkin tae ma cousin is that awrite?"

"No when we've got a game tae play."

As George moved past his uncle he caught him throwing Sean a seething glare. Sean had been on the brink of saying something, that was clear, and from the look on Davy's face it was something serious. George took a swig of the whisky as he sat down at the table, pondering.

Had tae dae it. Had tae happen...

He didn't want to even imagine what those words could mean. He took another swig of the whisky and gave his spinning head a shake as Davy appeared, followed by a sheepish looking Sean, staring down at the ground as he went. Someone had been on the end of a roasting, that much was obvious.

"Right. Where were we?" Davy gave Al a firm nudge as he sat there snoring away, but he wasn't budging.

"Looks like it's me an you then George, big Al's out fer the count. I can lay ye on another five to six hundred if ye want, but then it becomes a loan. And ye pay vig until it's paid off."

"It's a grand, Ah'm sure Ah'll be good fer it." George picked up his cards. Two queens. Finally some luck.

"Or we can make things a bit mair interestin. Raise the stakes a wee bit."

"What ye talkin aboot?"

"How about, the Vaults and The Gunner. Winner takes all? You lose I take your door at the Vaults. We take over the business in there and you step away. *You* win. And you keep yer door at the Vaults, plus ye get the deeds tae this place. Winner takes all. Ye man enough for it?"

George stared back across the table in disbelief as Davy focused on his hand.

"You're off yer heid." George looked towards the bar, where Sean was now sitting, staring into space with a walkman blaring into his ears.

"Nae point lookin at yer cousin. He's no interested. This is between me an you ma wee nephew. No got the balls fer it?"

"First of all, less ay the wee nephew. Yer back on the scene after fifteen year. Cunt Ah wis six year auld when you got put away. Ah dinnae ken ye. So ye've no earned the right tae refer tae me as yer wee nephew. Gordon's mair of an uncle than you. Far as Ah'm concerned yer just some guy that's waltzed back intae all our lives an started causin problems where there wisnae any before. And secondly," he looked around the place and laughed, "what the fuck would Ah want wae this shit tip? Come oan eh. Ma auld man flung ye this just tae keep ye from bitchin an moanin but fat lot ay good that done."

Davy placed the cards face down before rubbing his hands firmly together.

"Some mouth on you, son. Daddy no teach ye tae respect yer elders, naw?"

"How about we raise the stakes even higher then. How about – if Ah win, you walk away fae us altogether. Leave Muirhouse. Go an noise up some other folk an let me go back tae what Ah wis quite happily daein before you came along."

"You'd love that wouldn't ye. You and Dougie. That right tubsy?"

"What the fuck did you just call me?"

"What's wrong wae ye boy? Yer startin tae sweat."

George tried to shrug off the comment as he felt the rage growling away down below. He looked down to see the two queens crumpled in his right hand. And then looked up at his grinning uncle, who was clearly getting off on it. Like he was poking a bear in a cage.

"Just like a young Dougie. No quite sure how tae take being on the receiving end. Doesnae like it when the heat's on. Temper, temper son. Found yer weak spot have Ah? That very same weak spot as yer auld man."

"Maybe ye have. Just keep pushin at it an see what happens."

Davy smiled as he looked down at his hand. "Sean away an pit some chips oan. Looks starving, the fat cunt."

"AYE!" George hoisted the table off the ground, as bottles, money, cards, and glasses flew into the air.

Sean pounced in between to try and prevent Davy's head from getting torn off, whilst Al went flying backwards in his chair before scrambling out of harm's way.

"Get oot ma fuckin way Sean! NOW!"

"Settle doon George! This ends badly fer everyone, we both know this!"

"No giein a FUCK!" George barged his cousin out of the way just to find his uncle backing him off with a chair, wearing a pathetic grin on his face that George was itching to wipe off. He looked for an opportunity to lunge forward without catching a chair leg in the throat, forcing Davy backward as more tables and chairs toppled over in his path. It was time to put the old fossil in its place.

"Mon then tubs!"

"Drop the chair an let's go then!"

Davy dropped the chair and slipped behind the bar before coming back up with a shotgun, that he promptly backed George off with. Davy rose in stature, grinning, as George reluctantly backed away.

"Get the fuck outae ma boozer before Ah do somethin Ah might regret."

"Shitebag. Fuckin shitebag!"

"GET OUT!"

40

The following day Dougie turned up at the bookies, having already checked at The Gunner. As he approached the doorway deep in thought, he didn't notice his older brother walking briskly towards him until it was too late. They collided with each other. An envelope stuffed with notes fell to the ground. Dougie looked on as Davy knelt down, picked it up and rammed it inside his brown leather coat, snatching up a couple of twenties that had fallen out.

"You wantae watch where yer goin."

"What's wae the envelope?"

"Just some cash Ah lent tae Bob a couple ay weeks ago." Davy carried on walking hastily.

"Why the rush?"

"Ah'm a busy man Dougie, just like yersel."

"We need tae talk, pronto."

"Later. That son of yours wants tae watch his temper by the way." Davy jumped into his motor and started the car, grinding the gravel underneath the wheels into a cloud of dust that drifted past Dougie as he watched it disappear down the street.

When he opened the door to the back room of the bookies he caught a glimpse of Bob with his head in his hands looking deeply distressed. The moment he saw Dougie he straightened up and threw on a false looking smile. "There he is. Wasn't expectin you, Dougie."

Bob straightened up and started moving things around the table, clearly trying to act busy, but Dougie wasn't fooled for a second.

"How's things with you?"

"Fine. Yersel?"

"Ach, cannae complain, ye ken how it is."

"No. I don't."

Bob stopped what he was doing and looked back at Dougie. "What dae ye mean?"

"Well obviously I don't know how it is if yer havin to take loans off ay Davy waeout comin tae me first."

"Aye, Ah wis gonnae tell ye about that."

"Well. Now's yer chance." Dougie folded his arms and waited.

"It's just a bit ay cash tae help out wae the weddin an that."

"Ye've been savin up fer that fer aboot two year. Ye made it clear ye didnae want any loans, fae me or anyone else. Christ ye've been knockin back nights out left right an centre."

"Aye, but Ah kept on havin tae dip intae ma savings fer expenses an that."

"Well, why didn't ye come tae me if ye needed extra dough?"

"Ah jist didnae wantae bother ye wae it Dougie."

"So ye bothered Davy instead? A man who's had a vendetta against ye ever since he got ootae prison. Doesn't make sense, Robert. Elaborate." Dougie moved closer and sat on the edge of the table. He stared a hole right through the anxious expression Bob was uncomfortably wearing, watching him squirm and wriggle, fiddling with his hands the way he always did when he was telling a porkie. Was one of the benefits of working closely with someone you knew inside out. You knew instantly when something wasn't right.

"Och it's jist, ye've been so busy wae everythin that's been goin on an..."

"Bob listen tae me. Ma patience is wearing thin here. Ah want ye tae stop stutterin like a prick, cause yer no makin any sense, an Ah want answers. Now."

"Ah had nae-one else tae turn tae, Dougie."

"Ye had me!" Dougie stuck a thumb against his chest. "So Ah'm gonnae ask ye again, Robert. An this time Ah want the right answer. Ah want the truth! Why has my brother just walked outae here wae an envelope stuffed full ay cash!?"

Bob sat down on the chair, nearly losing his balance as he did. His head fell into his hands, as that same distressed expression broke through again.

"Spill it. NOW."

He broke down, the tears streaming down his scarlet face. Reminded Dougie of all the times he had had to bail him out in high school when he was in over his head with other kids.

"He's been robbin us Dougie! He's been robbin us fer weeks and weeks! When you telt him ye were wantin a cut eh everything he made on his loans he flipped out. Fuckin mowed me down in broad daylight wae his car! Telt me Ah'd have tae front up his end every time you asked for money, outae the safe. Started off payin um ootae ma weddin fund, an then..."

"Then what?"

"He got greedier an greedier. Started off just comin round now an then. Then it wis every other day. Ma weddin fund ran oot an Ah had tae start geein um money oot the safe. He demanded it, said he wanted your money, wanted one over oan ye. Dougie, Ah'm sorry! Sharon's left me!" Bob dropped his head face down on the table, sobbing uncontrollably. "Ah wanted tae come tae ye Dougie, but he telt me he'd murder me if Ah did!"

"How much? How much money is he intae us fer?"

"Must be aboot twenty grand by now. At the least, probably more. Ah'm sorry Dougie there was nowt Ah could dae! He's been a livin nightmare!"

Dougie felt his whole body go stiff as a feeling of dread washed over it. Bob looked up at him with those desperate, dog-like eyes, searching for pity that he didn't find as Dougie smacked him straight on the cheekbone with a solid open handed right, sending his head flying backward with such force it nearly hit the wall. On its way forward again he grabbed him by his shirt collar and yanked him off the chair. He sprawled across the floor as Dougie began kicking him furiously in the ribs with the point of his toe.

"Gies the key tae the safe. GIES THE KEY TAE THE FUCKIN SAFE!!"

Bob fumbled about in his pocket for his keys whilst trying desperately to cover up with his only free hand. Bob threw the keys down in front of him.

"Please Dougie, please. He said he'd murder me if Ah didnae carry on givin um the money. He said he'd shoot me Dougie, Ah swear!"

Dougie unlocked the safe, and threw it open. "COME HERE!!"

As Bob crawled over on his hands and knees like the stupid mutt he was,

Dougie grabbed him by the hair and rammed his head inside the safe before slamming the door against the side of his face. Bob let out a high pitched yelp, as it smashed into his jaw with a sickening crack. Dougie pushed Bob's head back further inside the safe and began forcing the door against it with all his might.

"Ye think Davy al kill ye, but Ah winnae!? Eh!? What am I, a fuckin SOFT TOUCH!?"

Bob tried to force out some words as drool began leaking out. Dougie leaned harder and harder on the safe door, furious, eager to force the point home that he was the brother to be afraid of, lifelong friendship or not. As he noticed Bob's neck changing colour and his left hand starting to fall limp, Dougie let go and stepped away. Bob dropped to the floor gasping for air, his body shaking horrendously. Dougie sat down, trying his hardest to cool off as he looked down at his own trembling hands. He walked over to the sink and poured Bob a drink before placing it on the floor in front of him. Dougie sat down again and lit up a fag as he rubbed at the stress lines etched into his forehead.

"Thirty odd years we've been friends Boab. Thirty years, an ye feel like ye cannae come tae me when yer in danger?"

Bob sipped some water through the uninjured side of his mouth, as he clutched the other side. It was obvious his jaw was badly broken and would likely need wired up. "Ah was scared Dougie," he said, forcing the drooling mumble out with serious difficulty. "Ah didn't know what to do. The last few months, they, they've been a livin hell."

He pulled himself up against the wall as his body continued to shake, his eyes wide with shock. "He said he was gonnae shoot me if I telt ye what was goin on, an he meant it. Ah swear on ma Mother's grave Dougie, he showed it to me in here. Put it tae ma heid one time, laughin, while Ah counted his money. He's a fuckin psycho, Dougie."

"Aye well dinnae worry about Davy anymair." Dougie stood up and sighed before pulling a roll of notes from his back tail. He looked down at his broken old pal, feeling some sympathy breaking through the walls of his hardened heart. "Get yersel tae the hospital. Tell thum ye goat mugged in the street by a gang, an knocked oot. That ye cannae remember what happened efter the first dig."

41

Sean woke with a start, drenched in sweat, heart pounding. Just a few seconds earlier he had been walking side by side with Willie on a hot summer day past Inverleith pond during school lunch hour. Laughing, joking, slagging off trench coat wearing freaks as they passed them by, looking about for a victim to push into the water.

Next thing he knew Willie had tumbled in, causing him to panic. He'd reached down to try to help him up but instead of pulling him out he'd found himself pushing him down kicking and screaming, deeper into the water until he stopped struggling.

As he stood up the water rapidly turned to ice, encasing Willie's lifeless body, eyes gone, staring back at him. As he looked up the trees at the top of the grassy embankment surrounding the pond began shrivelling up before his eyes, shedding themselves of all colour. He looked around to see that he was alone now, cold and vulnerable, alone with the guilt. He looked down at the ice right beneath his feet and watched as it began cracking all around him, until he plunged into the water himself, feeling himself dragged down kicking and screaming until he woke.

He clutched his tight chest as he tried to catch his breath, whilst instinctively grabbing hold of the steel bed frame, wary of toppling onto the floor. The nightmares were a daily occurrence now, well, on the days he actually managed to get any sleep that was.

Sean knew he had lost control. It wasn't like him. He had always prided himself on his ability to stay on point and composed when everyone around him seemed to be losing their heads, but that was gone now. He was freebasing frequently. His life had turned into a hazy blur of cocaine, women and hangers on. His vices were now consuming him.

He looked down at the slender frame of his latest conquest, as she lay face down. Didn't know what her name was, couldn't even remember how or where he'd met her. Kim had left him the moment she had found out he had a flat on the sly where he took all his bits on the side. Just so happened that since the wheels had came off the rails he had been using that flat a lot more. Didn't matter a fuck, the only women that meant anything to him were out of reach on the other side of the world, and oh how desperately he needed them.

He stood up and walked unsteadily over to his dresser, feeling spent. There was a Safeway bag full of coke that was spilling out. Who knows how much of it they had done. Sean would never normally leave all this shit lying about his flat. Used to give Willie pelters for leaving bags of gear lying about. Now he was the reckless one.

As he approached The Gunner doorway later that afternoon he was met by a sight he wasn't prepared for. Simon Lockhart skulking his way towards him. His Nike baseball cap was pulled down covering half those piercing reptile-like pupils, with his hands stuck inside his shell suit pockets in a manner that suggested he was ready to pull a blade on any passer by that happened to look at him the wrong way.

Since Ryan's incarceration for kidnap and attempted murder a couple of years earlier, Simon, being the second oldest and naturally next in line had taken it upon himself to assume the mantle of number one Lockhart. Simon had made his bones a year or so earlier by delivering a horrific Chelsea Smile to a local dealer who had been cutting Dougie's product in order to increase his share. This was a signal of his dedication to the cause that had endeared him to Dougie's good graces.

He had been instrumental in luring Willie away from Sean and into the clutches of other like minded jakies, and now both he and his younger brother Colin had assumed main control of the area's smack trade, as decreed by Dougie since Willie's demise. This meant that whilst Sean still ran the hash and speed for Dougie, he no longer got a piece of the lucrative heroin trade that both he and Willie had controlled for years. Instead this piece of shit that not too long ago would have stabbed his granny for some gear was now the main heroin dealer in the area, and that grated on Sean. The way he now swaggered around Muirhouse with a stink of pride and conceit, as if he now ran the show.

"Awrite Sean mate?" said Lockhart as he leaned against the wall, sparking a rollie between his dirty fingertips. For all the cash he was now making it hadn't made the slightest bit of difference to his appearance.

You're no fuckin mate pal...

"What's happenin?"

"Ach fuck all, ye ken me, just dodgin away gadgy. Was wonderin if yer auld man's havin one ay his card games the night?"

"How come?" Sean squinted his eyes at Lockhart with paranoid suspicion.

"Why dae ye think mate? Want in on the action don't Ah."`

"No the night Simon." As Sean tried to manoeuvre cautiously past Lockhart he stepped in front of him. They were now nose to nose and Sean could see his rancid yellow teeth, and smell his stinking breath. He felt his heart pounding again. This was the last fucking thing he needed.

"Sure aboot that? Yer no palmin me off are ye?"

Sean looked down his nose as he clenched his sweating fists and responded. "Naw Simon. Course no. Mate." Sean held his glare for several seconds, feeling the bitterness building within his cramped stomach.

Simon grinned and sniggered like he was part of a joke Sean wasn't in on.

"Crack on, eh." As he stepped aside, still grinning, Sean cautiously moved past, feeling the paranoia tearing right through him, wondering why Simon Lockhart was nosing about so deviously.

The old man was parked at the end of the bar with a whisky in hand laughing away. Carol Hunter, who had grown into a Gunner regular since she and Davy had become an item, was sitting next to him, screaming like a banshee at Davy's every joke. Sean wiped a layer of sweat from his forehead with the sleeve of his light grey Harrington as he approached, feeling his senses taking a pounding from Carol's verbal onslaught.

"Dad. A word in private please?"

Davy gave Carol some money to stick in the jukebox before leading the way through the back. Sean pulled a fag from his packet with his shaking hand and stuck it between his teeth as he began to pace restlessly.

"Ye look like shit Sean."

"Aye cheers."

He was right though. His nerves were on end, his brain was racing, he was wracked with anxiety at every turn and he could feel it spilling out of him. He needed the coke just to keep him on a level, even if it was a big part of the problem.

"What's eatin ye? Is it what happened the other night wae yer cousin?"

"What the fuck is Simon Lockhart daein askin if yer havin a poker game the night? Ah mean first George turns up unannounced, now we've got that fuckin waster nosin aboot askin if he can get in on the action. Somethin's up an Ah don't fuckin like it, Dad."

"They're fishin aboot fer something, clearly."

"Could it be Willie? They're ontae us aren't they? Fuck."

"Listen!" Davy rose from the wooden stool with a stiffened frame and gritted teeth forcing Sean to squirm backwards. "If Ah hear one mair word aboot fuckin Willie, son, so help me God you will feel the back of my hand an then some. It's done, ok? Over! Ye need tae get over it an pull yersel the gither. Fuckin gettin oot yer brain oan that shite twenty-four seven isnae helpin any cunt ye hear me?"

"It's no that though Dad, if they know aboot that or the coke we've been sellin behind their backs, or worse both..."

"Then what? Eh? Ye gonnae run an hide?" Davy sighed. "Listen. They might have their suspicions aboot Willie but that's all they are, fuckin suspicions. Can't prove shit. And as fer the coke, tell me why is it we're havin tae sell coke? If he had cut us both in on the smack rather than lettin the inbreds take it over would we even need tae be daein that? Naw, so fuck him, an fuck his suspicions."

Sean double drew the last part of his fag, leaving nothing but filter showing, and bounced it off the stone floor. He looked round at the old man who was now pinching his bottom lip, clearly deep in thought.

"Let Lockhart come."

"Eh?"

"Ah say let that fuck come. We strike first."

"What dae ye mean."

"Ah think it's about time we sent a message. Ah'll get word oot tae um that he's invited along. Then we'll show Dougie what we think about his little regime change. Do that bastard good an proper."

"Dad, if we do Simon Lockhart it will be like shakin up a hornet's nest. We'll have that whole family tae deal with, they're fuckin cut-throats. Ah'm goin oot ma way here tae keep stability, keep a war fae breakin out, keep business movin along, an you're just wantin tae turn the area intae the Wild West wae us on the front line. We don't have the back up. We cannae rely on folk fae Glasgow that might no even wantae get involved. If shit hits the fan we're fucked! Dae ye no get that?"

Davy launched himself at Sean, catching him by surprise, lifting him over the keg and wedging him into an uncomfortable position, his feet dangling in the air. Sean tried his hardest to struggle free, itching to fight back but he could only watch on as the old man snarled.

"Listen. Ok? Listen, an listen good, son. We've tried it your way. We've tried tae fly underneath the radar an keep the peace. Keep everythin nice an smooth, maintain the status quo for the greater good of family. But first Ah've got the son comin doon here tae tryin tae shout the odds. Now I've got Simon fuckin Lockhart threatenin tae invade ma card game, no doubt lookin tae raise some kind of hell. Now I didn't do fourteen years an come out the other side tae fly underneath the radar and accept the crumbs fae ma little brother's table wae a bowed head an a humble heart. I want what I deserve. An if he won't give it tae me, I will fucking take it, ye hear me? I'm responsible for his supply, and I will do everything in my power tae lift it from right underneath him if need be. An you, my son, are either with me or against me. No middle grounds, no straddlin the fence anymore, no grey areas! Just black and fucking white."

Davy released his grip, leaving Sean standing there staring him down, fists clenched. The blood was roaring in his ears, his heart was pounding even harder, every fibre in his body was standing on end ready to strangle the life out of his dad – or anyone else in his path.

"Ye wantae hit me? Hit me." Davy slapped himself hard across the jaw. "Anythin tae get the fire rumblin in that fuckin belly ay yours. We do that cunt tonight. Show Dougie we're tired of his dictatorship. Maybe then he'll see sense an we can sit down an sort this oot good an proper. If not we go tae John an we strike a deal. Shift the balance of power an take back what's ours."

42

That night, Sean looked down at the pile of envelopes. He wasn't sure why he had kept them all these years. He had sent his final letter around the age of eighteen, though the replies had continued for several years. Gradually over time they had slowed to the point where they only appeared on the odd birthday or Christmas, before eventually they dried up altogether.

Perhaps he had locked away a piece of his heart with these very envelopes.

He opened up the letter, the very last one he had received. He took a deep breath as he began to read.

My darling Sean,

No doubt you are a man now, and a handsome one at that. This will be my last letter. I'm going to respect your wishes and let you get on with your life since (as you said yourself three years ago) this has become too painful an exercise for me to continue. All this time I suppose I've been holding out hope that you would somehow change your mind, and find a way of joining me and your sisters over here in Canada. Come visit your aunties and uncles and perhaps even find a way to stay here with us. I can see now that Scotland is your home and your heart is in Edinburgh.

As I write this to you I am looking out of the window at Abby. She's so beautiful Sean; a young woman now, playing in the snow with your little cousin Max whom you've never met, with the Rocky Mountains in the background below a clear blue sky.

The door will always be open for you here, Sean. I want you to know that. You will always have a place here with me and your sisters. I need you to know that I didn't choose what happened, Sean. I tried my hardest to take you with us, but your father, well, you know what he's like, he wasn't having it, nor was Uncle Dougie. It isn't fair to continue this game of tug of war which is why I'm ending it now. Just please, please, be careful Sean, in everything you do.

Your loving Mother

Cindy

His eyes wandered to the bottom of the letter. An address in Calgary, Canada. He didn't know if they still lived there or if they'd moved on. It had been so long. Ten years.

43

Dad, I can't do this anymore...
   I'm going away for a while...
   It's all getting too much. I need time to think...
   It didn't matter what he said or how he said it, he was bracing himself for an onslaught. He was backing out and leaving his old man up shit-creek when he needed him the most.

He felt the jitters bouncing around his ribcage as he pushed the rusty key into the slot, applying pressure, just to feel the lock jam as it always did. After a couple of minutes of frustration and forcing, it gave way. The stubborn green door creaked open, revealing the dark and cramped kitchen area, a dim flickering bulb above the sink providing the only light.

As he stepped over two hefty boxes, out of the corner of his eye he thought he noticed a figure moving, forcing him to freeze. After peering about on the spot looking for signs of danger he shrugged it off as his mind playing tricks, and anxiously made his way toward the other side of the room, squeezing his way in between chip pans and tables as he went.

As he reached for the door handle he heard what sounded like a shuffling of feet behind him. "Hello? Is anyone there?" He placed a sweating hand inside his backtail and nervously took hold of the Stanley, whilst reaching for the light switch with his other hand. Then everything went blank.

The ceiling light was blinding, the back of his head was throbbing, he wasn't sure if he had slipped and fallen or what. Then as Simon Lockhart stepped over him with that sick grin, waving Sean's Stanley about in mid-air, it all became frighteningly clear. "Awrite Sean! Comin tae join the card game? Yer auld man's waitin oan ye."

As he felt himself getting dragged through the kitchen doorway and into the pub, he looked about for anything he could grab but it was useless. There were only tables and chairs and that was no good to him as he lay on his back getting dragged past fag ends and broken glass, the smell of stale bevy seeping up his nostrils. The haunting sound of his old man screaming in between heavy smacks was all he could hear as he closed his eyes and felt himself drift off again. In what seemed like a matter of seconds he was woken by a heavy slap, as he opened his eyes to an even more terrifying sight than before. Uncle Dougie crouched over him sleeves rolled up, hands covered in blood. "Ye with us Sean? Good. Sit him up. Ah want him tae have a ringside seat."

He felt himself hoisted up and then planted down on a chair, before looking to his right and seeing a stern faced Gordon Trevor standing by his side clenching his fists. In front of him his battered dad was slouched over a table, eyes swollen shut with blood and drool seeping out the side of his mouth as both Dougie and George stood over him puffing and panting.

He felt the urge to scream for help but he knew it wouldn't come. What he needed to be thinking about was damage limitation. He noticed Simon glaring at him with the Stanley in hand, looking to Dougie for the go ahead, and realised that if he was to have any hope of getting out of this situation in one piece he needed to use the sharpest tool at his disposal.

His mouth.

"Talk to me, Uncle Dougie. What's goin on here? Come on, talk tae me. We're family, we can sort this out. Whatever it is, we can sort it out. It's no too late."

Dougie smiled as he sat on the table in front of him and crossed his arms like he had appointed himself judge, jury and executioner. "Did you know? Did you know this was goin on? Were you part of it?"

"It's me, Uncle Dougie. It's Sean. Ah've always had yer back no matter what! What's goin on?"

"Naw Sean. No this time. He's gone too far. Stealin off his own, robbin me stinkin fer months! Ain't that right David?"

Davy lifted his battered head from the table and spat a mixture of blood and saliva. "Fuck you, Dougie."

Dougie stood up, causing Sean to flinch in his seat. He felt the sweat pouring down his neck as little black dots began to appear in front of his eyes.

"We'll get to your sins soon Sean, don't you worry. No havin ye feelin left out."

Dougie nodded at Gordon who began cracking his big knuckles as he towered over the old man's battered carcass.

"What dae ye mean he's been stealing from ye Uncle Dougie?" Sean offered faintly, feeling his powers of persuasion waning.

"It's awrite Sean!" yelled Davy as he lifted his horribly swollen face from the table. "Yer wastin yer breath son. Ah've been caught. Fuck him, he gave me no choice."

Dougie, sitting at the other side of the table from Davy, pulled a cigar from his pocket and lit it with blood-stained hands that were shaking with rage.

"Ah gave ye the pub. Ah let ye go about yer business uninterrupted. An what did ye dae? Ye shat all over me!"

"You gave me SHITE YA BASTARD! Taxin me like a mug," shouted Davy with spit flying from his mouth as he sat forward. "So what did Ah do? Ah TAXED YE BACK!" He burst into a bout of crazed laughter as Sean willed him to put a lid on it.

"Aye well, Ah'll teach you tae steal fae me ya bastard. Son?"

Sean gripped hold of the bottom of the seat and froze with terror as George pulled a long hammer from behind his belt. He planted the old man's hand down flat on the table whilst Gordon wrapped a big arm around his neck to restrain him. Sean felt the terror turn to fury as he stood up, just to feel the sharp Stanley slashing his forearm, forcing him to fall back into the chair like a scalded animal. He struggled to watch, holding his soaking arm as George lifted the hammer.

"AAAAAAAAAAAAAAGGGGGHHHHHH."

The scream did nothing to drown out the sound of bones cracking underneath the weight of the hammer. Every thud and crack reverberated around Sean's brain that was now buzzing, as he felt the piercing cries of his old man torturing him, laying witness to him whimpering like a little boy as George continued driving them in.

"Fuckin STOP IT GEORGE! He's had enough!"

George stopped and pointed the hammer squarely at Sean. "You fuckin killed Willie so keep that hole in yer face SHUT!"

As Sean tried to reply he caught a boot clean in the face from Lockhart that knocked him off his chair. He gnashed his teeth as he curled up into a ball on the floor and watched as Gordon took the right hand, the dealing hand, on the prompting of Dougie. Sean felt himself numbing inside as the screams, the thuds and the cracks increased in volume. After they were done with both hands, they hoisted the right leg up as he kicked and screamed in wild despair.

Sean closed his eyes and clenched them tight, clamping his hands against his ears in a desperate attempt to block it all out.

He tried his hardest but the faces of his mother and sisters were now gone, a distant fairytale fantasy ending that seemed utterly ludicrous and pathetic now. In its place was nothing but cold, hard vengeance.

44

"Mon Sean, up ye get."

He felt his whole body tremble at Dougie's command.

Now it was him looking back at his dad with pleading but he knew that he was in no position to save him. He sat up to the sight of that demon Simon Lockhart cooking up fluid in a spoon.

"No. NOOOOOOO!!"

"It's time fer you son. Tae take a dose of yer own medicine," said Dougie as George grabbed hold of him by the back of his head, dragged him up to his feet and shoved him back onto the seat. He felt himself growing dizzy again, but he needed to stay alert. Needed to find a way out of this somehow.

"Ye see Sean Ah knew. Too much of a coincidence. Then when George told me about yer mumblin's the other night Ah started askin about at the prison. An then it was confirmed." Dougie took a seat right in front of him, and eyeballed Sean with those searching eyes. "Ye should know by now, Sean. Nothin gets past me."

"He was gonnae grass us in Dougie! What would you have done! EH!? Ma best mate an he was gonnae serve me up on a fuckin platter! Ah had tae dae it, Ah had tae! Any cunt in here would've done the same! Ah learnt from the best didn't Ah?"

"Maybe so. But doesnae change the fact that ye let yerself get dragged doon wae him. An for all Ah know you were part of him robbing me aw this time."

"Was nothin tae do wae him Dougie. Leave um be," strained Davy in between tortured whimpers as he rolled onto his back with great difficulty, unable to use his mangled hands.

"No one's listenin tae you! Keep it down or yer face'll go on that table next. Simon! Do the honours, son."

"Time tae join the darts club Sean."

"NAAAAWWWW! Dougie! PLEASE!!"

As George and Gordon held him down, Simon Lockhart crouched over him with the needle in hand. That evil yellow toothed grin would be the last thing he ever saw. As he looked up to the ceiling, struggling hard and feeling himself gasp for air, flashbacks of his dream passed through his mind. Staring up at the cold sky overhead as he felt himself getting dragged down deeper into the lake, a premonition perhaps? Soon he would be taking the plunge for real he thought to himself as he muttered a desperate prayer and closed his eyes.

45

Sean wasn't sure how long he'd been out cold before waking up and spewing his load. Last thing he remembered was getting bundled into the back of the car half jaked, mind drifting, feeling like he was being driven to his imminent death. Felt like he could see the icy cold sky above him, just like in the dream. But as he wiped his mouth, clutching at his stinging forearm, caked in dry blood, and looked down at the bag of heroin on the glass table in front of him, it all became clear. Dougie wanted him down and out. Reduced to a junky, unable to function, right where he could keep his eye on him. If they had just killed the two of them and John found out, clearly he would be asking questions. If, however he was turning up in Glasgow to pick up gear on the regular, out his head on smack, something John *didn't* like, he might be asking questions of another kind, forcing him to distance himself, seeing him as a liability, less likely to support him and Davy should they try to turn the tables.

He shuddered as the sound of that hammer shattering the bones of his dad's hands and knee reverberated through him, and then just as he tried to block it out, it sent the contents of his stomach rising up in a projectile all over the floor again.

He wiped his mouth and took a deep breath before making for the kitchen. Once he had cleaned up the mess he had made, still feeling the wretched effects of the smack, he picked up the bag, took it through to the sink, opened it and poured the contents down the drain.

I'm no fucking junky...

There was only one thing left to do. Once he had grabbed the box from his room he emptied every letter, postcard, and envelope onto the fireplace.

There would be no running now.

46

Billy stared out the rear view window at the Forth Road Bridge as it towered across the dark night sky with its purple hue, the glistening water beneath reflecting dozens of shimmering lights. Thieving was one thing, dealing drugs, handing out the odd doing, sure – but murder?

All of a sudden he felt like an amateur, painfully out of his depth. Yet they had accepted half the cash up front, and anyway it wasn't in him to back away from anything, shitting it or not, and the way Jimmy was gnawing his knuckles to the bone suggested Billy wasn't the only one feeling the pressure.

"You ready fer this, mate?" said Billy.

"Aye. You?"

"Fuck aye," said Billy.

His attention drifted out to the Forth Road Bridge again. Such a massive presence in the distance, looming as large as that contract in front of them. They had no plan, not really. All they knew was they didn't want any witnesses, so the only real idea was to follow the fucker until they had him on his own and then give him it, hard and fast.

Clark was true to his word. Goddard was so at ease in his little manor that he went about without any protection, meaning it would hopefully be a two-on-one situation. The car they were in was completely untraceable. The shotguns they had acquired also untraceable, or so he hoped.

Billy looked at him standing behind the counter of his chip shop, grinning, completely oblivious, as some drunk stumbled in for a supper on his way home. He didn't look much. Long black sideburns clung to his face like thick patches of carpet. He wore the appearance of someone who at one time was built like a brick-house, with a physique that had gradually shrunk into its frame over the years, leaving a sagging sack of shit in its place.

Of course, the other possible motivation was that he was supposedly a beast. This was according to Clark himself, who probably had his own reasons for spinning that line.

As the purple hue in the sky slowly faded to black, Billy felt that knot in his stomach tightening.

Shitebag. Weak. No got it in ye. Call yersel a Wright?

Billy shook his head to rid it of Jack's negative taunts. He had abstained from the gear until now, figuring better to have a straight head on his shoulders to avoid doing anything too rash or making mistakes, but out of the corner of his eye he caught Jimmy gubbing more bass and he gave in. "Gies some ay that, mate."

"Looks like he's oan the move eh," said Jimmy as the lights were switched off one by one in the shop.

Billy brushed away the residue from his fingers and pulled on his leather gloves as he felt his heart pounding like fuck.

"Let's just do um in front ay the shop," said Jimmy. "Git it over an done wae."

"Jimmy, there's a polis station right roond the corner. Let's follow um, see where he goes."

"We did that last night an got naewhere. We might no git a chance tae get um on his own. We've got the balaclavas there so nae cunt can ID us."

Now Billy felt backed into a corner by Jimmy's burst of reckless courage. He didn't want to look like the shitebag but at the same time he was determined to wait till the right moment, and as Goddard laughed and joked with a young lassie and a middle-aged woman right in front of chip shop, this clearly wasn't it.

Billy had to stick to his guns. Had to go with his instincts and keep from getting pulled in by Jimmy's impulsiveness. If it went south and they wound up taking out one or worse both of the women out in the open, they'd be lucky to reach the A90. If they got Goddard on his own, hopefully it would be seen as what it was, a gangland hit.

"We wait, mate. Trust me on this. Mental enough agreein tae this as it is, wantae dae it right. Got a fuckin baby oan the way mate, Ah'm no watchin um grow up fae behind bars."

Jimmy sighed, clearly growing restless. Billy could understand it to an extent as the longer they left it the more chance of hesitation and nerves creeping in. More chance they might choke when it came time.

Goddard climbed into his car and started the engine as the two women disappeared down the street. As his car moved off, Billy slowly crept past the old church on his right, making sure there was enough distance between them.

The previous night Goddard had gone straight to the boozer on the main street. This time he was going in the opposite direction, away from the bright cobbled streets lit up by the rail bridge. Instead he was venturing into the growing darkness of the night, with the Road Bridge beyond them in all its competing shades of grey.

As Billy continued down the street, he suddenly found himself having to slow down to a crawl as Goddard pulled in at a grassy verge directly underneath the bridge. Billy pulled in behind another car just shy of the grass where Goddard had parked, and slowed to a halt. He stopped and stared as their target calmly exited his vehicle, quickly glanced left and right, and made for a stone staircase that appeared to lead up into nothingness.

Billy and Jimmy looked at each other. They had been waiting agonisingly for their opportunity and now Goddard appeared to be presenting them with one that was perfect. Was it a trap? Had he been playing them all this time like the pair of amateurs Billy feared they might be? As the wheels began turning in Billy's mind he slammed a leather clad hand on the dashboard to stop them in their tracks.

The time for caution was over, it was time to get it done, and get the fuck out of there.

Billy strode purposely across the grass, tightening his grip on the shotgun as Goddard disappeared into the nothingness. A heavy vehicle passed overhead shaking the bridge as it went, with little drops of water showering down.

Billy's senses were heightened, everything intensified. Even the cars sounded like trucks to him, and his heartbeat felt as heavy and loud as anything on that bridge. The staircase was steep and imposing. The smooth stone steps were wet, and covered in moss. Not ideal given the fact they had no idea what they were walking into, and if it was a trap they didn't want to be sliding into it. At the top of the steps, Billy's eyes quickly adjusted to take in a dirt track to the right that sprawled round into a small maze, with scores of jagged, angry looking branches tied together in bunches, marking the track. To the left was another path that led past a bunch of trees, appearing to wind round to the right underneath the bridge.

The moment Billy's chewing gum hit the wet stone in front of him, he heard talking coming from the left. He glanced round at Jimmy to see if he had heard it or whether it was just his mind playing tricks.

"Hear that?"

"Naw.

"Come oan."

They emerged on the other side of the path to the sight of the road bridge's massive arches lined up in front of them dominating the black sky, beneath which lay the dark, murky looking Forth.

As they walked up the gravelly pathway towards the closest arch they passed a collapsed wall, with massive boulders lying all over the place and piles of black soot on the other side of them. The ground at the foot of the arch was covered in empty cans and fag ends, with the last ashes of a fire blowing about in the wind, remnants of a gathering. The Rail Bridge was now just a faint image in the distance, obscured by its partner, a line of trees and the derelict wasteland they were walking on.

There was no sign of Goddard as they cautiously edged forward, and now Billy could feel the potential danger on all sides. They were boxed in, surrounded by overgrowth. Now all Billy could hear was the ominous whistling of the wind in the trees, as he slowed his pace, wondering if someone was luring them closer. There it was again, that whispering, except much closer this time. As they backed up behind the grainy stone arch, he heard heavy breathing. Billy looked at Jimmy and this time received a look of recognition in return. It was coming from the other side of the arch. Billy tightened his grip on the shotgun as he peered round the corner of the arch, wracked with screaming paranoia. He looked at Jimmy and motioned for him to take the other side.

A young laddie fell backwards into the dirt covering his face with fear as they appeared from both sides with their shotguns aimed. Goddard froze, his eyes bulging with panic, before frantically trying to conceal the fact his fly was open.

"You dirty bastard," said Billy, as Goddard raised a hand in desperation.

Billy shook his head, and gritted his teeth as Goddard panted for breath. "So. It was true then? That'll make this a bit easier."

"Who sent ye?"

"Doesnae matter who fuckin sent us does it? You've just been caught wae yer pants doon ya beasty bastard!" screamed Jimmy in anger.

"It's ma son! Awrite? It's no how it looks! Colin tell thum. Come oan son."

Billy looked at the young lad as he crept to his feet and dusted some dirt from his trousers, school trousers at that. He looked at Billy and nodded his head, as he fiddled nervously with his hands.

"See? Just out fer a walk that's it! Nothin dodgy goin on here. Was jist takin a leak. When ye need tae go ye need tae go eh!"

Billy looked back at the boy whose hate filled expression betrayed the pathetic protest of innocence Goddard was making as he stood there caught in the act.

Billy knew it was true, he sensed it in the boy's eyes. Reckoned the poor laddie had been suffering this unspeakable fate for years. Crawling into a corner in his room, squeezing his face between his legs, rocking back and forth, willing it to end. Praying for someone to save him. Longing for the day when he would be old enough to overpower the bastard and push him off a cliff, hit him in the head with something heavy, anything to make it stop. Billy could also see that defiance, that undying will to rise above it, shining through the hatred in his eyes. All those years and all those hammerings Billy had suffered week in week out. Smacked upside down, battered with that stick, lashed with a belt buckle. All those batterings multiplied by a thousand wouldn't come anywhere near what this laddie had suffered.

"Ah've got money. Take it all. Whatever they're payin ye, I'll double it, triple it even!"

"Your own flesh an blood. Your own fuckin son of all people." Billy tensed his grip, slugged him in the stomach, and then watched as he fell backwards into the arch with confusion in his eyes. He slumped to the deck clutching at the contents that were spilling from his stomach, looking round at his son, his mouth uttering something he didn't have the strength to say. It looked like a sorry, but it was too little too late. Jimmy stepped out of the shadows, pointed the shotgun at his chest and blasted him into the dirt.

Another car passed overhead as a train sounded in the distance from the Rail Bridge that no longer seemed so imposing. Billy had built the moment up in his mind so much, scared deep down that he wouldn't have the minerals. Worried that he would prove the old man right, that he would be too weak. But as he looked down at Goddard's limp, tangled up body, lying in front of the blood spattered arch he realised it hadn't been that big a deal after all, taking a life. Certainly not this one.

He turned to the son who wore an expression of pure relief and calm, clearly unfazed by it. The days of getting buggered underneath the bridge by this monster who called himself Dad were over.

"You good wae this?" said Billy.

"Yes."

"So when the police find the body, and start askin about?"

"I was down by the water. Watching the boats come in."

"Good lad." Billy pulled a wad of notes from his pocket, counted several out and offered them to him.

The boy looked up at him and calmly shook his head before disappearing down the path and into the blackness.

47

Billy took a deep, laboured breath as he looked out onto the waters of Cramond, that were far calmer than his turbulent thoughts. The sun was setting with an incredible pink glow permeated by striking yellows and oranges that reflected in the shallow puddles scattering the sand. He focused his weary eyes on the sunset in a futile effort to ease the tension that had settled on his brain like a murky fog. Losing himself in reflection, or at least trying to, was a welcome rest from the events of the previous twenty-four hours. Had they left anything that could incriminate them? Had anyone seen them pull up or leave? Would the laddie keep his mouth shut? Images of father and son engaged in an act so horrible – it was too much to bear.

Billy had never been one for planning, he could never see far enough. He was all about making cash, living for the weekend, confronting danger head on, living at a hundred miles an hour whilst looking over his shoulder every step of the way. No wonder he needed a few eccies to cut loose and escape from time to time.

Well, now everything had changed. If the revelation that he was to be a father wasn't a watershed moment, the murder certainly was. He couldn't risk spending his bairn's upbringing behind bars. His luck would surely run out sooner or later. He didn't want his child to have to dodge broken glass and used needles when he fell off his bike or tripped in the street. He wanted his bairn's childhood to be so far removed from his own that a completely new brand of Wright was formed. One that was free of the anger and bitter residue of past generations.

It was time to start planning an exit strategy.

"Someone looks deep in thought." Brian Clark dropped the bag on the ground as he took his seat on the wooden bench, pulled his knee-length cashmere closed, and quickly adjusted his specs.

"What a sky eh?" said Clark.

"Ah ken."

"So. Job done?"

"Well, he's no breathin."

"Good man. I won't forget this favour in a hurry. It's all there, the other twenty grand."

"You can keep that."

"Come again?"

"It's time tae expand. I want to quadruple the next batch. Take advantage of these yellow crowns you've got comin in."

"Gonna be the strongest pills on the market."

"Aye. If they're as good as Ah'm hearin, there's at least five local dealers that will be interested in takin a load on the regular, already been puttin the feelers out. No tae mention these raves you can get us access too. Seven months. Seven months till ma bairn's due then Ah'm out. If Ah keep ma heid doon between now and then, focus on makin money rather than gettin blitzed, Ah'll be set up, an ready tae split."

"Ye might want tae think of cleanin some of that money in the meantime. Putting it through a business, anythin rich in cash. If you get captured, you want to be able to declare your earnings as something other than the obvious or they'll take you to the cleaners. I mean seriously, how does a young guy with no source of income justify sitting on a wad of cash? Yer a clever guy, don't make the same mistake so many stupid fuckers currently residing in her Majesty's establishment have made."

Billy pulled a joint from his cardigan pocket, bit the end off and spat it on the ground as he toyed with the clipper between his fingers. "Maybe if Ah was plannin on hangin about. But 7 months, an am outae here. Need tae keep ma money where Ah can get at it immediately no tied up in fuckin businesses."

"Ok then." Clark stood up and glanced over his shoulder to the hulking figure behind casting a large shadow against the illuminated concrete. "For now business continues, and increases. I'll be in touch soon. I'll leave you to enjoy that sky."

Billy lit the joint and let it hang between his lips as he gazed back out onto the water. There was another area of his existence that had been weighing heavily on him for too long. It was time to do something about it.

48

Billy walked into the living room to the sight of the old man hunched over the coffee table, gazing out the window through strained eyes. The living room hadn't seen a single lick of paint since Billy was young, felt like it was frozen in a time he would rather forget. Still the same peeling nicotine-stained cream wallpaper. Still the same horrible brown curtains with the intertwined flowers winding their way up to the ceiling, looking like they could spiral on forever. Just like the tired old house was crying out for a change so was Mum, Billy thought to himself.

Jack was clutching hold of a brandy like his life depended on it. His back looked more arched than ever, no doubt weighed down by the pressures his hard labouring trade was placing on his aging bones.

Billy wondered if that twisted old spine was equally weighed down by the bitter, cruel nature that had probably sucked all the marrow out of it by now. He might have been in his late forties but Jack wore the look of a tired, miserable old man now. The zigzagged stress lines were etched even deeper into his forehead, creating a permanent frown, with a layer of fur-like grey hair that had settled all over his torn face, along with various second prizes, scars that he had earned over the years when finding that some folk weren't as easily bullied as his wife. Billy did wonder whether he felt any regret, guilt or remorse over the way he had treated his family. He wondered whether the memories kept him up at night.

"What you wantin?" said Jack, a look of increasing discomfort on his face with every step Billy took towards him. Maybe the memories really did haunt the bastard. He squirmed in his chair and picked up his brandy with a shaking hand as Billy sat down.

They sat there, in silence, for what felt like an age, soaking in the uncomfortable reminiscence of it all. Just as Billy felt it creeping up his body hairs and threatening to choke him, he forced himself to speak, pulling at his collar as he felt a tight squeeze. "Disturb ye did Ah? Look like yer havin a great old time, sittin here on yer own, starin oot the windae. Some life eh?" Billy smiled.

"Aw aye an what's so fuckin rosy about your life? Eh? Never worked a day. Expelled fae two schools. Dealin drugs now. Bloody waster that's all ye are. A waster."

Billy looked his Dad square in the eye. "Least I've made somethin ay masel. Might no be much but it's somethin. Ah'm someone. People ken me, people respect me. You, on the other hand..." Billy looked him up and down with disdain. "What's your legacy? Eh? Sittin here on yer ain. Nae real pals, a wife that's fuckin feared ay ye. That ye've reduced tae nothin but a nervous wreck, a fuckin zombie, scared tae have an opinion on anythin."

Jack shook his head as he drained the rest of his brandy. "Made somethin of yersel? A bloody drug dealer? Let me tell you son, you're on borrowed time. The enemies you've made?" Jack sniggered to himself. "An now the boy's gonnae be a father umself eh? Ye think ye've got it in ye dae ye? Think yer ready fer it? No bloody chance."

"Be a better father than you anyway."

"Aye we'll see. Ye wantae come round here an try an gloat because Ah skelped ye aboot when ye were a bairn?" He sat forward in his chair and looked Billy square in the eye for the first time. "That's what happens son. That's what happened tae me. That's what happened tae yer Grandad tae. It's called teachin manners, respect. Fat lot ay bloody good it did. Might as well have let ye run wild. All you bams runnin aboot stabbin an slashin each other. In ma day ye used these!" Jack clenched his fists, his eyes widening.

"Funny that. See fae what Ah can remember you used a stick on me. Big long one wae a sharp end. Used tae huv tae pick the splinters oot ma shoulders in the mornin before Ah went tae school. Here, look."

Billy pulled his jumper down over his shoulder and pushed it toward his father, who recoiled in his seat, back within his shell, clearly finding it difficult to witness his handiwork.

"Still got the scars. Wantae see them naw? Discipline's one thing, Ah used tae take a leatherin fer breathin, fer darin tae exist." Billy shook his head. "Then there was that belt buckle. Can mind one time ye hit me so hard wae that ma wee heid was still spinnin in the mornin. Sure ye'd use yer hands fae time tae time tae. But the way ye set aboot me wae those fists ye wouldae thought Ah was a grown man. Nothin tae say now naw?"

Jack let out a deep groan before pouring himself another brandy.

"Well ye ken somethin? Dad? Ye did do me a favour. You made me fuckin fearless. Scared ay nae cunt. Took all that abuse fer all those years, sucked it up an still standin. LOOK!!"

He stood up with outstretched arms and watched his father shrink even further into his seat. "Still fuckin standin! Walkin tall! An look at you, eh? Just a miserable wee man. Drinkin yer nights away. Who came oot better? You tell me!"

Jack sat forward and rubbed at his tired looking eyes. "What ur ye wantin? Must be a reason why yer here."

"Where's Mum?"

"She's away oot."

Billy pulled the envelope out of his jeans pocket and dropped it on the coffee table, before sitting down again. "Open it."

Jack picked it up and opened it before looking back at Billy. "This some kind of joke?"

"Ten grand in there."

Jack dropped the envelope on the table and gave his head a shake.

"Ah did come here lookin fer Mum. Was gonnae try an tempt her intae goin away. Somewhere far away fae you. But thinkin about it now, there's not a hope in hell. Too fuckin scared in't she? So what Ah'm askin you tae dae is - go through yer room. Pack a bag. Go tae the train station, or the airport. And go as far away fae here as possible. On me. On yer only fucking son, ma treat. This is your chance tae escape this life that makes you so fuckin miserable, along with everyone around ye."

Billy sat forward and pointed a finger in his old man's face. "An Ah don't want you tae have any part in your gran-kid's life. An Ah don't want you tae have anything tae dae wae Mum. Anymair. Ye hear me?"

Jack smiled as he shook his head in clear disbelief. "What, you think Ah'm gonnae take orders fae you dae ye? That I'll just up an leave like that? Who would support yer Mum, eh? You?"

"Aye fuckin me. Ah make mair in a week than you make in a month shovellin bricks and boulders."

"So you're gonnae pay yer Mother's rent, and support a kid, all on drug money? You live in cloud bloody cuckoo land son. Soon yer gonnae touch doon wae a bang, mark my words."

"Awrite." Billy had been waiting for this moment. He pulled the stick out of his back tail and slammed it down on the table. He wasn't sure why he had kept it all these years, having retrieved it before moving out. A memento of youth. Perhaps he had kept it as a reminder of where and what he had come from. A symbol of what he never, ever wanted to return to. Never again would he be bullied or belittled.

"You choose. Take the money an run. Or you get that stick."

Jack looked back at his son with an expression of bewilderment. "Is this for real? What ye gonnae do wae that? Return the favour? You really have lost it eh? One too many bloody drugs. Move on. Get bloody well over it eh! Go on, take yer money an fuck off! Cause Ah'm no goin naewhere. Ye wantae talk about what Ah've put yer mother through, what about you? Runnin aboot the area fae the age ay twelve. Tannin windaes, stealin. Lifted every week, all the rumours about yer exploits wae the rest of the bams from the area. Dole dosser, drug dealer, blade merchant! Ah was the one supportin her as she cried intae her pillae every night about what her only son had become. Ye dinnae ken that side dae ye!? A somebody, ha! You're nothin! Ye hear me!? NOTHIN! Ye never were!"

Jack grabbed the stick and stood up with authority, glowering over Billy like he was still that helpless twelve year old.

"Ah should give you a fuckin hidin jist like when ye were a laddie. Fer darin tae come in here an shout the odds at me!"

Billy felt it come rapidly like a spear through his chest. That old fear, that unwelcome companion that he hadn't spent time with in so long. Maybe it was the surroundings, maybe it was that dreaded stick, back within the old man's grasp as he stood poised over him, ready to strike like a rattlesnake. It was all rushing back with a vengeance, forcing his heart to race as he felt himself shrink inside. Then the face of that young boy flashed through his mind. Falling into the dirt underneath the bridge. Sitting there helpless beneath the domineering spectre of a father figure who had crushed his spirit in such disgusting and despicable fashion.

Billy wasn't that boy anymore. He wasn't helpless, afraid, or bullied by anyone, not least the coward standing over him, who need not hold any power, not these days. He stood up and grew in stature as he looked down on a father that was now a good couple of inches shorter. He stared a hole right through his angry skull and watched him slowly wilt back into his decrepit frame. A bully. That's all he was. That's all he ever had been. Nothing but a fucking coward. Unable to stand the heat the moment it was turned back on him.

Billy grabbed the stick, wrenched it from his grasp and watched the venom evaporate from his father's eyes as he realised the power he had once held was long gone. With one hand Billy shoved him back into his seat. With his other hand Billy dragged his jumper up over his head and dumped it on the seat behind him. He took a step forward and tensed his arms and shoulders, his eyes wild as he stood over the old man, forcing him to look up.

"Gimme a fuckin hidin aye? Like when Ah wis a laddie? Ah'll save ye the bother." He gritted his teeth and took the stinging blows as he whacked himself with all his might, in the ribs, over the shoulder, across the neck. The pain was worth it, worth every second of terror that he could see in Jack's face as he flinched and jumped again and again.

"SEE!? Nae bother tae me!! NO ANYMAIR!!"

Billy stood right above him and pressed the sharp end of the stick hard into Jack's chest.

"Maybe Ah should just drive this right through your black heart. Dae ye a fuckin favour. Put ye oot yer misery."

"Awrite! Awrite! Ah'll take the money an leave! Ah'll never come back, ye'll never see me again! Just settle doon eh!?"

He continued to apply pressure as Jack gripped hold of the hand rests, eyes bulging, frozen into his seat at the mercy of his only son.

"SON!!"

His mother's yell brought him quickly to his senses. He hadn't noticed her coming in. His eyes met with Jack's in a moment of recognition that he had been saved just in the nick of time. The smell of pure fear was enough to leave Billy satisfied, yet he wasn't sure whether he would have been able to stop himself had his Mum not walked through that door when she did. He dropped the stick on the table and turned around.

Angie looked even more tired and worn out than Jack, her wiry hair ravaged by a forty a day smoking habit, her sagging eyes full of anxiety, spirit broken long ago by such a toxic attachment.

It needed to end.

"Dad's leavin, Mum. For good." He turned back to Jack. "Aren't ye Dad?" There was a pause as Jack looked down at the envelope. "WELL!?"

"Is someone gonnae tell me what's goin on here!?"

"Yer son wants me tae leave. Don't ye son? Well, I think we should let yer mother decide."

"Mum, he's a bully and a coward. Ah cannae bare tae see him grind you down any longer. Look at me Mum. It needs tae end. You know it does."

She looked back at him helplessly, before breaking down and falling to her knees.

"Well well." Said Jack. "Look what you've done. Haven't you put her through enough? I think you should leave. Stay out of *our* lives."

His sneering expression tore at Billy so much he had to look away. He turned his back on him and offered comfort to his mum, placing a hand on her back as he felt her body tremble under the weight of it all.

"Don't you want this Mum. A new start. A chance at happiness?"

She looked up at him helplessly. "I don't know anything else, Son. This is my life. Fer better or worse."

Billy felt his heart sink.

"You heard her. She's made her choice, now away ye go an leave us in bloody peace will ye?"

Billy watched the old man shrink back into his chair as he turned and stalked towards him, grabbing the stick again as he went. "Just remember this you twisted fuck. If I ever see so much as the smallest mark on her face again. If I even see a hair out of place at your hands then there won't be any more threats. I'll kill you stone dead right where you sit."

After flinging on his jumper, Billy snatched the envelope from the table and offered it to his Mum as he passed her.

"This is for you Mum. Ah want ye tae hold ontae it and think about what I've said. It's never too late. Ah love ye Mum."

She squeezed hold of his hand, filling him with a glimmer of hope.

"She doesn't want yer drug money. *We* don't want yer drug money. Take it an go. And never come back, ye hear me?"

Billy felt his whole body tense up again as it swallowed up the doorway.

"You've been warned. And you should thank Mum fer walkin in when she did. Next time you might no be so lucky."

As he walked away from the old house he stopped and looked at the stick. He snapped it over his knee and dropped it on the pavement. Time to let go of the scared wee boy that cowered in the corner all those years ago. To let go of the ghost that had followed him all these years, just like that wee laddie disappeared into the night, not for a second looking back, freed from the shackles of an evil tyrant. It was time to shed the skin and move forward with fatherhood in sight. And with it a chance to break the cycle.

About the Author

Stephen Scarcliffe spent ten years as a singer-songwriter for Edinburgh rock band The Number 9's before turning his main focus to crime fiction writing. He grew up in and around north Edinburgh, where his novel is set, lending authenticity to the story and its characters. When Irvine Welsh provided positive feedback for one of his early short stories after a chance meeting in the mid-2000's it planted a seed that has now grown into Pure Angst, the first of a three-part book series.

Read more at www.stephenscarcliffe.co.uk.

23805002R00128

Printed in Great Britain
by Amazon